Outstanding praise for Emmeline Duncan and her Ground Rules mysteries!

Fresh Brewed Murder
"Coffee lovers, this book is for you. A fresh take on the cozy mystery genre. This is a great debut!"
—*Criminal Element*

"Portland's beloved food carts provide a tantalizing backdrop for a new cozy mystery by Portland author Emmeline Duncan. . . . A creative way to address both the quirkiness and the more dismaying aspects of life in contemporary Portland."
—*The Sunday Oregonian*

Double Shot Death
"The possible killers and motives are well juggled, and Duncan's writing is fresh and realistic. Readers will look forward to more with Sage and her coffee cart friends and family."
—*First Clue*

"Solid prose, a well-crafted plot, and plenty of coffee lore draw the reader in. A socially liberal vibe—Bax happily mixes with his ex-wife, their young son, and her husband—sets this cozy apart."
—*Publishers Weekly*

Flat White Fatality
"Tips on coffee and a touch of romance combine in a mystery with a strong West Coast vibe."
—*Kirkus Reviews*

Books by Emmeline Duncan

Ground Rules Mysteries

FRESH BREWED MURDER
DOUBLE SHOT DEATH
FLAT WHITE FATALITY
DEATH UNFILTERED
FATAL BROUHAHA

Halloween Bookshop Mysteries

CHAOS AT THE LAZY BONES BOOKSHOP

Published by Kensington Publishing Corp.

FATAL BROUHAHA

Emmeline Duncan

Kensington Publishing Corp.
kensingtonbooks.com

To all of the readers who've followed Sage's journey from the beginning or joined us along the way

Chapter 1

It's always fun when decisions from over a year ago come to fruition. My coffee empire, Ground Rules, had partnered with a local company, Doyle's Oregon Whiskey, to create a canned Irish coffee. We provided the coffee grounds and expertise; they distilled the whiskey, procured the locally sourced cream, and managed the canning part of the manufacturing process. Doyle's Irish-To-Go tasted smooth, with the perfect balance of coffee and Irish-style whiskey distilled by the Doyle brothers, Tierney and Shay.

We were celebrating the product launch with a makers' fair-slash-festival at the distillery over the Fourth of July weekend, on the Doyles' property in the Columbia Gorge with a view of the mighty Columbia River. Twenty local companies were set up, all selling locally made products, with a collection of food carts and the Ground Rules coffee cart stationed on the edge of the paved parking lot. We had a busy schedule of cornhole tournaments, a Connect Four tournament for children, a series of bands performing on the stage in the meadow, and everything would finish with a holiday barbecue leading to the annual fireworks display.

In addition to our cart, Ground Rules partnered with Hannah Clyde at Stonefield Beach Teas to run a booth in the makers' fair. So I'd scheduled a selection of baristas to staff either the cart or our booth.

But as everyone knows, even on sunny days, you might see storm clouds approaching. And I saw a big thunderstorm swaggering my way.

Mark Jeffries. If I had main character energy, he'd be the wannabe antagonist in my coffee journey. I do my best to never think of Mark, and I hadn't seen him for a few months.

And here he was, bearing down on me, during the setup of a festival he'd applied to attend but had been turned down for. He'd tried to complain, but I'd been in the Doyles' distillery when Tierney had bluntly told him they had one coffee vendor and didn't need a second.

Mark looked the same as he had for years, with a moka pot tattoo on his right ropey forearm. A trucker's cap with the name of his coffee company, Left Coast Grinds, reminded me of the hats that Ground Rules had introduced earlier in the year. I'd been hesitant, but two of my baristas had insisted they'd be big sellers, so I'd trusted them.

And once I had one of the trucker hats in my hands, or rather on my head, I liked the laid-back hat, especially in the summer.

The blue collapsible wagon Mark pulled behind him detracted from his usual air of hipness.

Mark smirked when he saw me. "You didn't think you'd be the only coffee company here, did you?"

I straightened my back as I glared at him. "Actually, that's what I thought." It had been part of my agreement with the Doyles, and it was logical. We were partners in the canned cocktail, after all.

"Sorry, Princess." Mark walked past me. The wheel of his wagon caught on a divot in the grass, and the boxes in his cart rattled. He soldiered on.

Glass? Why was Mark here with glasses?

I shot Tierney Doyle a quick text. *Did Left Coast Grinds sign up for a booth after all?* I'd vetted the vendor applications with Tierney and was sure he would've contacted me if someone dropped out and he'd needed to fill a last-minute spot.

Plus, I'd heard the phone call between them, which had been on speaker. Tierney had sounded firm with Mark, like he'd never budge.

There wasn't anything I could do about Mark right now, so I continued checking out the booths at the craft fair. The leather booth that specializes in cosplay had a suite of armor in their tent, along with chest plates and gear that was sure to make fans of franchises like *The Lord of the Rings* and *The Witcher* drool. I waved to the owner of a local one-woman business that made bags out of Pendleton fabric, canvas, or leather and showed her that I was carrying one of her bags. One of my favorites from her shop, with an owl print that was perfect for summer. I also knew that if I stopped at her shop, I'd buy another one of her bags, despite already owning three. Or was it four? My friend Zarek was hard at work setting up his booth with artisanal vegan energy bars, so we only waved hello, as we'd have time to catch up later.

I halted.

Mark was adding a display of bottles on one side of a booth. The sign on the other half of the table said DULCINEA CHOCOLATES & GOURMET CANDIES, and their display case was empty. Like most vendors, they'd set up the booth to encourage customers to walk inside, under the shade, instead of browsing at a table along the front.

The name of the company jogged a memory. I remembered reviewing the owner, Dulcie's, festival application; she'd just launched her chocolate shop last winter. She already had shelf space in several local grocery chains and opened a small storefront in Southeast Portland. After we'd offered her a spot in the makers' fair, I'd dropped by and purchased a mix of her products and left a Ground Rules sample behind, in case she decided to start offering coffee in her tiny chocolate café. I hadn't known she had any sort of connection to Left Coast Grinds.

My phone beeped. Tierney. *No, of course not.*

I texted back. *LCG is setting up in the Dulcinea booth.*

On it.

I wondered how Dulcie's chocolates would fare in the summer

heat, but then I noticed the coolers on her side. But that had to introduce a whole new host of problems, because if moisture ends up trapped with the chocolate, like in a fridge, the sugar in the chocolate can "bloom." Which results in a white coating on the chocolate that's safe to eat but looks terrible and can also affect the taste. Which is one of the reasons I prefer working with coffee. Coffee can be temperamental, but chocolate is a whole different, melty, but delicious ball game.

My eyes wandered back to Mark's setup. The bottles he was lining up were small, maybe eight ounces. He'd also added a few products, like coffee mugs and beanies, all branded with Left Coast Grinds's logo.

Mark's smirk my way could count as a reason for justifiable homicide. "It's my newest product. It's the newest, hippest alternative to cold brew."

"Hmm," I said. Hippest didn't always mean the best, although I was curious where he was going with this.

"You just need to add one tablespoon to water or milk to get the best cup of coffee in your life."

"Interesting." I moved on like I was bored. But Mark's presence did rankle, like a seemingly inconsequential blister waiting to ruin an entire backpacking trip.

I paused by a local soda company's booth, because I saw Tierney heading my way, decked out in an official Doyle's Oregon Whiskey T-shirt, which featured the text in a retro script over a line drawing of the Cascade Mountains.

"Left Coast Grinds took over Dulcie's booth?" Tierney asked. He knew some of the history between Mark Jeffries and my business partner, Harley, and me.

"It looks like he took over half of the booth. Dulcie's also selling chocolate, supposedly." Maybe the empty case held invisible truffles.

"Is Left Coast Grinds selling drinks?"

I shook my head. "Just bottled coffee juice and gear."

Tierney's eyebrows scrunched together. "Juice?"

"Coffee concentrate, if you want to be precise." On a normal day, one of Dulcie's chocolates would've sounded like the perfect afternoon pick-me-up, at least once she was set up and ready to sell. But seeing Mark next to her would turn me off of her products, showing my petty side.

"Do you want me to kick him out?" Tierney asked.

"The idea is tempting. If he stays, Mark is just making a fool out of himself. But if you kick him out, you'll let him play the victim," I said. A weekend of him watching Ground Rules's success would be more of a punishment. He'd be jealous when he saw customers browsing the craft fair with cups of Ground Rules cold brew in their hands.

Although I'd love to see him forced to leave with his tail between his legs, pulling his cart of rattling bottles of coffee juice behind him.

"Mark being here annoys me. And I'm trying to remember what, exactly, we said about subletting space in the rental agreements for the festival." Tierney's lips scrunched up slightly as he thought. Both of the Doyle brothers look similar. Both are fairly tall, about six feet, with brown hair, blue eyes, and sturdy builds. Tierney is the taller of the two and more gregarious. Shay was more taciturn, but when he said something, I knew I should pay attention. Shay was also the distiller, while Tierney handled the business side. He could schmooze with the best when needed, but he was always honest, and I never felt like he was trying to get something over on me.

My thoughts clicked together into a decision, and as I spoke, I wondered if I'd regret it. "Don't kick Mark out of the festival on Ground Rules's behalf. Like I said, I don't want to turn him into a victim. You don't need the drama during your product launch."

"I'll warn him to be on his best behavior." Tierney looked like he wasn't happy with his decision. "But I'm annoyed he's here. You heard me tell him the decision to deny his application was final."

One of the festival bouncers swaggered up, wearing one of the official bright-orange T-shirts that said DOYLE'S on the front and SE-CURITY on the back. He wore a headset with a black receiver on his hip. He'd finished off his look with black cargo pants and heavy boots with a law enforcement air that must be murder in the summer heat. The other bouncers I'd seen had been more casual with less military cosplay.

"Problem, boss?" the security guard said. I would've guessed he was in his early forties. He looked muscular with a slight belly and rocked a close-trim haircut.

"Sort of, Trevor, and in a moment, I'll need you to come with me. Right after I introduce you to Sage Caplin, one of the Ground Rules owners and coffee purveyor extraordinaire. Sage, this is Trevor, our head of security for the festival."

"Hi," I said. We awkwardly shook hands. Then Tierney led Trevor away toward Left Coast Grinds's illicit booth, and I continued on my roundabout way through the festival, meandering toward the joint Stonefield Beach Tea and Ground Rules booth.

I scanned the lineup of businesses in the second row. Tierney had stationed a local cheese company next to a vegan cheese operation. I wondered if they'd rumble later.

A collection of local artists shared a booth, and the mix of paintings and illustrations caught my eye, so I told myself to come back later. Ditto the booth for a local hot sauce company and the local refugee organization selling baked goods, which were stationed side by side. And the artisan ginger beer stand almost made me detour.

Then I reached my destination.

The Ground Rules half of the booth was fully set up. Our coffee bean displays were stocked, along with the merch selection of camp mugs, tumblers, pour-over cones, and other quality coffee gear, plus hats and T-shirts. We'd last-minute added a bucket hat perfect for sunny days that, fingers crossed, would appeal to festivalgoers spending the long weekend in the sun.

Hannah mumbled to herself as she set up the Stonefield Beach side of the extra-large corner booth. She carefully put her rather fancy folding knife down in a wooden tray before turning and picking up a large box and rummaging through it.

Hannah had a vintage-looking apothecary unit with carefully labeled drawers on one side. She'd create on-the-spot tea blends based on someone's taste using words, feelings, or even fandoms as inspiration. A display of ready-made tea blends was stacked on a table with movable shelves that looked like they were made of reclaimed pipe and old wood. The artwork on her tea canisters was top-notch. A sign on one end of the table highlighted how Hannah and her sister, Josie, grew or foraged for tea ingredients at their family farm on the Oregon Coast.

"Do you need any help?" I asked.

"I'm good," Hannah said. Her eyes were focused on the box she was rummaging through. She pulled out a white card reader and then sighed, like she'd been afraid she'd left it behind. She finally made eye contact with me. "Your barista offered to help me finish my setup, but I sent her away. I appreciate that both of you offered to help. That's kind of you."

Hannah's curly brown hair was pulled into a high ponytail, and her striking green eyes caught my attention, as they always did. She was tall, about five foot ten, with a sturdy build and a love of vintage-looking baseball tees. Today's was medium gray with red sleeves, which she'd pushed above her elbows, showing off the small tattoo of a teapot pouring stars into a cup and saucer on the inside of her elbow.

She paused and picked up her stainless-steel water bottle, which had a sticker with her tea company's logo on the side. "I hope this festival is as busy as you claim."

"The advance ticket sales are strong, which will hopefully lead to strong craft fair sales, although I can't make any promises," I said. Attendees had to buy tickets to enter the festival's fenced-off music zone, although the craft fair was open to everyone, and we hoped to attract shoppers who hadn't bought a ticket in addition to regular festivalgoers.

The distillery's tasting room, which had bottles of Doyle's Whiskey for sale plus the new canned cocktail, was open to everyone old enough to drink. The distillery had one side patio open to all, but their primary, and enormous, patio facing the meadow, and therefore the bands, required a festival ticket.

"I wish I could've gotten Josie to join us, but she's in full recluse mood at the farm on the coast. In her defense, the weather is much nicer."

"It'd be lovely to meet her. It's, what, supposed to be sixty degrees on the coast this weekend? I can't blame her for staying away from the heat," I said. Summers on the Oregon Coast are frequently hoodie weather, which is always a relief when the Willamette Valley has a heat wave.

"High of sixty-five, so it's basically tropical." Hannah grinned.

"I'll let you get back to work, but let me know if you need help. We're happy to assist." I adjusted my crossover bag so it felt more secure against my hip.

"Yeah, I know, but I have to organize this so I know where everything is, or else I'll be confused all weekend." Hannah turned to her boxes of tea leaves, like she was reading the future.

I left and finished scoping out the last row of the craft fair before finishing my circle, which took me back to where I started.

As I walked up to the Ground Rules cart, Kendall and Sophie were sitting in camp chairs outside. I was about to call out to them when a voice said my name.

I turned.

Dulcie the chocolate maker. She hustled up to me. She was a few years younger than me, which I knew because one of the articles about her business in the local paper had highlighted how she was only twenty-three when she launched her company last winter. Her dark brown hair was pulled into a high bun. The straps of a cheerful yellow sundress peeked out under her retro flowered apron, with DULCINEA embroidered on the front.

"You're Sage, right? We've met," Dulcie said.

"Yep, at your shop." The last person I'd known to wear an apron like Dulcie's while working had hidden a dark side under her craft-loving exterior. But I shouldn't let that affect my opinion of the choc-olatier.

"I can't wait to try your collaboration with the Doyles," Dulcie said. "It sounds delightful."

"Canned cocktails are still on the upswing." As beer lost some of its luster and some of its sales, drinkers switched to cocktails. So, the market for canned cocktails was expanding, at least for now. Some-thing else would be trendy in a few years, but hopefully, the canned cocktail would be established enough to be a trend-proof classic by then.

"It was smart to diversify. It must be fun seeing your logo on the drinks," Dulcie said. "Are coffee sales consistent in general? I'm still debating adding coffee drinks to my café."

"I'm surprised you haven't asked Mark, since he's sharing your booth," I said. My tone was acerbic, and Dulcie's eyes widened slightly.

"That sounded mean. What's your problem with Left Coast Grinds, anyway? It's a totally good coffee company, but I can understand if you just don't like hanging out with your competition," Dulcie asked.

My tension with Mark Jeffries was more than just being competi-tors. Should I tell her that Harley and I had worked there as college students, although I'd quit when Mark had propositioned me? Or how Harley had become his primary roaster, only for Mark to steal the glory and, more importantly, credit for her award-winning blend at the regional coffee championships? Or how he'd blackmailed one of my former baristas into spying on us? She hadn't sabotaged us, al-though if we hadn't found out about the blackmail when we did, who knows how far it would've gone?

Simple is always best. "It's a long story."

"I hope Mark being here isn't stepping on your toes. My assistant manager had to leave town unexpectedly, and she's so organized that

I knew I'd struggle to run the booth alone all weekend. So when Mark offered to take over half of my booth, it seemed like a great chance to get coverage so I could use the bathroom and leave the booth in his hands part of the time. I'm so worried I won't make a profit. I didn't think through the logistics of bringing chocolate to a festival when it's this sunny and hot."

"Chocolate and the heat are tricky." It was supposed to be in the upper eighties all weekend, which was relatively mild compared to the end of July and August, when we'd most likely have a few odd 100-degree stretches. Although we'd had a few early heat waves in the past few years, including a handful of miserable heat domes. So this weekend's weather felt lucky.

"I should stick to indoor events, like Crafty Wonderland. It's much easier to plan for," Dulcie said. She tilted her head slightly and looked at me. "Have you tried Mark's new coffee product?"

I shook my head.

Dulcie pulled a small bottle out of the pocket in her vintage apron. "Here, this is on me as an apology. It's a bit harsh for my taste, but Mark thinks this is the wave of the future for coffee drinkers that want an affordable option at home but don't want to deal with brewing their own coffee."

Something told me Dulcie's words were a direct quote. And why had she brought the bottle with her? As I took the bottle from her, I wondered if Mark had sent her my way. If he was trying to knock me off of my game and make me worry that his product really was revolutionary.

I looked at the two-ounce bottle, which had the Left Coast Grinds logo on one side and instructions on the back. "So this is for lazy coffee drinkers."

"Mark has a point. Sometimes, you just want a coffee without having to grind beans or clean up a French press or whatever later. Not everyone has the skills to make a good cup, too. My sister can ruin coffee just by touching it, no matter how hard she tries."

"This is like instant hot chocolate made with water," I said. I'd noticed the house-made drinking chocolate blends that Dulcie had sold in her shop, with a note that they'd taste best with milk; the higher the fat, the better.

"Point taken. But truth be told, I've made my nieces cheap hot chocolate before because that's what they like, versus a proper *chocolat chaud*. And sometimes, easy is best."

I worked through the drink database in my brain before placing it. A *chocolat chaud* is an intensely rich Parisienne style of hot chocolate.

"Thanks, I'll try this." I slipped the coffee juice bottle into my bag, nestling it inside one of the inner pockets next to my lip balm.

"And like I said, I hope I didn't offend you."

"You should probably talk to Tierney or Shay," I said.

"Who?"

"The festival organizers."

Dulcie blinked, as if she hadn't realized the people she'd signed a contract with might have issues with her breaking it. "Do you think they'll mind?"

"Like I said, talk to them."

Dulcie scurried away, and I finally made it all the way back to the comfort of the coffee cart, which felt like a second home.

"You going to read us the riot act, boss, for sitting on the job?" Sophie asked. Her curly red hair peeked out from underneath one of our teal Ground Rules bucket hats, and she'd placed her chair in the shade of the cart. Kendall had also gone for one of our hats, but he'd opted for one of the trucker versions with a mesh back that he'd lobbied us to add to the product lineup. They both wore Ground Rules T-shirts, just like I did. We all wore shorts and sneakers, since we required everyone to wear closed-toe shoes while working, and I did my best to lead by example.

"Is the cart fully set up?" I asked.

"Yes," Kendall said. He didn't tell me I knew it was set up, as I'd done it with him, only leaving him with the final steps, like setting up cups and getting the condiments tray ready.

Even though I'd already visited the booth, I asked, "Is the booth set up?"

"Yes. I finished it with Hannah, then came back to make sure the cart didn't need any help," Sophie said. "She said she'd text if she needs to leave the booth."

"Then why would I chastise you?"

Kendall offered me his chair and grabbed the third collapsible camp chair we'd stashed in the cart before setting out for our long holiday weekend in the gorge.

"Technically, we need to take one of these chairs over to the booth, so there is one thing we need to finish," Kendall said.

"Oh, you're fired, you slacker," I said.

Kendall laughed.

I glanced at Sophie. "Everything in the booth looks great. Thanks for getting things set up so quickly."

"We're a well-oiled machine, boss," Kendall said.

I wasn't sure when, exactly, all of my staff had started calling me boss. It still felt slightly odd, like I was a kid playing dress-up, but I enjoyed it.

"Have you seen Harley yet?" I asked. My business partner had been finishing up a project in the roastery when we'd left for the festival.

My baristas shook their heads in tandem.

We were quiet for a moment. "How are the wedding plans going?" Sophie asked.

I covered my face with my hands. "Don't remind me."

My wedding was in three weeks.

Twenty-two days. Over 450 hours. I didn't need to calculate the time to the exact minute again, but I was tempted.

Based on the shared spreadsheet Bax and I had created, everything was in control. We had our vendors lined up, along with the venue. My seamstress had done my final dress fitting last week, although I had one final fitting the week of the wedding. I'd chosen a color for my bridesmaids and let them pick out their own dresses, and they'd all texted me photos of them in their new duds.

Based on my gut feeling, I needed to panic and double-check all of my plans. We'd missed something.

The event would fail. Epically.

Except it wouldn't. Perfection is an illusion, and as long as Bax and I ended up married, that's all that would matter.

Two voices shouting caught my attention, and I swiveled around. I couldn't quite make out the words, but I knew one of the yellers.

Harley, my business partner.

And she was faced off against Mark.

Chapter 2

As I hustled over to Harley, I realized Kendall was beside me.

And Trevor, the security guard I'd met earlier, was also marching over with a stern look on his face.

But I got there first.

"Hey, guys," I said. Both Mark and Harley turned toward me.

Harley looked so angry that tears were starting to form in the corners of her eyes, while Mark crossed his arms over his chest.

"The clown and the con artist," Mark said.

"Get it right. Con artist's daughter."

I'd kept my biological relationship with my mom quiet from most people in my life. But it'd become somewhat public knowledge last spring, despite my best efforts, due to a true-crime podcast that talked about my mother's rumored demise. Which hadn't been true, as my mother had sent me a congratulatory bottle of champagne shortly afterward, congratulating me on my engagement. Which led to a few more interviews with one of the FBI agents hunting for dear old mom.

Hmm, maybe I should invite the FBI agent to the wedding. We spoke more often than I see some of my college friends.

But my mother's criminal past wasn't my problem, at least right now.

"Do I need to break this up?" a strident voice asked.

Oh, great. Trevor had officially arrived, complete with a self-important tone.

Although, since he was the person in charge of festival security, I couldn't fault him for rushing over. Breaking up fights before they spun out of control must be proactive in his world.

"You could kick these two frauds out of the festival," Mark said. "Barring that, you can run along."

"Back at you, buddy. May you have the festival you deserve," I said. I pulled Harley away. Kendall followed and stayed between us and Mark.

"What's he doing here, anyway?" Harley asked once we'd retreated to the Ground Rules cart.

But I looked back the way we came. Trevor and Mark were talking intently. Mark had crossed his arms over his chest and was shaking his head.

"Mark's illicitly splitting a booth. I told Tierney not to kick him out of the makers' festival, but I've changed my mind. I'll text him."

"Mark's such a jerk." Harley picked at one of her nails.

"What was that about?" I asked.

"Mark was just being Mark." Harley looked away from me.

"Meaning?" I eyed her side profile. Harley has a high bridged nose and a round face. Her shiny black hair was loose over her shoulders. She's taller than me, but not by much.

"He was his usual jerk self, comparing me to a child playing dress-up," she said.

"Mark must be really envious of us," I said.

"I wish he'd go be jealous someplace else," Harley said softly.

Sophie walked up. Kendall stood at the cart's edge, facing Mark, who was walking away. Trevor turned and headed in the opposite direction.

"Come on, Harley, let's go look at our booth at the festival," Sophie said. "I hope you'll like the way I set it up. I think it looks sharp."

Sophie carried one of the camp chairs with them as they walked away. A woman in her early twenties caught my eye, as she was filming the cart. She turned and moved on, filming our neighbors.

People are weird.

But at least my baristas are lovely.

Later that day, the craft fair portion of the festival was shutting down as attendees streamed through the gates to hear the music. The food carts were hopping, with lines of people buying food. I'd left Ground Rules in the steady hands of Kendall and Sophie, since I had somewhere to be.

Before the first band was scheduled to play, it was showtime for Ground Rules, and therefore, Harley and me. As we stood to the side of the stage, where a rock band was preparing to go on, my business partner looked a bit stressed. I couldn't tell if it was from her earlier argument with Mark or because we were about to have the festival crowd's eyes upon us. Harley prefers to be in the background. While I could fake being comfortable with the attention for the next thirty minutes, although I didn't mind operating in the shadows.

Tierney and Shay were already onstage, with the microphone in Tierney's hands. Shay stood next to him like a statue. I could almost swear he wasn't even blinking, just gazing off into space above the fence that separated the music venue from the rest of the grounds as his brother worked the crowd. DJ Helios, one of the newer DJs at a local radio station, was acting as emcee tonight and stood to the side. The DJ was ready to take over when Tierney was done and it was time to get the crowd jazzed for the first band to take the stage.

"Thanks, everyone, for coming out to our inaugural Doyle's Oregon Whiskey Fourth of July Extravaganza," Tierney said into a microphone. The crowd cheered.

I peeked out and noted the meadow was more than half-full, with more people streaming in.

Not too bad for almost five p.m. on the Friday of a holiday weekend.

Tierney continued, and the audience was focused on him. He had the right sort of charisma for an event like this. Plus, they were the first people onstage today, so the crowd wasn't fatigued. "And this is a special year for us, as it's not just our first festival, but the launch of our brand-new Irish-To-Go canned cocktail. So I'd like to invite our business partners onto the stage. We couldn't have done this without Sage Caplin and Harley Yamazaki, the proprietors of our favorite local coffee company, Ground Rules. Come on up here, Sage and Harley."

"Why does everyone say your name first?" Harley asked as we climbed the stairs up to the stage.

"I have no idea. Maybe it's because my first name has fewer syllables? Or maybe he went alphabetical?" I said.

Harley half-smiled. Her hands fidgeted, and she kept pulling the hem of her T-shirt down. If we hadn't had so many people gazing our way, I would've asked her if she was all right.

As we stopped on the stage next to Tierney and Shay, I noticed the influencer who'd been wandering around earlier was filming us. We have security cameras at the shop and at the main Ground Rules cart. But it's still weird to know I can be filmed virtually everywhere in public and potentially pop up on the social media app of the moment at any time. I knew I'd be in the spotlight now, so it's not like I could complain, especially since I'd taken a moment to touch up the light dusting of makeup on my face. But would anyone who wasn't at this event really care about Tierney's opening remarks?

In an hour, would the crowd still remember, let alone care?

Tierney turned to me. "I feel so lucky that Sage and Ground Rules partnered with us. It's not just because Harley's special roast pairs so well with our whiskey, but because they brought incredible energy and helpful ideas to the process. They could've just dropped off the coffee beans, but instead, they became friends and valued business allies."

The crowd clapped, and I wondered how many people just wanted the music to start but were polite enough to treat their festival hosts with respect. But I smiled and waved, and then the four of us walked off, ceding the stage to DJ Helios, who introduced the waiting band, who rushed out to play.

"That went well," Tierney said, as we walked down the fence that separated the backstage from the crowd, heading toward the gate to watch the music from the back.

A woman stepped forward to say something to Shay, and I noticed the man leaning against the fence with his arms crossed over his chest.

Mark Jeffries.

And he looked pissed.

"You stole some of my best roasts when you abruptly quit Left Coast Grinds," Mark said. His low tone pulsed with anger. His glare at Harley didn't waver.

"Just can it, Mark!" Harley screamed back.

"You're a copycat. And a thief."

I stepped between them, but that didn't stop their voices from traveling over my head. Their vocabulary, which made them sound like six-year-olds fighting, didn't help. Part of me waited for one of them to say, "Yeah? Well, I'm rubber, and you're glue."

The band started playing an upbeat, and loud, number, so the people who'd swiveled to face Harley and Mark turned back to the stage.

"Why would I steal any ideas from you? I'm the better roaster," Harley said. "And you absolutely did not invent Guatemalan coffee. It's existed longer than you. It will continue to exist long after your body has turned into worm food."

"Keep telling yourself that," Mark said.

I held out my hands in a calming gesture toward both of them. "Are you trying to claim you invented Central American countries, Mark?" I said. "And trying to get yourself banned from the festival?"

"Trying? Mark's now banned. Leave, and don't come back," Tierney said.

Mark smirked, and I wondered if he'd wanted this. Maybe his

whole goal of coming this weekend was to be a proverbial thorn in our side until we forced him out.

Trevor showed up. Tierney or Shay must have messaged him.

"Please escort this gentleman out and ensure he does not return to the festival grounds," Tierney said.

"Come with me." Trevor looked at Mark, who gave him a lazy smile and walked out with him.

I turned to Harley, but before I could say anything, she said, "Please let me be, Sage. I'm heading home, and we can talk tomorrow."

Harley scurried off.

I glanced at Tierney, whose half-smile was part grimace. "That was exciting."

"I should've said yes, kick him out, when Mark showed up earlier today."

We walked and took reserved spots alongside the patio to the distillery.

"Your reasoning was good. I can't fault you."

We chatted as we listened to the bands. But I couldn't lose myself in the moment, even though the music was perfect.

I felt like something still wasn't right.

DJ Helios was smooth as he introduced the bands. He subscribed to the minimalism camp of public speaking, keeping his comments short and snappy.

"After the last few weeks, I'm relieved to see this actually happening. I was beginning to think it was a dream," Tierney told me. We sat watching the bands, with a couple of burritos and bottles of water.

"Today has been the bomb! I can't wait until the cornhole tournament starts tomorrow!" A thirtysomething-year-old stopped by our table. He was one in a long line of excited festivalgoers who'd told us they were having a great time.

"I hope you bring your cornhole game face," I said. "The competition will be fierce."

"Really?" he said.

I laughed. "Maybe? You know the winner gets bragging rights."

"You had me scared. I wondered if I needed to watch my back, afraid of a Nancy and Tonya situation."

Hopefully, no one would take the competition that seriously. Although I appreciated and winced at the reference to Oregon's former US champion figure skater whose fall from grace had spawned criminal charges, documentaries, and movies after her husband hired someone, according to Tonya without her knowledge, to (unsuccessfully) kneecap her opponent. Which goes to show, whenever a group of people are passionate about something, someone will always go too far in the desire to win (or help a loved one succeed).

During a moment of quiet, I texted Harley. *Are you okay?* But I didn't hear back.

I exchanged a few texts with Bax, who was finishing something up at work before spending the long weekend at the festival.

"You sure you don't want a drink?" Tierney asked. Like me, he'd stuck to water, except for a lone bottle of artisanal ginger beer.

I shook my head. "It's going to be a long weekend, so I plan to start off slow." I took a sip of water.

"Smart choice. And it's not like you haven't sampled the Irish-To-Go many times."

Tierney and Shay had invited us in to try different versions of the canned cocktail and give them feedback until they'd chosen their final recipe.

We chatted for a while. Our gaps in conversation were also comfortable, especially since we were both watching the band. I'd heard the Banshee Blues multiple times, and the lead singer was a talented musician who'd also written scores for my fiancé's video game studio. The band was still working on their big break, but they sounded like a million bucks.

When the last band neared the end of their set, I said farewell and headed to the coffee cart. Kendall and Sophie should have started closing the cart, so I headed to help.

They both paused working when they saw me.

"Did Mark and Harley really yell at each other? I've never seen Harley raise her voice," Kendall said as we worked. Well, as I stood in the doorway, overseeing the operation.

"Same. But everyone has a breaking point." And Mark knew how to push Harley's buttons.

"Did Harley really slap Mark?" Sophie asked.

"No! Who told you that?"

"We've heard so many different versions of what happened," Sophie said.

"The best was Harley raked Mark's face with her long talon nails, making him need stitches," Kendall added.

Great. We were already in the rumor mill.

"How long did Harley and Mark work together?" Kendall asked. He resumed closing the cart, and Sophie followed along.

I stood at the door to the cart. "Good question. About a decade, I think, or a little longer. Harley started as a barista at Left Coast Grinds when she was in high school and stayed after she graduated. We worked together for a while, but she moved into roasting, so we didn't see each other every shift. But we stayed in touch." I smiled. "Harley actually trained me. I barely knew how to make a cup of drip coffee when I started working with her. But by the time she was done, I could go toe-to-toe with any barista in the world."

"And then the apprentice exceeded the master," Kendall said.

"I wouldn't say that. Harley pulls a mean shot. Get her to make you a latte sometime. You'll wonder how she makes something so amazing with the same milk and coffee beans you use."

"Harley made me a drink once when she was filling in at the cart. I know she's legit."

"Her palate is amazing. I'm no slouch, but she could be one of those experts who taste something and can immediately tell you all of the ingredients. Then she'll follow up with the origin and provenance."

The crowd streamed past us toward the parking lots, and I mentally clicked off day one of the festival. Despite a few hiccups, it'd been a success. Especially since the bands were terrific. The Doyles had done a fantastic job.

Sophie ran the cart's trash to the garbage bins as I double-checked that we'd completed the closing task list. But my thoughts kept wandering to how Sophie and Kendall made a good team when they worked together. Kendall is naturally calm, which is reflected in his customer service skills. His natural equilibrium and easygoing smile stay consistent, even when we're slammed with business. While Harley does better in the back half of the coffee cart or shop, making drinks while Kendall charms the customers. When he works with Sophie, they take turns handling the order window and making drinks.

Harley excelling at crafting drinks in the cart but preferring to let someone else work the order window isn't dissimilar to how we run Ground Rules. We eventually split the corporate accounts, but I handle the initial outreach and contract negotiations. Once she gets to know our customers, Harley generally takes over the brunt of day-to-day customer relations and order fulfillment, becoming a resource with deep knowledge that customers rely on. And she'll move mountains to ensure we can serve their needs, like when a hotel had a kitchen fire. She showed up with filled Ground Carafes for their guests, since no one should face a day after a traumatic night without caffeine. That hotel had expanded, and upped their Ground Rules orders to cover all of their branches.

"Looks like we're done," Kendall said. He glanced around.

"Except for Sophie." She'd left to empty the garbage, leaving behind empty space that should contain recycling, compost, and garbage bins, and a Sophie-sized hole in the cart.

"The problem child is on her way back," Kendall said in a level a few ticks before a shout. I wasn't surprised to see Sophie approaching the cart with the empty bins.

"Is Kendall looking in the mirror again? We can't keep that boy from gazing at his reflection," Sophie said. She brushed past me and said, "Don't forget this!" She rummaged under the counter and emerged with the booth's tablet and cashbox.

After checking the cashbox—which still only had the original cash to make change that we'd started with, since most people pay with cards—I switched the envelope with money into my bag. I tucked the tablet into my bag alongside the one we'd use in the cart. I stashed the cashbox back under the counter. Once, at this cart's first festival, a stray cat had adopted this cubbyhole as his favorite nap spot. The cat went home with me. Well, technically, the cat went home with my fiancé Bax, and I moved in later. But we still call the cubby the "Kaldi spot" in honor of our temporary kitty barista.

After I locked the cart, we were ready to go. So we walked as a group toward the Ground Rules Subaru, which was parked downhill in the first of several lots. The parking spots closest to the carts were designated handicapped, and about half were full.

"Thanks for giving me a ride to my car," Sophie said. While Kendall had tagged along with me earlier today, Sophie had driven herself after a summer school class at her college. So she'd parked in the farthest general lot and hiked in.

"It's so beautiful out here," Sophie said, looking up at the stars dotting the clear night sky. The air was cooling off, reminding me to bring a light hoodie to wear when watching the evening bands. It was starting to feel chilly. But it was gorgeous, and it promised to be a fantastic weekend.

As we walked up to the Ground Rules Subaru, my steps paused. A set of shoes was on the ground next to the driver's side of our ride. A pair of worn gray Chuck Taylors.

And there were ankles, along with the shoes, poking out of a cuff of denim.

Which were connected to legs encased in jeans.

I gasped when I saw his face.

Mark Jeffries.

He was still. Too still.

Sophie screamed. I held out my hand when Kendall tried to rush past me.

"Try not to disturb the scene," I said.

I'd been around way too many homicide investigations, and the thought layered on top of the queasiness that had already invaded my stomach.

Sophie took a few steps away and puked, bumping a dark SUV. A series of loud beeps filled the previously quiet night air.

Such a useful car alarm.

"I'll see if Mark's alive." Kendall sounded grim.

I dropped my hand, and he stepped forward carefully and leaned beside Mark. He carefully touched Mark's throat. Kendall looked back at me and shook his head.

I pulled out my phone and dialed 911.

"What's your emergency?"

"We need police and an ambulance at the festival at the Doyle's Distillery," I said.

Trevor pulled up in a golf cart. "What's going on here?" he asked.

I dropped my phone a few inches and said, "I have nine-one-one on the line. Can you tell them how to find us here at the festival?"

"You should have let me call," Trevor said, but accepted my phone. "This is Trevor Bright, head of security at the festival."

I didn't want to look at Mark, but even when I looked away, I could see the image of his sprawled body in my mind.

This was a nightmare.

But I was awake.

Chapter 3

The first police officers to arrive wore Multnomah County Sheriff's Department uniforms. The festival was east of the Portland city limits but still in Multnomah County, near the "virtual ghost town" of Bridal Veil, Oregon. Once a company mill town, the place has a still-working post office popular with couples about to marry, who like to mail their wedding invitations from town to get the Bridal Veil postmark. The post office and the cemetery are the only things left. Mail, and ghosts. What a legacy.

This part of the county feels like a different world from the city and suburbs despite being a short drive away. But the shift from urban to rural didn't stop crime—because people are people. No matter where they live.

Standing here in the steadily cooling night air made me shiver, but my entire soul felt cold. I texted Bax that I was running late and not to wait up, although I didn't tell him the bad news.

A handful of stragglers rubbernecked as they avoided the crime scene, with a few pausing and asking the uniformed officers on the edge of the tape what was happening.

"Please move along," was the standard response. And if the person didn't move, Trevor harassed them into moving. He had set up his own security perimeter after giving the 911 operator directions on how to find us. The police officers had quickly dismissed him to wait with me, Tierney, and my baristas in our spot on the edge of the parking lot. Tierney and one of the security guards had brought over a couple of chairs. Which Trevor didn't use and instead paced back and forth.

Gotta get your steps in, right?

I wrapped my arms around myself again, wishing I'd brought a hoodie. Maybe if I were warm, I'd feel less cynical.

When two additional police officers—whom I'd bet were detectives from the Multnomah County Sheriff's Office—walked up, I felt guilty for hoping we could leave soon.

Both were dressed in black shirts with olive cargo pants, and for some reason, I remembered the old emerald-green pants with the lighter green shirts the county force used to wear. I'd read about their change in uniform in the local paper years ago. It must've been a slowish news day.

The younger of the two officers was female, in her early thirties, with black hair pulled back in a ponytail, and lightly tanned skin. The second officer was older, probably in his late forties, with graying hair and a world-weary air. Or he was just tired; it was late.

When he saw the detectives, Trevor stopped pacing and walked toward them.

"Please wait with everyone else," one of the police officers barked out. Trevor held up his hands in a calm-down gesture but backed up. He stood at attention, staring at the detectives while they huddled for an intent conversation with one of the police officers who'd first responded.

"This is a nightmare," Tierney said.

I glanced at him. He sat with his elbows on his knees and his hands propping up his forehead.

Would Tierney regret partnering with us? Would he think we brought a Ground Rules curse to his business and festival?

"Should we cancel the festival?" Tierney asked.

"Maybe," I said. "But you don't have to make a decision right now. Maybe wait and see what the police say? Maybe this was just an accident, and Mark fell in the dark and hit his head."

But as I said the words, I doubted it was true. The little voice inside me told me that Mark's death wasn't a fluke. And since Harley had argued with Mark not long before he died, I knew she'd seem like a prime suspect. If, or I suspected once, they dug into Mark and Harley's history, they'd find out the two had clashed multiple times. Which might also help Harley, since if she'd wanted to harm Mark, she would've had incentive to do it earlier. There wasn't a reason for her to explode now.

All of us perked up when the detectives walked over.

"You're Sage Caplin? You made the initial nine-one-one call?" the female detective asked. Her eyes zeroed in on me.

"Yes." My older brother, Jackson, had told me multiple times that when speaking to police, I should only answer what was asked. Refrain from embellishing or providing context, even if I want to be helpful. He'd been annoyed I hadn't already called him to babysit me during this interview.

If the police talked to me again after tonight, I'd call my brother.

"I'm Detective Ortega, and this is Detective Moore," the female detective said. She handed me her business card. "Please come over here and talk to us?"

She led me to a spot about one hundred feet from where I'd been sitting, which felt like a long distance.

Detective Ortega turned and faced me. "Can you walk us through what happened tonight?"

"Sure." I told her about shutting down the coffee cart with my baristas and finding Mark's body. "Ground Rules has a coffee cart set up with the rest of the food vendors, so we're here for the whole festival."

"What were you doing before you shut down the cart?"

I reiterated that I'd been with Tierney in the "pavilion" off to the bar, watching the music.

"You knew who the victim was right away?" Detective Ortega

asked. She held her notebook and pen ready. She reminded me of an eager high-school student ready to impress everyone with her note-taking abilities.

Beside her, the male detective seemed to hold in a yawn. But his gaze didn't waver.

"Yes, I did," I said. Mark's crumpled body flashed through my mind, and my stomach roiled.

"How?" Detective Ortega eyed me like I was sketchy.

"When I was in college, I worked in one of Mark's coffee shops," I said.

"Coffee shops?"

"He owns Left Coast Grinds." I was ready to give them a quick rundown.

"Oh, I know them. I used to go to their shop on Northeast Alberta, but then it closed," Detective Ortega said.

I nodded. I didn't tell the detective that the Left Coast Grinds shop on Northeast Alberta was just one of many closures. I hadn't been keeping track, but I'd heard through the coffee grapevine that Mark had closed or was going to close several of his shops, with the one on Northeast Alberta being the first. But I wasn't sure if the information was accurate.

The male detective made a slight grunting noise. I couldn't tell if he was tired, annoyed, or just done with life.

"Had you stayed in touch with the victim?"

"Not exactly." I'd walked out of my job at Left Coast Grinds mid-shift, saying if I never saw him again, it'd be too soon. "Mark wasn't happy when we started Ground Rules, and he was a proverbial thorn in our sides for a few months. But a cease-and-desist letter from my attorney cooled things off. I hadn't even thought of Mark for months."

"You didn't think highly of him." The detective stared at me again.

"When I worked for Mark, I didn't appreciate how he crept on younger female employees, so I quit. Ask around, and you'll find disgruntled employees who didn't like how he treated them. And you know, I remember how one of his former employees used to get into it with him back when I worked there, and she's working at one of the booths in the craft festival. And he might be up on revenge-porn charges from him trying to blackmail a former employee."

I didn't mention I knew about those potential charges because he'd blackmailed one of his former employees to spy on Ground Rules, presumably intending to sabotage us. But Nina, his former employee, hadn't been able to keep the façade. We'd let her go from Ground Rules, and I also introduced her to a detective with the Portland Police with strong opinions about revenge porn. Last I heard, Nina was pursuing criminal charges, but I hadn't followed up with her.

Hopefully, the police would realize there were more suspects than Harley, because I knew they would look her way. It was inevitable.

Detective Ortega had perked up when I mentioned potential criminal charges, so I told her to contact Detective Leto with the Portland Police Bureau.

"I know her," the detective said. She scribbled the notes down, then glanced at Detective Moore, who nodded at her. He looked faintly bored, but I could tell he'd been paying close attention to the interview. Something told me his air wasn't indifference, even if it could be read that way, and to not underestimate him.

"Do you know why Mark Jeffries was at the festival?" Detective Ortega asked.

"Maybe he wanted to hear the music? It turns out Mark agreed to sublet half of a booth to sell a new coffee product he'd developed, which surprised the festival organizers, since they'd turned down his original vendor application, and never approved his addition. You could talk to Dulcie at Dulcinea Chocolates to see how that came about."

"Did that make you angry? You're here as the coffee vendor, right?" Detective Ortega asked.

"If I had to describe how I felt about it, I wouldn't have said angry, because we're selling drinks on site. While Mark had products for home use. But yes, it was awkward. I just planned to ignore him, since the weekend should be busy. I decided to worry about my coffee cart and let everything else sort itself out." Technically, his booth conflicted with our combined coffee and tea booth, but that hadn't worried me.

Although I hadn't expected things to sort out the way everything had played out. I'd been expecting a farce, not a tragedy.

"You can leave now. We'll let you know if we have any other questions," Detective Ortega said.

As I walked away, my thoughts were in turmoil. If Mark had died a few years ago, when he was in the prime position in Portland, his death would've created a vacuum at the top of the coffee grounds. But his brand had been faltering for a while, and Ground Rules had steadily carved out our niche fueled by the same sort of good reviews and brand loyalty that had propped up Left Coast Grinds on their way up.

Given Harley's history with Mark, she had to be a suspect. Even if there was no way she would harm Mark.

Should I have mentioned Mark and Harley's very public arguments today? Would the detectives think not mentioning it was suspicious, like I knew Harley had something to hide?

Trevor paced on the edge of the police line while the detectives called Sophie over. Tierney was typing on his phone, while Kendall raised his eyebrows at me.

I glanced at the police officer standing with us, then back at Kendall. I sat down in the camp chair. While I'd love to leave, the car I'd driven here was part of the crime scene, so Sophie had offered to give Kendall and me rides home.

We sat silently, and eventually, Sophie came back. The police interviewed Kendall. Trevor continued to pace, while Tierney furiously texted.

Tierney glanced at me. "Shay's worried about the liability of holding a festival when someone died in the parking lot."

"Maybe talk with your lawyer?" I'd once looked up deaths at music festivals, and it wasn't as uncommon as I'd hoped, and those festivals were still going strong. But the deaths weren't caused by the festival directly. Just like how Mark's death most likely wasn't caused by the festival itself, although he wouldn't have had a reason to be here, on the Doyle's Oregon Whiskey grounds, without it.

"This is a nightmare." Tierney turned back to his phone.

Sympathy coursed through me. Tierney wouldn't want his fledgling business and new festival to be associated with murder any more than I wished Ground Rules to be known as the wrong kind of killer coffee. Hopefully, no one would make a graph of the murder rate in Portland versus the number of bodies I've found.

Maybe I was the problem. Why was murder attracted to my presence? Or was I just unlucky?

Kendall returned, and the police called Tierney over, so we nodded goodbye as he followed the female detective.

"I'll text if we cancel the festival," he called over his shoulder. "If that happens, I'll contact everyone before we're scheduled to open."

"Let me know if I can help," I said, then turned to my employees.

Finally, my baristas and I were free and started walking to Sophie's car.

"I can't believe the police haven't interviewed me yet," Trevor muttered as we walked past.

Even though I was tempted, I didn't tell Trevor to chill out; he'd get his chance to talk to the police.

Something told me they'd want to talk to all of us multiple times.

And maybe I'd be able to block out the image of Mark from my brain someday. But I suspected I'd see his body in my nightmares. A reassuring small part of me said I'd be more worried if the sight of a dead body didn't freak me out.

If Tierney canceled the festival, it would be painful for the makers' fair booths, which had all signed on to join us, hoping for a vibrant weekend of sales in the sunshine.

If the festival was canceled, I wouldn't blame Tierney for severing our business deal. Since it felt like, somehow, Ground Rules was at fault for Mark's death. Even if none of us had committed the actual murder. Something told me our presence drew him here, leading to his demise.

Even if we found the murderer, I knew I'd always feel a sliver of guilt.

If the murderer went free, that sliver would grow into a wedge that would bother me forever.

Chapter 4

"Have either of you heard from Harley?" I asked. We walked away from the crime scene, hiking to the parking lot Sophie had used, which was four whole lots away.

"I haven't seen her since this afternoon, and she didn't respond to my text," Kendall said.

"Ditto." Sophie's tone was grim. "What's the story between Mark and Harley, exactly?"

We walked along the middle gravel parking area, which was empty, save for a late-model Honda parked smack-dab in the middle of the lot. I glanced around; no one was in sight. "You know how Harley used to work at Left Coast Grinds? She started as a barista and eventually convinced Mark to let her become a trainee roaster. She eventually became his head roaster."

"Because she's that awesome," Kendall said.

"Exactly. And to give him his full credit, Mark is—Mark *was*—a decent roaster himself. But he recognized that Harley was something special. Someone greater to be developed. It seemed like a good fit for a few years, with Harley taking on more responsibility in the roastery, and their reputation soared alongside the increase in quality. But then Mark made a decision Harley couldn't live with, and their relationship crumbled." I paused. Anger for the way Harley had been treated coursed through me, causing my hands to clench.

"You can't leave us hanging," Kendall said.

"Looking back, the final straw for Harley was so on brand for Mark," I said. "He entered some of her work in the regional coffee championship under the Left Coast Grinds label, which was fair, since she'd roasted them for Mark's company. Including a special roast she'd developed for the competition. But then Harley's special roast took first place."

"Not a surprise."

From the way Kendall nodded, he agreed with Sophie.

"But when Mark accepted the award on behalf of Left Coast Grinds, he took all of the credit. He didn't even mention Harley. And he doubled down in interviews afterward. He even posted about the win and credited himself on the Left Coast Grinds website. He claimed responsibility. That it was his personal creation. His inspiration and hard work."

"That's rude."

Kendall shook his head. "If Harley had punched Mark in front of the whole crowd then, no one would've blamed her."

"Not so fast," I said. "Before the competition, Harley told some of the other roasters that she'd roasted the beans Left Coast Grinds was entering. But when Mark took the credit, some of the other roasters accused Harley of lying and were jerks about it. But others supported her. So Harley quit Left Coast Grinds."

"Please tell me she flounced out in style."

"Legend has it she told Mark good luck defending his title without her. And Mark didn't even place at the championship, although, to be fair, the new roaster that took first was awesome, and I'm so sad they were only in town for two years before moving on."

"So what'd Harley do then? Did one of the supportive coffee companies hire her?" Sophie asked.

"She took a job as a barista at a chain coffee shop," I said.

Sophie gasped, mostly joking, like I knew she would. "Blasphemy."

I took a deep breath and let it out. "Then, when I was out with Harley and some friends, I joked that we should start a coffee business. I was at loose ends, 'cause I'd just gotten home after volunteering overseas for a year, and I was debating my next steps. Harley took me seriously, and I realized it could work if we partnered. So we set up Ground Rules, worked out a business plan, and found an investor—my uncle—since neither of us had the capital to launch on our own. He agreed to invest, and six months later, we launched."

"This is me," Sophie said. She stopped by an older sedan with a music-note bumper sticker on the back. It was the only car left in the makeshift parking lot closest to the road. The night sky above us was brilliant with stars, which promised that tomorrow would be a clear, beautiful day, despite the horrors of this evening.

After a brief "no, you" discussion with Kendall, I ended up in the front passenger seat, and he sprawled in the back.

"How did Mark react when you started Ground Rules?" Sophie asked. She carefully reversed into the empty parking lot.

Was she always this careful, or was she paranoid having her boss next to her?

Memories slid through my mind. "Mark started showing up not long after we launched, and acted like we were little kids playing coffee shop. He was clearly concerned we'd be competition."

"Does he show up at all of the grand openings of roasters around town, glowering?" Kendall asked from the back.

Kendall said "does." It was hard to think of Mark in past tense now. That he wouldn't show up at the Rail Yard again and glower at the coffee cart (although to give him credit, he'd respected the cease-and-desist I'd sent him and had seemed to avoid our coffee cart.) It was hard to believe I wouldn't randomly bump into him again, or see him at industry events.

"Did he act like he would cast a spell on them so they'd fail?" Sophie said.

"You know, I remember Mark being buddy-buddy with Flynn of the Clinton Street Roasters when they launched. He was all 'let

me know if you need any help' with them. So maybe he only hated
us," I said. Flynn was nice, and his focus was specific. He wasn't looking to expand; he just ran a beloved neighborhood coffeehouse with
made-to-order donuts served alongside micro-roasts of single-origin
coffees.

"You have a history with Mark, too, right?" the peanut gallery
asked from the back seat.

"Yes, as I mentioned, Harley and I met when she trained me as a
barista at Left Coast Grinds. It seemed like the perfect job in my student days."

"I thought you worked at your uncle's bar as an undergrad?" Sophie asked.

Which was a good question; I'd found Sophie a part-time job
barbacking at my uncle's bar, the Tav, to help her make ends meet
when her free housing had fallen through when she moved to Portland. She had been struggling to make ends meet working for
Ground Rules part-time while also starting her graduate program.
Somehow, she'd managed to work both jobs and attend school.

"I did work at the Tav, doing the same job you do." I'd started
working at the Tav as a young-looking senior in college, with quite a
few patrons asking if I was still in high school. Thankfully, while I
still looked young for my age, no one questioned if I was old enough
to drive anymore.

"Actually, I've started picking up some bartending shifts," Sophie
said. She sounded proud.

"Oh, that's awesome! But I worked for Mark before I started at
the Tav. I walked out of a job at Left Coast Grinds when Mark
made a pass at me." The feeling of revulsion had shocked me at the
time. I'd felt hesitant to work at the Tav, even if my beloved cousin
Miles had been the manager for years. But it'd been a wonderful
place to work, with supportive coworkers and management that
had worried about us as people. My experience with Mark and then
the Tav helped me develop my theory for how to treat my Ground
Rules employees.

"You know, my friend Naomi used to work for Left Coast Grinds. She just left, and still talks highly of Mark," Kendall said.

"Dude, read the room," Sophie said. "Naomi not complaining doesn't mean Mark didn't hit on Sage."

"That's not what I'm saying. I'm just curious what Mark's like now. Did he learn his lesson, or was he still slimy?"

"You mean like when he sent someone in to spy on us?" Sophie said.

"Whoa, let's take a moment to take a few deep breaths," I said.

"I didn't mean to offend you, Sophie," Kendall said. "I just meant my friend might have insight into the current state of Left Coast Grinds. Since she works elsewhere, she might be willing to be honest."

"I'm sorry for snapping. I'm just tired," Sophie said.

We quieted down, and I wondered why, exactly, Mark had had it in for us. Was it just because Harley had rage-quit? Had he enjoyed hovering over the background of our lives like a *Scooby-Doo* villain, muttering he would have gotten away with it if it hadn't been for us meddling kids?

Or had we started Ground Rules at the same time his business began to decline, and instead of looking deeply at why, it was easier to get angry with us? Especially since losing Harley as a roaster had to have hurt.

As Sophie exited from I-84 and headed toward the house Kendall rented in Northeast Portland with four of his closest friends, I sent out a few messages to former coworkers from my Left Coast Grinds days. One of them, Austen, had run their flagship café in downtown Portland until about a year ago when it'd closed. The LCG official statement blamed a host of urban issues for why they'd closed and said they were focusing on their neighborhood stores. But I'd heard rumors that LCG was in financial trouble. One rumor claimed their wholesale accounts had lost significant market share, including a national one. Losing shelf space in retailers is always painful, and if Mark had counted on the sales forecast when setting his budget, it could be ruinous.

Although the possibility of the Left Coast Grounds flagship store struggling in downtown in a post-Covid world with more employees working from home and higher than pre-pandemic office vacancy rates felt authentic.

Austen had moved on to a new café in St. Helens, a small town that wasn't too far of a drive from Portland on the Columbia River but felt like a world away.

Ramona, the daughter of a mother who'd been obsessed with Oregon's own Beverly Cleary, had worked in the roastery side of the business with Harley. She'd overlapped with me as a barista from my college days. From a quick glance at her social media, Ramona might still be with Left Coast Grinds. If she'd left, there was no sign. But her postings were infrequent, and not everyone documents every step of their life online. So I sent her a message asking her to call me.

Then, I took a deep breath and texted one of my former employees. Nina was the first Ground Rules hire I'd utterly failed with. I'd had another barista leave when he was accepted to grad school out of state, and he knew the Ground Rules door was open in the future. We'd celebrated his leaving with cupcakes, and a couple of regulars had banded together and bought him a gift card for school supplies.

When I hired her, Nina had looked fantastic on paper, with excellent experience and references. She'd backed it up with the ability to craft a mean cappuccino.

But she'd turned out to be an unwilling spy for Mark Jeffries. He'd been blackmailing her with the sort of intimate videos no one wants to be forced to share, and she and Mark had filmed them when Nina was already dating her then-fiancé, now husband. When it all came to light, I'd introduced Nina to a youngish female detective with the Portland Police Department who'd taken the revenge porn-slash-blackmailing allegation seriously. But I hadn't heard anything since.

Was Mark facing deserved criminal charges? Was Nina the only person he'd blackmailed? Or were there more people out there who'd served as Mark's unwilling dupes?

After I sent the text, I pulled up Nina's social media.

Darn. Set to private, and if we'd even been social media friends, she'd dropped me. Going private was a smart move on her behalf, but I wondered what was happening in her life.

And hey, she hadn't blocked me, so hopefully she'd respond to my text.

"Thanks for the ride. I'll see you in the morning," Kendall said as he climbed out of Sophie's car.

And then there were two.

"I'll see you tomorrow at ten," I said, as Sophie pulled up to the house I share with Bax in Southeast Portland. She'd volunteered to drive Kendall and me back to the festival tomorrow, since the Ground Rules Subaru was part of a crime scene. The thought of the car surrounded by crime-scene tape still didn't quite feel real, although the impact of Mark's death was feeling more painful to me by the second.

"See you tomorrow." She waved and then waited as I walked up the walkway, clearly waiting until I was inside to leave, even if she clearly wanted to go home. I owed Sophie something as a thank-you. The front porch light glowed like a beacon.

And I wished the festival were an easy bike ride away. My morning bike commutes always help me focus and pull on my Ground Rules persona, like a favorite sweater that sometimes feels like a suit of armor.

Sophie zoomed off when I opened the door. The house was quiet as I stepped inside, but it was long after Niko's bedtime.

Bax had bought the bungalow long before he'd met me. When I moved in, he carved out space for me, including a shelf in the closet in the room we use as a joint home office. I headed for it.

Kaldi appeared out of nowhere with a chirp and followed alongside me. Evidently, my project fit in with his busy cat schedule.

I pulled a bin out of the closet, hoping this was what I was looking for and that I wouldn't have to troll through my brother's basement looking for a box I'd left behind. I sat on the area rug in the middle of the room, and Kaldi promptly jumped in my lap. I popped the top of the box off.

Score. I pulled out a collection of photos from my college days. I sorted through them, noting the time I'd try rocking a dyed-black pixie cut, which had made me slightly vampirish. I'd awkwardly grown it out, cut out the black, and never dyed my hair again, even though I wondered how I'd look as a redhead instead of my natural light blond.

"Was that for Halloween?" Bax asked, making me jump.

Kaldi let out an annoyed "mer," chastising me for jostling him. He settled back down on my leg.

"You scared me," I said. "If you keep doing that, you'll need to wear a bell."

Bax sat down next to me and put his arm around my shoulder. He watched as I sorted through the pictures.

"And you have to do this now because?" Bax finally asked.

I finally found the batch of photos I'd been looking for. "Because of this."

Harley and college-aged me, wearing matching Left Coast Grinds aprons and holding espresso shots with our pinkies out. One of me pulling a shot of espresso with one of my old coworkers, a blur in the background. The photo had been part of the profile of Left Coast Grinds by a local magazine that focused on human interest and soft news. My photographer friend Erin had been interning at the magazine, so she'd made copies of the photos for me.

Erin had taken some of the photos, and all of them, including a group shot from the café with Mark Jeffries in the center, like a king surrounded by his serfs, were perfectly balanced. Then I uncovered an issue of the magazine, and my eyes scanned the cover article.

Portland's Left Coast Grinds Serves a Cup Above the Rest.

Clearly, hard-hitting journalism. But it was a lovely article, full of hope for the future.

"This is relevant now, why? Was Mark annoying you at the festival?" Bax asked.

"Mark's dead," I said. The words felt strange on my lips. I realized if I added the word "baby" to the statement, I could almost quote *Pulp Fiction*.

I must be more tired than I thought.

"For real?"

"Sophie, Kendall, and I found his body when we left the festival." The words felt stark in this otherwise cozy room.

"Was it an accident, or . . ." Bax's voice trailed off.

"I believe the correct phrase right now is suspicious death. But yes, it looked murder-y."

"Are you okay?" He rubbed my shoulder, while Kaldi made a few biscuits on my thigh in solidarity.

"Join Ground Rules, and in addition to brewing world-class coffee, you can stumble over bodies." We could rework our slogan to attract lovers of macabre.

"Maybe I shouldn't invite you to join at the comic-con booth," Bax said. He nudged me, letting me know he was joking. I leaned into him.

"Hopefully, no one dies on our honeymoon," I said.

"It's not your fault, even if it feels horribly unlucky," Bax said. He nodded at the photos. "So is this you reminiscing?"

"I just wonder why his death happened now. What led to it? Maybe the answers are in the past."

"Or maybe he made someone angry tonight, and the past is just a distraction from thinking about what happened," Bax said.

I winced. Like Harley. Mark had picked several public arguments with her. Even if those arguments were rooted in the past, they were conflict from the present.

"C'mon, this will all look better in the morning." Bax stood up, then held out his hand and, once I'd dislodged Kaldi, pulled me up. We headed upstairs, and he went back to bed.

Before I brushed my teeth, I realized there was someone else I needed to contact.

My Uncle Jimmy—technically great-uncle—isn't a huge fan of

texting but has accepted it's part of modern life. So, I sent him a quick recap of the day.

His response was almost immediate.

You're okay?

I'm fine. I still need to touch base with Harley.

Keep me posted. And talk to your brother.

Of course, he'd want me to loop Jackson in. But it was a good idea, so I texted my brother with the same summary I'd sent my uncle, then sent it to my father. Hopefully I didn't wake any of them up.

Then, I decided it was time to call it a day and head to bed.

Tomorrow would be here soon enough.

And I knew it'd be a scorcher in more ways than simply the weather.

Chapter 5

My phone alarm went off way too early for a Saturday. Beside me, Bax groaned, even though I turned my alarm off as quickly as possible.

"Rise and grind!" I said. My voice was way too chirpy to my own ears. Given the way Bax covered his ears, he agreed.

Kaldi meowed at me and moved from my stomach to perch on Bax's shoulder, letting his tail fall across Bax's nose. I held in a laugh as I crawled out of bed. Bax and Niko planned to join me at the festival later today. But I was heading to the roastery to meet Sophie and Kendall to stock Sophie's car with things we might need at the cart, like extra cups, since the Ground Rules Subaru, as far as I knew, was still part of a crime scene. No one had texted me otherwise.

As I got ready, last night's events kept flashing through my brain. But no matter how I tried, I couldn't make the different pieces fit into a logical pattern.

I knew I should leave the investigating to the police, but I didn't want the specter of Mark's death hovering over us, and especially around Harley. It was inevitable that the police would hear about their arguments.

As I ate a quick breakfast, I paused. There were security cameras on the festival grounds, and the influencer I'd noticed seemed to be filming nonstop. There were probably hundreds of videos taken last night.

Maybe, if I could get ahold of enough video or photos, I could create a timeline of Mark's movements to prove no one at Ground Rules caused his death. I doubted his death was captured on any social media feeds, or else someone would've called for help.

Hopefully, someone hadn't watched Mark's murder without doing something, like calling 911 if they couldn't intervene. I've only read a little bit about the Bystander Effect, mostly in my Psychology 101 class ages ago as an undergraduate, which says the bigger the crowd, the less likely one person is to call 911, because they assume someone else will call. The original example of Kitty Genovese, who was murdered in New York City in 1964, is now considered to be a flawed example of the Bystander Effect with a lot of inaccurate data, which makes it slightly reassuring that multiple people didn't ignore the twenty-eight-year-old's pleas for help at three o'clock in the morning. But a podcast I listened to said that in recent experiments, people taking an exam in a room slowly filling with smoke were likely to notify an instructor or other authority figure if they were alone, but were more likely to ignore the smoke if there were other students in the room. Only ten percent of the people in a group in the study reported the smoke. I'd like to believe I'd be one of the ten percent. That I wouldn't assume someone else would step in during an accident, turning an event into a tragedy. But maybe I haven't been tested.

And I couldn't believe multiple people had watched Mark be murdered and ignored it. But if Mark had died while the bands played, maybe nobody would have heard the struggle. If he struggled.

But that didn't feel right. Had anyone seen Mark's body in the parking lot and not called for help? How long had his body lay on the ground by my company car? Had his murder happened in the narrow window of time after the festival grounds cleared out, but before my baristas and I had finished closing the cart?

Most people at the festival had been watching the bands after the craft fair portion had closed down, followed later by the food carts, who had stayed open, and busy, until the final bands started.

Had any of the booth owners been hanging out in the craft area? A few booths had brought tents with zippered fronts that could be opened during the day and closed at night, and others had brought various types of ways to secure their merchandise overnight. For our combined coffee-and-tea booth, we'd brought several locking bins to store expensive products in overnight with anything we'd hate to lose, like the tablet we used for purchases; these would be locked inside the coffee cart once the booth closed, along with the cashbox, and I'd take them home with me. If anyone paid with cash—a rarity these days, with more and more of our customers paying with their phones versus breaking out their credit or debit cards—I'd deposit it into our corporate bank account on the way home.

My first steps were clear. Sometime today, I'd work on getting as much footage as possible. I bet I could sweet-talk Tierney into providing the festival's security recordings.

One question kept popping up in my head: why had Mark been next to the Ground Rules Subaru? Had he snuck back on site to key our car? Was it just a chance? Or did he have some other reason?

Or maybe Mark never left the festival. How far had security escorted him off the property? Just to the gates to the music area? Or all the way off? Had they escorted him to his car and watched him drive off?

I'd need to find a way to chat with Trevor about how the security staff had handled Mark.

The roastery felt normal. Right. The scent of coffee beans filled the air as I parked my bike in its usual spot by the back door. I double-checked that the door behind me was locked, and I heard a few people walking to the gym in the back of the building.

Life goes on.

The kitchen was spotless, with just a couple of mugs on the drying rack, which I put away before pulling out a couple of the sturdy square totes we use when transporting extra supplies to the carts. The official Ground Rules car was stocked with extra cups, sugar packets, bags of coffee beans, nondairy milk, and everything else we could possibly need.

Hopefully, we'd regain access to the car today. For now, I filled the totes with a smaller amount of the same supplies I'd packed yesterday. If we ran out, I'd need to head to the grocery wholesaler for everything except coffee beans.

Thankfully, we had enough of our standards, like Puddle Jumper, a medium roast with notes of dark berries and spiced dates that we use as our house coffee, and our espresso roast, Twelve Bridge Racer. Plus, a few extra bags of our Concrete Blonde, a light roast building its own following, and a mix of single-origin options, all neatly bagged and ready for sale.

Sophie showed up promptly at ten, with Kendall in tow. The three of us carried the tote bags to Sophie's car in one trip.

"Sure you can handle all of those heavy bags?" Sophie asked Kendall, who was carrying one bag in each hand while Sophie had six.

Kendall curled the bag as if he were lifting weights in a gym. "I think I got it."

Considering he was carrying quarts of nondairy milk, the bags were probably enough weight for a solid set of bicep curls.

We dropped by the bakery to pick out our special festival order for the cart and had barely started driving to the gorge when Sophie said, "Can we talk?"

Uh-oh. "Is everything all right?" I glanced at my barista, whose eyes carefully scanned the streets around us as she stopped at a red light.

"Kendall and I talked earlier, and we want to help."

"Help work the festival? You've already scheduled." They'd called dibs on the long weekend in the gorge.

Sophie glanced over at me and smiled, then faced the road again. "Help figure out what happened, so Harley doesn't get in trouble."

"We know you're going to get involved in the investigation. Considering the best prediction of future behavior is past performance in a similar situation and all," Kendall said from the back seat.

"Just because I've solved a few suspicious deaths doesn't mean I'll get involved . . ." I couldn't even finish the sentence.

"The first festival I worked at with you involved you solving a double murder over the course of a long weekend. We have faith in you," Kendall said.

"And we can help you if you tell us how," Sophie added.

They believed in me, and I felt my face blush. "I'm not going to do anything stupid, but I have a few ideas and people I can talk to. We can at least throw up enough questions so it will be obvious Harley isn't the only person who had issues with Mark."

"And meanwhile, how can we help?"

I thought for a moment. "Do your jobs well so I can leave the business in both of your capable hands and investigate. It will be useful if both of you listen carefully to any comments about Mark. People might talk about what happened. Most of the gossip will be trash, but there could be a few useful kernels amidst the rumors."

"I can be a verbal trash panda," Kendall said. "I love gossip."

I needed to make one point. "But if you need help, and I'm off somewhere, don't be afraid to ask me to come back. Ground Rules, and you, have to be my priority." Ground Rules came first.

"If Harley is arrested for murder, that affects all of us, plus Ground Rules," Sophie said. "And I don't want to see Harley in jail for something she didn't do. She'd hate jail. You'd do better. You'd subtly have the whole prison following your orders in no time—"

"You'd be a world-class prison boss."

"—But Harley . . ."

"Wouldn't cope, to put it mildly," Kendall said.

I wasn't quite sure how to react to my baristas claiming I'd make a world-class prison boss, to quote Kendall. But their faith in me made me feel a bit warm inside.

"Do you know where you're going to start investigating?"

Trying to sweet-talk security footage from Trevor? Or chatting with one of the Left Coast Grinds's former employees I knew? I needed to decide, but I settled for saying, "I sent out a few messages to people I know who work with Mark, and hopefully, I'll start hearing back soon."

"My ex-girlfriend—the one I mentioned last night—worked for Left Coast Grinds until a few weeks ago. I checked in with her, and she's happy to chat," Kendall said. "She's cool."

"Your ex? The one with the obsession with pickling everything?" I asked. Kendall had said friend last night, not ex-girlfriend.

"Hey, her watermelon refrigerator pickles were addictive. And I miss her kombucha," Kendall said.

"You didn't tell me you broke up with Naomi," Sophie said.

"She broke up with me," Kendall muttered. I sensed a story there but refrained from poking at it for now.

Sophie turned into the driveway for the festival. The first lots were empty, and she pulled into the spot in the same lot as the Ground Rules Subaru, which was still surrounded by yellow police tape. A golf cart idling just outside of the tape started rolling our way.

The golf cart pulled up beside us, and Trevor, the driver, motioned for Sophie to roll down her window.

"The festival isn't open yet. You'll need to leave," Trevor said.

"We're here to open the coffee cart!" Sophie's tone was overly chipper. You had to know her to hear the sarcasm layered inside.

Or maybe you didn't, as Trevor's eyebrows tightened. "Your car isn't on the official list."

I leaned over to look Trevor in the eyes. "Do you want me to text Tierney?"

"No." Trevor rolled away.

"Weirdo," Sophie muttered.

After we exited the car and started walking toward the coffee cart, Sophie handed me a Newfoundland Growlers keychain with a single key on it. "That's my spare, so please don't lose it. But this way, you can get the extra supplies from the car without me."

"So take it for a joyride, check." I tucked the key into a pocket inside my bag.

"If you do, just bring me back a burrito."

I handed Sophie the cashbox, tablet, and spare charger for the booth we were sharing with Stonefield Beach Tea. "Let us know if you need any help from us to set up the booth."

Sophie smiled. "I should be fine getting our half set up. I can't speak for Hannah."

"Harley should be here soon, as well." Harley was scheduled to work the closing shift at the cart, but if she stuck with the plan she'd told me yesterday, she'd show up sooner rather than later to help out at the booth. Although she'd told me her schedule before her fights with Mark.

And she hadn't responded to my texts, which worried me.

I let go of my worries and worked with Kendall to set up the coffee cart for the day.

I'd let my worries handle themselves, at least for now.

Chapter 6

The first customer of the day caused an exasperated smile to cross my face.

Brown hair. Usual RBF, except in Jackson's case, the acronym stands for Resting Brother Face. My older brother, and sometimes my lawyer—even though on the rare occasion he does anything related to criminal law—he represented children being adjudicated in juvenile court versus adults facing sentences in the big house.

And he has a default annoyed face, regardless of how he feels inside.

As Kendall made his cappuccino, I stepped out of the cart.

"You're already here?" I said.

"It sounds like you need me around if the police question you."

Never speak to the police without a lawyer was Jackson's number-one rule for me. I nodded.

"And you know, Bax and I are going to dominate the cornhole tournament." One thing I hadn't known when I started dating Bax was that he and my brother would develop a bromance that, once in a while, left me standing outside, peeking in.

"No Piper today?" I asked, referring to Jackson's girlfriend.

"She's going to try to swing by later, but she had to go into the office, and she has a red-eye flight tonight."

Piper is a US Attorney based in the local office, so I knew not to ask for specifics of what she was working on if Jackson didn't offer it.

"I haven't seen the police around yet today, although I'm sure they're going to show up." I rubbed the toe of my sneaker against the cart's floor.

"But you're worried about something."

I didn't want to say the words, but they spilled out anyway. "I haven't heard from Harley. I texted her last night and this morning, and nothing."

"Do you think something happened to her, too?"

Now, instead of wondering if Harley was avoiding talking to me because she knew something about Mark's death, I had a new worry: "I hadn't even thought of that. Is there someone gunning for Portland coffee roasters?" But as I spoke, I knew I was wrong. The real answer would be much more mundane versus someone systematically searching out local coffee figures to assassinate.

"So you're afraid she did it?" my brother asked.

I glanced at Jackson. "If Harley had wanted to kill Mark, she would've done it years ago when she quit Left Coast Grinds in a huff. But Harley's not violent."

"Anyone can snap under duress." From the grimness in my brother's voice, I could tell he was thinking of a few real people he'd dealt with, real families that had been torn apart.

"That's true."

I handed Jackson his cappuccino, and went back into the cart as he wandered away when a few more customers walked up on a caffeine hunt. But I knew I'd see him again. And not just because I'd already agreed to watch his and Bax's cornhole matches. He'd check in again, fueled by worry and the need for an afternoon pick-me-up.

Trevor, the security guard, swaggered up to the order window. He glanced at the Ground Rules menu, then into the cart, and tapped something in his phone.

"You in the market for coffee?" I asked.

"Ugh, I don't do stimulants. They mess with my focus," Trevor said. "And my body is a temple. It doesn't need drugs."

"There are proven health benefits with a moderate intake of caffeine and coffee," I said. The words were almost automatic, and I was telling the truth. But moderation was one of the keywords.

"Golden milk is as close as I get," Trevor said.

"We offer that sometimes," I said. I'd played around with making a syrup of turmeric, cinnamon, and a dash of black pepper, lightly sweetened with maple syrup, as a special in the shop, that we'd blend with milk, although it was easier to just steam the ingredients together.

Tierney walked up. "Hey, can I get a large coffee? I'm exhausted. I didn't get to sleep until three, and I was sadly up by seven. It's not like I expected to get a full eight hours during the festival, but this is not how I expected everything to kick off."

I knew the unspoken: Mark's death could cause a whole host of problems for the Doyle brothers and the festival, the sort of issues that could sink their entire business.

"Yes, you can have the largest-size coffee we have, and I can even add an espresso shot to it if you can do something for me," I said.

Tierney laughed. "What?"

I glanced at Trevor, who watched us intently, like he'd be graded on this later. His gaze swiveled back to his boss. "Can I get copies of the security footage from last night? Starting with your opening speech, until the body was found?"

"You're in your Trixie Belden mode? Did you bring an extra-large magnifying glass?" Tierney asked.

"Trixie what?" Trevor said.

"Did Trixie Belden even carry a magnifying glass? For the record, I'm just curious. Plus, if Ground Rules as a company somehow gets dragged in legally, it'll be good for our attorneys to have copies if we face anything, liabilities-wise. Our name is prominently listed in the event marketing."

"This isn't your property. No one would have a reason to sue you," Trevor said. His condescending tone made me want to dump a glass of evil caffeinated iced coffee over his head.

I stared directly at Trevor. "If you're included in a lawsuit, even when you shouldn't have been, you know you still need to hire a lawyer to get yourself clear, right? Even stupid and pointless lawsuits can be expensive. And someone died."

He blinked and looked away first.

"We can get you copies, no problem," Tierney said. "Trevor, please ensure Sage gets all of the footage from last night from every camera. Get it to her by the end of today."

"But then she'll know where all the cameras are, and my security setup will be for nothing." Trevor crossed his arms over his chest.

"You heard me," Tierney said. He turned back to me. "And can I get a muffin?"

"Marionberry or carrot-cake surprise?"

"Poison," Trevor muttered.

"What's the surprise in the carrot cake?" Tierney asked.

"A sweetened cream-cheese center. It's delish." It was perfect, adding a not-too-sweet element to a muffin that tasted enough like carrot cake to feel decadent.

"Sold." Tierney turned to Trevor. "Don't you have somewhere to be?"

"I can't believe you're going to eat that much white flour," Trevor said before sloping off.

"At least the muffins contain a decent amount of shredded carrots," I said, but Trevor didn't acknowledge me. I swiveled my gaze back to Tierney, and he must've gathered the direction of my thoughts.

"Trevor's actually good at his job, even if he can be obnoxious," Tierney said. "He's very proactive. Unbelievably dedicated. The everyday security system he implemented when we're not in the middle of events really is thoughtful, and he went all out for the festival."

I didn't agree that Trevor seemed obnoxious, because that would have been stating the obvious. But I did ask, "Do you have any female security guards this weekend?"

Tierney paused. "No. I don't think I've seen any on his company's staff list."

"You might want to think about that."

"Point taken. Good luck solving the case. All of our fates might rest on you." Tierney saluted me with his coffee. He split, carrying his caffeine and muffin breakfast, heading toward the distillery.

His words weren't fully a joke, although he hadn't been entirely serious, either. But there was a kernel of truth in his words. If left unsolved, Mark's death would forever follow us around, like a ghost we wanted to exorcise, but couldn't.

I'd had enough of Mark Jeffries in my life and refused to let him sink my future.

A while later, something in my chest relaxed.

Harley walked up, wearing a red T-shirt instead of the teal Ground Rules shirt the rest of our employees, including me, were wearing. Her hair was pulled back into a ponytail. If she wasn't wearing the same navy corduroy shorts as yesterday, she has an identical pair, which I wouldn't put past her. She knows what she likes.

I hopped out of the cart, leaving Kendall to help the two women walking up.

"You didn't respond to my texts." Or calls.

"Oh, my phone's battery died. I really need a new phone. My current battery life is terrible." Harley glanced around. "So, how's the cart? The festival looks busier than I thought it would this early."

"You don't know?" I said.

She crinkled her eyebrows. "Know what?"

"Come over here."

I led Harley to the shade next to the barn, away from the growing festival crowd. I handed her my spare phone block. "Charge your phone. When you turn it on, you're going to have a ton of missed texts and calls. We've been worried about you," I said. I took a deep breath to steady myself, then let it out and said, "Mark Jeffries was murdered last night."

"Mark . . . what?" She paused as she plugged her phone into the charger.

"Mark was murdered. Here at the festival. Next to the Ground Rules Subaru, to be specific."

Harley turned her hands palm side up. "Are you pranking me?"

"No, he's really dead, and—"

"How did he—" Harley started to say.

"—the police will want to talk to you," I said.

"Why me?" The pitch of Harley's voice went up to a level just below screechy.

"Because of the highly public argument the two of you had yesterday. The one that led to Mark being kicked out of the festival. Plus the earlier argument. I'm sure I'm not the only one who noticed it."

Harley closed her eyes.

"What did you do last night after we left the stage? Did you see Mark again?"

She shook her head, causing her ponytail to brush back and forth. "I left here and went to my sister's house in Hood River. We stayed up late talking. She was trying to talk me down from the ledge. Mark made me so angry."

Harley's the youngest of three, and her older sisters are awesome. If I remember correctly, her oldest sister worked as an ER physician in Hood River, a charming town of about 8,000, about thirty-five miles east of us on the Columbia River, known as the windsurfing capital of the world.

"I can't believe I let Mark rankle me the way he did. I thought I was over him being able to trigger me like that. But of course, he knew what buttons to push," Harley said.

Harley's phone beeped as a flood of text messages were delivered.

"You're not joking."

"No."

"This isn't a bad dream." She looked at her phone. "I'm guessing these voicemails are the police."

"The police, but also Kendall, Sophie, and me."

Harley covered her eyes with her hand. "I'm going to call my other sister—"

"The attorney?" One thing Harley and I have in common: being the younger siblings of accomplished older siblings who'd excelled at school. Her sister worked in real estate law, but if she was anything like Jackson, she'd known people in other specialties.

"Yeah."

"Do that."

Harley looked at her phone again. "I'm going to do that now. Let me know if I can do anything to help out with Ground Rules when I'm done."

"Let me know if you can think of any reason why someone would kill Mark," I said.

"You mean other than everyone he ever talked to?" she said. Harley looked around, presumably looking for a calm spot to call. She slipped an earbud into her ear.

But her eyes widened, and she froze in place.

"Sage Caplin? We'd like to speak to you again," a female voice said.

I turned. Detective Ortega, followed by her slouching shadow. His name clicked into place. Detective Moore.

Detective Ortega eyed Harley. "Is this your business partner, Harley Yamazaki?" she asked.

"I'm Harley." My business partner's voice sounded uncertain, as if she were starting to realize how much potential trouble was staring us in the face.

"Where were you last night after you left the stage following the opening words of the festival and argued viciously with Mark Jeffries?"

Detective Moore winced, like he wanted to edit his partner's phrasing of that question.

Harley blinked. "Umm, when I walked away after the opening ceremony, I headed to my car and went for a drive."

"Did you stop anywhere?"

"No, why would I?" Harley turned to me. "I need to call my sister."

She bolted and was quickly lost in the crowds of the craft fair.

Detective Ortega watched her disappear with a frown; then she turned to me, and her scowl deepened. "You didn't tell us about the argument between your business partner and Mark Jeffries last night."

"I answered the questions you asked," I said.

"Is there a reason you hid that argument?"

"I didn't hide it. I'd found Mark's body, which was very traumatic. I focused on answering your questions so I could go home." I was mostly telling the truth.

"What sort of knives do you have in your cart?" Detective Ortega asked.

"Umm, we have a multi-tool in the cashbox." I also carried one around in my bag most of the time. The knife was shorter than my pinky finger.

"I would like to see it."

Her tone was basically a warning sign flashing danger in front of me. I made my voice sound bored. "You can once I see your warrant."

"Is it true your mother is a wanted felon?" The younger detective eyed me, while Detective Moore yawned in the background.

"Not exactly." The ground beneath me threatened to turn to quicksand.

"Your mother isn't Saffron Jones?"

"That's my mother's name. But she's not a felon. As far as I know, she's never been convicted of a crime. I'm under the impression that felons have been convicted of certain types of criminal acts, although I could be mistaken. I'm not the lawyer in my family."

Detective Moore stepped forward. He gave a chastising glance at

Detective Ortega, then turned to me. "Did you say, 'May you have the festival you deserve' to Mark Jeffries?"

I nodded. "I did say that, but it wasn't a threat."

"What was it supposed to mean?"

"That I hoped he received the sort of energy back that he was putting out into the world. That Mark should stop and analyze what he was doing since I didn't think, if he reflected on it, that he was doing things that would make him feel proud. Or happy." Maybe Mark's behavior had made him get caught up in a misery loop that he wanted to share with the world.

"So you're saying he deserved to die," Detective Ortega said.

"That is not what I was saying at all. You know, if you want to talk to me, you can do so with my lawyer present," I said. I turned toward my cart.

"If you don't have anything to hide, you should answer my questions," Detective Ortega said.

I turned back and made eye contact with her. "And I will, just with my attorney by my side, since I don't trust you."

Harley running away couldn't have looked good, but at least she hadn't said something too awkward in front of the detectives.

I couldn't say the same thing about me.

Chapter 7

Not long after I returned to the cart after talking to Harley, my phone rang. After glancing at the caller, I looked over at my barista.

"I need to take this," I said. "I'm sorry for ditching you again."

"I can handle the crowd," Kendall said.

Kendall snagged his water from the cart fridge as I walked out of the cart. We were in a lull after a steady stream of customers, so a quick hydration break was a great idea. The cart was starting to feel warm as the day heated up, so it was time to switch our mini-split AC.

"Hi, Nina," I said as I answered my phone.

"Why do you need to talk to me?" my former barista asked. The sound of a baby's "ba da ba da da!" in the background caught my attention. When Harley, Nina, and I had agreed Nina should leave Ground Rules because she was there as a reluctant corporate spy, she'd been in the early stages of pregnancy.

Nina was the first employee I felt I'd failed with, and I'd never entirely shaken the sense that I should've known earlier. I should've been able to tell she was half-heartedly trying to spy on us and that her questionable performance wasn't just a lack of work ethic, since I knew her skills as a barista were solid.

Since Nina was going for the brutally direct conversational route,

I responded in kind. "I'm curious about the status of your revenge-porn case against Mark Jeffries."

"Why are you asking?" Nina said.

"What I'm about to tell you isn't public news yet," I said. At least, it had yet to make the local news sites when I scrolled through them over breakfast.

"Is Mark dead or something?" Nina said.

When I didn't respond, she said in a quieter voice, "He's dead?"

"Please keep that to yourself. It would be a tragedy if Mark's family heard it from the gossip mill instead of official sources." Did Mark have a family? I tried to remember if he'd ever mentioned kids, his parents, or a beloved sibling. But my memory was blank. Had he really not spoken of them, or had I forgotten?

"I can't believe it. How?"

"The answer to that is still being investigated."

"And you think someone killed him because I refused to testify against him?"

"Back up. You refused to testify?"

"There's no way I could proceed with the charges without blowing up my life. My husband doesn't know the full story, so, as far as I know, Mark skated away. I hoped he'd be smart enough to let it go."

The memory of Nina telling me about her history with Mark, including that she was already dating her now-husband while hooking up with Mark, bubbled up in my mind. Mark had blackmailed her with videos.

Wait, had Mark been married at the time? If he was, had his wife known about the affair? Or affairs, I suspected.

Something told me that Nina should've told her husband the unabridged truth versus living with a metaphorical ticking time bomb waiting to blow up her domestic life.

However, keeping her secret under wraps would be easier with Mark dead.

And now he was.

If Nina had been at the festival yesterday, she'd be a suspect. It was possible she'd been here and I hadn't seen her, although that might be reaching.

"Is there anything else?" Nina asked.

I stopped myself from asking her where she'd been last night. "I was just curious about his court case."

"I gotta go." Nina hung up.

Mark wasn't facing criminal charges; that added a few more details to my understanding of his life.

Part of me wondered if Nina had gone forward with the criminal case, if the news would've made more former employees come out of the woodwork with similar tales, or if Nina was a one-off. I suspected she wasn't, although she might have been the first to be blackmailed.

But he might have had intimate videos of other employees he'd been involved with, and I could see someone harming Mark to keep those sorts of videos from being released.

As I stepped back into the cart, I remembered something. I slid one of the cart's drawers open and pulled out the small bottle Dulcie had given me yesterday.

It was time to try Mark's coffee juice in a mini in-memory-of moment.

"Is that the coffee juice?" Kendall asked.

I nodded. "We should try it."

"How exactly are we supposed to use it again? Other than mixing it with water?"

I reread the instructions on the back. "Supposedly, dilute one tablespoon in eight to twelve ounces of ice water or hot water."

"So you're saying?"

"In the spirit of science, we need to do a controlled experiment."

"I'll get the kettle going if you set up the ice water." Kendall filled the gooseneck kettle.

When we cup coffee in the roastery, it takes on the trappings of a sacred ritual. We bring out specific porcelain bowls designed for the experience. We carefully grind the coffee beans, weigh out an exact amount of grounds in each cup, and boil fresh water to just below boiling at about 205 degrees Fahrenheit before adding it to the bowls, letting a coffee crust form on top. We carefully note the aroma of the coffee and then the taste while analyzing the coffee. Breaking through the crust atop the bowl is always my favorite part.

This coffee concentrate wasn't up for the whole cupping experience, but we could be methodical. Give it an honest, as unbiased as possible taste.

A few minutes later, we had three iced coffees and three hot coffees in front of us, in a set of eight-, ten-, and twelve-ounce pours.

I poured a shot of the smallest iced coffee into a small glass and took a sip, while Kendall followed my lead.

A slightly bitter brew covered my tongue, but it wasn't bad. But I didn't love it, either.

"It'd be better with milk," Kendall said. He added a splash of cream to his glass, and I followed along. He was right; it cut the flavor, and it tasted drinkable.

We tried the next-size iced coffee, and then the largest, which was the most diluted.

"It's not terrible," Kendall said.

"If I worked at a regular day job and wanted easy coffee in the morning, something like a basic drip, but didn't want to go through the production of making a decent coffee, this could work," I said.

"High praise," Kendall said. And he wasn't being sarcastic. "And I agree. It's better than some cold brews I've tried, although it's not as good as the best."

Mark's product had potential. It felt like a pivot from his origins in upscale, third-wave coffee, but it also seemed like a way to bring decent coffee to the masses who wanted a quick cup, provided the price point was reasonable.

And it was better than the instant coffees I'd tried.

Maybe Mark had been onto a winner.

But now he'd never know.

Chapter 8

About half an hour before I expected the lunch crowds to descend, I'd sent Kendall out on a break when a gentleman wearing a jaunty fedora strolled up to the cart.

"Did you forget your trench coat?" I asked.

"Dad said I would be too hot if I wore it, but I did bring my cape," Niko said. He glanced over his shoulder at his dad, who'd gone with a trucker cap advertising his latest video game launch in contrast to his son's dapper hat.

Bax shrugged. "That's true."

"But I brought all of my gear to investigate." Niko patted the faux leather satchel that he wore over one shoulder. The bag's Indiana Jones vibe had been perfect for his Halloween costume a few years back, and he adopted it for everyday use. It was starting to look tattered, so I made a note to see if I could find a new one for him for Christmas.

His jean shorts and hunter green T-shirt didn't quite match the aesthetic of the fedora but were weather-appropriate for the festival. His green eyes were just like Bax's. But Niko was still a few years away from developing into a prototypical romance hero, always dressed to impress and presumably wearing cologne with sandalwood notes along with his vintage-inspired fedora. But he was getting closer each day.

"Investigate?" I said.

Niko nodded. "You know about how I'm writing my comic?"

Niko had been working on his comic for months and regularly showed me illustrated pages about a cat, Kaldi, and a goat, Ben, a crime-fighting duo who solved mysteries at a pumpkin farm. "Yes, I remember."

"I'm putting my skills to the test and will help you out this weekend as you solve the murder."

I glanced at Bax, who shrugged, but I could read a note of worry in his eyes.

"Why do you think I'm going to get involved?" I asked.

"Are you saying that you're not going to investigate?" Niko asked.

Niko's tone reminded me of my brother Jackson. It must have been the note of skepticism.

"We should leave the investigation to the police. Investigating can be dangerous," I said. I heard the irony, considering I'd already contacted multiple people who'd worked with Mark, showing I was already sticking my nose into the situation, although in a low-key way. It's not like I tried to work the crime scene.

It's not like I had the forensic skills, after all.

And if I tried to grill too many people about Mark, they'd walk away.

"Don't worry, I'll keep an eye on him," Bax said.

Niko held up his hand. "I'm way too savvy to get myself into trouble."

Famous last words from an elementary schooler. "But will investigating get in the way of your goal of winning the cornhole tournament?"

Niko was in the Corn Chips children's bracket, while Bax was in the Last Bag Standing adult division. Plus, Niko was signed up for the Connect Four tournament.

"I can do both." Niko sounded confident.

Behind him, Bax pointed at his eyes, then at his son.

"Do you need an espresso to help you investigate?" I asked.

Niko scrunched up his nose. "Eww, no."

"I would love one, but maybe stained with milk?" Bax said.

I grinned. I love it when Bax uses coffee lingo correctly. "One cortado coming right up."

We chatted for a little while, and then Bax and Niko left to explore the festival, and I returned to work.

The thought of Niko investigating worried me, but he was just a kid.

No one would take him seriously, right?

A familiar woman strode up to the cart shortly after the lunch rush slowed. Her curly hair was pulled back into a ponytail, and she wore a flowered headband that matched her dusty blue T-shirt. She finished the boho look off with a tiered maxi-skirt that looked perfect for a summer festival in the sun. Her leather camera bag–style purse looked familiar.

Her name clicked into place as she walked up.

"Hi, Ramona," I said. She was one of the Left Coast Grinds employees I texted last night. I hadn't seen her in person for years, but her phone number had been in my address book, automatically uploaded along with the rest of my phone book to the handful of new phones I'd acquired over the years, a small sign of the past I'd carried with me.

"Hi, Sage; you wanted to talk to me?" Ramona said.

I noticed her eyes were red, like she'd been crying. "Would you want something to drink first?"

After pouring an iced coffee for Ramona and telling Kendall I was leaving the cart in his hands, I sat with her outside in the shade at a nearby picnic table.

"I assume you want to talk about Mark?" Ramona said. She swirled the coffee cup in her hand, making the ice rattle.

"You've heard?"

"One of my coworkers talked to the police. He texted me about it a few minutes ago." Ramona quit fiddling with her cup and put her hands in her lap.

"Are you still with Left Coast Grinds?" I asked.

She nodded. "My fifteenth anniversary there was just a few months ago."

"Are you still in the warehouse?"

"Yes, I've been leading the distribution side of the business for a few years now. So are you looking to buy out Left Coast now that the owner's dead, or what's going on?"

Buying Mark's old company hadn't even crossed my mind. Who would own it now? Would his heirs want to sell it? More importantly, who'd be interested in buying it? Would some local entrepreneur see the potential to buy a locally grown company with history and try to restore it to its former glory? Or would a larger brand see a chance to add it to their larger portfolio and move the jobs out of state but keep the branding?

Would someone have wanted Mark's company so bad they would have murdered him, like in a Golden-Age murder mystery?

I looked at Ramona. "No, buying Left Coast Grinds hadn't even crossed my mind," I said. "But I found Mark's body, and I'm worried the police are going to look at me and Harley, and I wanted to—"

"Because of the fight? Yeah, I've heard about that. It looks bad for Harley," she said.

"—find out who would've had it out for Mark enough to harm him."

Ramona half-smiled at me. "Other than your business partner? Let me think." Her gaze looked above my head.

"What about his ex-wife?" I asked. I hated thinking about other people's divorces as I planned my wedding. Because those marriages had started out with hope, only to become unsalvageable.

"Oh, Melissa wouldn't hurt a fly, although I don't know if I would say the same thing about Jocelyn. But Mark maybe brought out the harpy in her, and she's usually not a raving brat." Ramona must've noticed the skeptical look I was sending her way. "Mark sure was good at riling Harley up."

"She's not the only one—"

Ramona held up her hand. "I know Mark rubbed some people the wrong way. He fed on conflict."

"Yet you worked with him for years." The idea sounded exhausting to me.

Ramona glanced away again. "The medical benefits kept me around. Mark and I generally got along, especially when he realized I wasn't in the running to become ex-wife number three. I just didn't engage when he got testy, which made him chill out around me, which was the best way to deal with him. Harley never learned that, and their arguments were legendary. And yes, we've had an . . . issues . . . with quality staff retention. Has anyone told you about when Mark outsourced HR? They were horrified, so he dropped them and found a bookkeeper willing to serve as HR in-house. She's nice, but it's sort of a joke."

Ramona paused. "You know, I remember for a while, someone unhinged kept calling the main phone number and asking for Mark. She refused to leave a message. We never put her through, and she yelled at us. I asked Mark about it once, and he pretended like he didn't know who could be calling him. But I didn't believe him."

"Hmm."

"You could talk to Mark's ex-wives one and two. Maybe one of them was calling, although I never heard their voices, just heard about her from colleagues. Supposedly, his second divorce was more bitter than the worst coffee. But that's just a shot in the dark." Ramona smiled briefly at her own puns. "Or maybe it was connected to the nightclub fire. Mark didn't like to mention it, but he was involved, somehow, with that fire. Someone came by the warehouse asking about it the other day."

Nightclub fire. The words rang a bell in the back of my mind.

Years ago, when I was in high school, a dance club in a warehouse in an industrial area of North Portland had caught fire, causing a stampede. Several people had died, and over fifty were injured. It wasn't as bad as the Cromañón nightclub fire in Argentina, which had led to 194 deaths and almost fifteen hundred injuries, or the Station nightclub or Coconut Grove fires, but it'd been traumatic.

I could google the fire, or I could consult my personal source for Portland business news and gossip.

"Thanks for the coffee, but I need to get back to work," Ramona said. She stood up.

"Work?" Was she covering the Left Coast Grinds booth?

"I'm here with my side hustle. Otherwise, I would've spent the day at home, relaxing after working doubles for weeks." When she spoke again, her voice was tight with tears. "I can't believe Mark's gone."

She bustled off, and I felt for her. She'd clearly liked Mark, even if there'd been an edge to her comments about him.

Before going back to work, I texted my Uncle Jimmy. *What do you know about the NoPo nightclub fire that happened when I was a teen? Do you know who owned the business? Did anyone face criminal charges?*

Then I sent my father a text, asking him the same thing. He'd been with the Portland Police Bureau then, although he'd recently retired and turned into the Ground Rules's warehouse employee when we needed help.

Something else Ramona said struck me. Two ex-wives? Could either of them be here?

But why would they choose to harm him now?

Chapter 9

Not long after Ramona walked away and I'd returned to work, I spotted the woman I'd pegged as an influencer walk by. She was filming the food carts, and I clocked a few people who gave her an annoyed glance when they suspected they were being filmed.

"I'll be back," I said to Kendall. I left the cart just as the situation caught fire.

"Why are you filming my kids?" A woman marched up to the influencer, leaving two kids sitting at a picnic table with the remains of their lunch. She looked to be in her late thirties, dressed in bright pink capris and a loose tank top.

"I'm just filming vibes from the festival," the influencer said.

"You do not have permission to film me or my kids, so you better put that camera away, or—"

"Or what? You'll stop me? You know that's assault, right?"

As I hustled up, I realized the influencer was still filming. I stepped between them. Hopefully, the camera wasn't filming an unflattering view of the underside of my chin.

"Everyone, let's take a deep breath," I said.

"This person was filming my kids."

"I was filming the food carts, not you. Which is my right."

Up close, the influencer was probably in her mid-twenties, with dark hair pulled back into an artful braid. Her yellow muscle shirt and swishy striped skirt looked perfect for the sunny weather. Her trendy tote looked heavy, as if she were carrying additional equipment.

The mother swore. "I did not give you permission to film my kids."

Okay, broken record. I made my tone sound calm. "She has a point. I checked once, and Oregon law doesn't prohibit filming in public spaces unless there's a reason the person being filmed would have a reasonable expectation of privacy, like in a public restroom. So eating in a public area is fair game, even if it's highly annoying."

"That doesn't give her—"

I cut the mother off. "And there were signs on the way into the festival pointing out that you might be filmed while on these premises." Granted, the signs referred to the security cameras covering the festival and the licensed film crew that the Doyles had hired to make an ad with festival footage.

I glanced at the influencer. "But that doesn't mean filming random people enjoying their lunch is cool. And arguably, the grounds are private property, so you should check in with the property owner for permission."

The mother finally realized she didn't know who I was, even if I acted like I had some authority in this situation. "And who, exactly, are you?"

"I'm Sage. My company, Ground Rules, is part of the reason for this festival."

The influencer's face lit up. "Oh, that's why you looked familiar. I saw you on the stage last night. The canned Irish coffee is amazing. Can I interview you later about it?"

Great. The last time I became heavily involved with a social media star, murder followed.

Trevor strode up with his shoulders back. "Is there a problem here?" he snapped out, as if he expected us to stand up straight and salute him.

The mother turned to him with a look of relief. Like finally, someone official was here to take charge.

"We're good, Trevor," I said.

One of the kids had walked over. "Mommy," she said, and tugged on her mother's hand. She pointed in the direction of their table.

The other child, whom I guessed was about two, had removed his clothing and was rolling around in the lone patch of mud behind one of the carts. The ground was otherwise dry, so someone must have spilled something. Hopefully, it was just water.

"Oh, no," the mother said. She turned and snapped, "You better not film that," before rushing over to her son with the girl following behind.

"Like I'd want to," the influencer said. She glanced back at me. "Karens gotta Karen."

"That's not fair. The woman has a point: not everyone wants their kids on social media." A pang of sympathy for anyone named Karen, who now had to deal with their name being turned into shorthand for someone of any gender who is entitled and uses their privilege to police other people's behaviors, flowed through me. At least my name hadn't turned into a meme. Although if I kept falling over bodies, maybe someday.

The influencer let out a long breath. "Honestly, I would've cut the footage with the kids out. It's way too problematic to post footage with kids. And even if I used the footage, they're in the shade, and I was focused on the sunlight hitting off the carts, so they're not really visible. They're also not in a spot I wanted to feature, so I didn't linger on them. Which I would've told the mom if she hadn't been so rude. Hopefully my time in the music zone will be less stressful."

"You're not allowed to film in the music area," Trevor barked. He must have felt neglected.

The influencer half-smiled and pulled a press pass out of her tote bag. "I did check in with the property owners, and Tierney gave me permission to film the crowd during the music fest and to take limited footage of the bands."

Trevor scowled at the press pass as if it insulted his mother.

The influencer laughed. "Although, unless you confiscate everyone's phone, footage of the festival will end up online. It's inevitable. But my footage shouldn't trip any copyright violations."

"Does that happen?" I asked.

"When music is involved, definitely. I heard about a kid who was upset at her family filming her whole life for their vlog, and she started playing Disney music whenever she saw a camera pointed her way. Which is a surefire way to make the footage unusable, since Disney does not play around. They excel at getting videos with their music taken down on all major platforms."

"So I should blast 'Let It Go' from the cart if I'm ever annoyed about being filmed?"

"Yes, or you could, you know, let it go since it's part of our world, whether you like it or not."

I laughed, while Trevor glared at us both.

She handed me a business card. "I really would love to interview you."

"I should get back to my cart, but come by later." I glanced at the card.

Astrid Clementine. The influencer's name was Astrid Clementine.

Or at least, that's the name she uses. Last week, I overheard a conversation of a group of college students debating which names they should go by, since none of them liked their given names. Their take on names was more fluid than that of my former classmates, although I liked to think we'd laid the groundwork for a world that accepts their differences.

Or, as I glanced at Trevor's scowling face, maybe I was delusional.

"Is this a good time to get to the security footage?" I asked him.

"Maybe this afternoon," he said. He looked like he wanted to say something else, but his walkie-talkie crackled. He flipped something on the black box jutting out on his hip. "Hold on, I'll move to a quieter spot," he said into it.

He walked away, and I headed back to my cart.

"Good timing with breaking that up, boss. I was totally ready to run to your aid, but you had it covered," Kendall said from the order window of the cart as I walked up. "It's like you are psychic. You knew just when to rush out."

"Just lucky," I said.

I paused outside of the door of the cart and used my phone to take a glance at Astrid's social media accounts. She focused on travel, with lots of fun reels and short videos highlighting beautiful scenery and places that looked perfect to visit on vacation. She focused on small food and boutiques, and I recognized footage on one reel from a quirky "art" inn on the Oregon Coast, just a few blocks from one of my favorite bookstores on the beach. Her photos of food were artful, with careful lighting. She balanced glamorous with offbeat and approachable remarkably well. Nothing in her account stood out to me, but given her number of followers, likes, and more importantly, comments on her posts, she had developed a loyal group of followers. A quick check told me she included regularly sponsored posts, meaning a company had paid her to post about them. But plenty of her travel posts also made it clear she was giving her honest opinion; I laughed when she commented on one post that she'd used her compensation from a hotel to eat her way through the surrounding city.

I wondered if she'd ever thought she'd end up at a festival in the middle of a murder investigation. It wasn't the sort of travel memory I'd want to make.

A while later, while we were serving a steady line of customers, Detective Ortega walked up to the coffee cart. "Have you seen Harley Yamazaki?" she asked me.

"She's around, but I'm not sure where," I said. If I were looking for her, I'd start with the Ground Rules booth. While Harley might have left the festival, she was scheduled to close the cart today and hand over the cashbox and tablet to me at the end of the day to bring back tomorrow when we started all over again.

"If you see her, please let her know the detectives on the case would like to speak with her." Detective Ortega left.

Would knowing the police wanted to talk to her make her want to leave or seek out the detectives? Jackson would tell Harley not to speak to the police, to never, ever, voluntarily visit a police station, and to absolutely not speak to them without a lawyer. Given her public arguments with Mark, she had to be one of the primary suspects. Her alibi of leaving and driving home alone wasn't the best, and hopefully, a road camera or two caught her, showing she was telling the truth.

I did my best to forget the detective and focus on taking orders for another collection of drinks, mostly iced. Kendall and I worked in tandem to get the coffees into the hands of eager festivalgoers.

Our lull started when one of the bands started playing. We'd guessed our biggest bursts of customers would be in the breaks between bands. But it was nice because we could hear the music inside the coffee cart, even if the sound was faded.

My phone dinged with a text.

Sophie. *Boss, can we chat for a minute? Hannah can watch the booth.*

After conferring with Kendall, I replied, *on my way.*

Sophie met me between the coffee cart and booth, next to a non-alcoholic cocktail company handing out free samples. We walked out of the craft fair together and paused next to the fence separating the music from the rest of the festival. The music was louder here, like being part of the action. A few people were eating lunch next to the "outside" part of the fence.

"What's up?" I asked.

"I got the lowdown on Dulcie," Sophie said. "It's just gossip, but it's interesting. Maybe."

"Is this stuff you overheard?"

Sophie nodded. "Two of Dulcie's high-school classmates came through the booth, and they must've just run into her. They were hardcore gossiping. I started chatting with them, and they just went off, like they enjoyed having an audience. I wish I could've recorded them so you could hear it yourself."

"Don't leave me in suspense."

Sophie adjusted her teal Ground Rules bucket hat. "Supposedly,

Dulcie's parents are loaded, like legit rich with generational wealth. Dulcie was the baby of her family, which was unexpected, because her next oldest sister was either fifteen or seventeen when Dulcie was born. Supposedly, her parents spoiled her rotten. They—Dulcie and the girls I talked to—went to a fancy private school from kindergarten through high school, and it sounds like they used to know each other well."

I could think of a couple of local schools that fit that description. "It might have been the sort of school when you know everyone," I said.

"They claim Dulcie was a 'total party girl' in high school. She wasn't dumb, but she didn't try very hard. One of the girls said this was frustrating to their teachers, because they track the metrics of where their graduates go to college, and Dulcie was messing that up for their class. According to one of the girls, Dulcie's dad even got into a very loud fight with the school principal about Dulcie's college prospects at a basketball game. He wanted his daughter in the Ivy League; supposedly, the principal suggested community college. Although her friend said no, the principal suggested one of the smaller state colleges. Which, to these girls, that was a slam. Which is ridiculous, but as we know, the rich live in a different world."

"Maybe that was Dulcie's rebellion," I said. When I thought back to my college application days, one of my main memories was the stressful feeling that had tied me up in knots. I'd been afraid I'd make a bad decision and ruin the rest of my life. But I'd gotten into several state schools, and a local college had offered me a good scholarship, so I'd stayed in town. But I'd wondered then if I should've been braver and gone out of state versus staying in the same city as my family. But for a girl with heavy expectations, rebelling could be failing, or at least not trying.

If you don't try, you can't fail, after all.

And looking down on community and the smaller state colleges annoyed me, too.

"Maybe," Sophie agreed. "Both girls agreed that Dulcie hadn't done much after high school, and her parents eventually funded her chocolate business to try to get launched since she'd barely scraped by with a degree in something. They couldn't agree if she studied theater or communication. They did agree that she tried to choose the easiest path possible, and her GPA wasn't good enough for law school."

"Interesting."

"I hope that helps. I'll see what else I hear," Sophie said.

"Everything helps at this point," I said. "Have you seen Harley?"

Sophie shook her head, and a worried look invaded her eyes. "Is she still MIA? Should we contact someone? Her family?"

"Harley dropped by the cart earlier today, but I haven't seen her since."

"Oh, good, she's alive," Sophie said, then winced. "Bad choice of words. Is Harley still going to close the cart tonight?"

"Hopefully."

"Let me know if she can't; I can stay."

"I don't want to overload you."

Sophie grinned. "I'd love the overtime, and I don't have school because of the holiday, so this is prime earning time."

"How's working the booth with Hannah?"

"It's fine. Hannah seems distracted and a bit irritable but lights up whenever someone wants a custom tea blend. I suspect she's hungover." Sophie shook her head.

"Want me to ask my dad to help out in the booth? He's around this weekend and said he might drop by to hear the music."

Sophie thought for a moment. "That'd be overkill."

We both flinched at her words.

"I really need to think before speaking," Sophie said. "I just meant it's rarely busy enough for us to need a third set of hands, but we are selling steadily."

"Let me know if you need help," I said, and we split up.

It wouldn't surprise me if the rumor that Dulcie's family had funded her company was true. Her marketing and website looked great from the outside, with slick designs that implied a good design firm.

My feet stopped by one of the other candy vendors. She Sells Candy Sea Shells has a booth at some of the same farmers' markets as Ground Rules. I remembered trying one of their chocolate seashells, which had been ribboned with pistachio butter and tasted delightful. But today, they'd focused on lollipops, cocoa marshmallows, and hard candies, all with nautical flair. Plus, sugar cookies cut like seashells with beachy pastel icing.

They also had cute bottles of chocolate "potions" that I saw, after looking at the bottle, were chocolate sauce meant to be drizzled, and jars of a chocolate hazelnut spread using Oregon-grown nuts.

I appreciated that they'd decked out their booth with a beach theme. They'd brought their A game.

I picked up one of their order forms, which listed products for pickup that weren't part of their festival offerings, like the chocolate shells I'd tried before.

"Can I help you with anything?" the woman running the booth asked.

"I'm just checking things out. I'm with Ground Rules, the coffee cart," I said.

"Oh, yeah, I saw you onstage during the opening celebration."

We chatted for a moment. "I tried one of your chocolate seashells last winter."

"Those are our best sellers, and if you're ever interested in ordering them, we can schedule a pickup time from our commissary kitchen. Or we can deliver them for a fee. We also sell in a few shops around town, which are listed here." She handed me a postcard.

"Have you thought of opening a storefront?" I asked.

"That's the goal, but I want to be positive I'm ready and able to afford a full shop. I might open up a pop-up inside a larger makers' hall this fall and see how that goes."

She smiled. "I might have a lead on a small storefront in a small town about twenty miles out of Portland, but I'm not sure I want to leave the city. Mainly because I don't want to give up on my current retail accounts who've been so supportive, but it'd quadruple my delivery distances."

We chatted about the logistics of owning a shop for a while before I took my leave.

"I should check in on my coffee cart," I said.

After leaving the cart, I glanced at the company's website. Their owner, whom I'd just met, had a lengthy list of chocolate-related experiences in her bio. She'd even completed an apprenticeship in Belgium after getting a culinary degree with a focus in bakery and pastry arts.

Something told me that if I were forced to bet on which chocolate company would be here next year between She Sells Candy Sea Shells and Dulcinea, I'd have to vote for the chocolate sea shells, despite the tongue-twister name.

Then I remembered the "Varsity Blues" college admissions scandal, in which elites across the country paid to get their children into exclusive universities by recruiting them as athletes for sports they didn't play or having someone take the SATs or other entrance exams on behalf of their offspring so they'd get high enough scores.

But Dulcie had parents willing to prop up her business. Would they eventually cut their losses and make her close the shop if it wasn't doing well? Or would they hire someone to run the company with Dulcie as a figurehead?

And maybe this wasn't something I should think about.

I should get back to work.

Chapter 10

But getting back to my cart wasn't going to happen, at least not yet. Ramona flagged me down as I passed a booth selling locally made leather purses. "Sage, do you have a moment?"

I glanced around the booth. The bags were in all the colors of the rainbow, as well as classic browns and blacks. "Why are you hanging out here?"

"Working part-time for Bagatha, doing their social media, is my side hustle. I'm saving up to buy a condo, and you know housing prices are ridiculous," Ramona said.

I barely stopped myself from asking if she would focus her condo search on Northeast Klickitat Street. Or maybe Northwest Quimby. Since I was sure Ramona had heard those jokes before.

Ramona kept talking. "Maybe if Left Coast Grinds goes belly up with everything that's happened, I can convince Agatha—one of the owners—to let me update their warehouse procedures. Their shipping methods are so inefficient. It'd take me a week to get them running faster and leaner."

"They'd be lucky to have you." Actually, I had no idea if that were true, but it felt like the right thing to say.

Ramona smiled. "But come with me. I want to introduce you to someone. You'll need to be gentle, because this is Mark's first ex-wife. She still loves him."

She led me to the next booth. The sign at the back of the booth said, FRESH PINES STYLE BY MELISSA, with an image of three pine trees along with a tagline: "Locally, ethically made clothing with boho flair." The booth was lined by two racks of clothing with an earthy vibe.

The woman in the booth was tall and willowy and dressed in baggy orange hemp overalls with embroidery on the straps, layered over a tight white crop that showed off the lean sides of her stomach. She had an angular face with strong features. She was striking, I decided, with the perfect face for avant-garde makeup. I bet my photographer friend would love to have her as a subject. Her light brown hair was the same shade as the liquid caramel sauce we used in the cart. She wore it loose over her shoulders. I'd guess she was in her mid-forties, like Mark.

Ramona motioned me over. "Sage, this is my friend Melissa. Melissa, this is Sage."

Melissa glanced at me, then back to Ramona. "I thought you said you knew someone who could get justice for Mark."

"Don't let the air of sweetness around her fool you. She's solved several murders."

I noted Ramona didn't mention my close connection to Harley.

"If you can get justice for my Mark, I'll tell you anything," Melissa said. Her tone was bordering on angry.

"I'll watch your booth. Why don't the two of you go talk." Ramona shooed us out of the booth.

Should I send Melissa to the detectives who were actually investigating Mark's death?

But this was an excellent opportunity, so I decided to start easy. If I approached this right, Melissa could be a great source of background on Mark. "I'm sorry for your loss."

"Thank you."

"How did Mark decide to open Left Coast Grinds?"

Melissa smiled, but it was sad. "Mark was always obsessive when he became interested in something. He thought about opening a brewery and then a bar for a while. His dad had left Mark a small trust fund, and when it came under his control when he turned twenty-five, he wanted to make it count. So he played around with investing in a few different ventures, but he was looking for the right company of his own to launch."

"Did it take him a while to find his calling?" I asked.

"Even though he drinks pots of coffee each day, he didn't think about opening a roastery until we visited one of the oldest coffee shops in Seattle. That was the lightbulb-over-his-head moment. When we came home, we visited a local micro-roaster, and Mark realized he could do that, too. He had a good palate, which he refined over time. He roasted so many batches of coffee at home until he found his first job in the industry. He always dreamed of opening a shop that would become the neighborhood living room, where people would feel like friends, even if it was their first visit."

"That sounds like a lovely dream."

"I remember when Mark opened his first shop," Melissa said. "It was full of couches, and the space was odd, with a few hidden corners and surprise rooms you couldn't see from the front. It was the perfect neighborhood space Mark had dreamed of. It really felt like a home away from home.

"Then, when Left Coast Grinds started getting hip, he turned his focus into being in every neighborhood in Portland—well, at least the upscale ones. He remodeled his stores to be sleek and started chasing national distribution."

"So you were with him for all the grunt work when he opened his business?" Her stride was longer than mine, but I didn't have any problems keeping up.

"We broke up not long after Mark opened his first shop, although we stayed in touch. He asked for my design advice, although I don't really like the ultra-modern approach he ran with. It's sterile. Boring. It doesn't say Portland to me."

"Why'd you break up?" I asked.

"It was an age-old reason: we were married too young." Melissa twisted a silver band on her ring finger. She must've realized I noticed, because she said, "I don't usually wear my old wedding band. But when I heard about Mark, I went on a treasure hunt and found it in the back of my jewelry box. I felt like I had to wear it. It comforts me. I can't believe I won't see Mark again."

"How old were you when you started dating?"

"We were fourteen. My family, as obnoxious as they can be, was a safe haven for Mark. His father died when he was in elementary school, and his mom's new husband was an absolute tool. He made sure Mark knew he was barely tolerated, and when his mother wasn't around, his stepdad was actively mean. Like, cruel. But never with witnesses, which is even worse, you know? At least be honest."

Melissa pulled her hair off her neck, back into a ponytail, then let it drop, causing it to flow back to her shoulders. "My family was loud and chaotic. Our family motto is there's always room for one more at the table. So, as I fell in love with the deep first-time sort of way, my family basically adopted Mark. He just seemed like part of my life. Running off and getting married to him at nineteen just felt right. Even if I later realized we didn't know what we were doing. We both had a lot of growing up to do. It turned out it was better for both of us to do some of that growing up apart. But I always hoped we'd find our way back to each other again, maybe when we were old and gray. Now I have to face that's a dream that wasn't meant to be."

I felt sorrow for Melissa and her dreams that were never meant to be. Part of me wondered if Mark had agreed with her. Had he dreamt of reuniting?

Melissa gave her ring one final turn before dropping her hand. "Mark still came home to us for Christmas, even after he married the harpy," Melissa said.

"The harpy?"

"Jocelyn, his second wife. She was intense in an awful, discordant way. She brought out the turbulent part of Mark's personality. Really, they brought out the worst in each other. I was glad for both of their sakes when they split. Which didn't stop her from doing anything she could to ruin Mark's life."

"What did she do?" After looking at Melissa, I wondered what Jocelyn looked like. While they didn't look alike, there was a similar vibe to both Melissa and my former employee Nina. Maybe Mark had had a type.

"Jocelyn threw a fit when Mark celebrated Christmas with our family instead of driving out to nowhere on the middle of the Oregon Coast. She wanted him to spend the holidays with her parents. She kept texting nasty comments all day, threatening divorce, threatening that she'd do everything she could to make his life miserable."

In some ways, I could sympathize with Jocelyn. Even though I liked Niko's mom, I wouldn't be happy if Bax had ignored either of our families to spend the holidays with his ex, even if he did it for Niko's sake. And I wouldn't have texted threats. It sounded like Melissa's family had become Mark's, even if they weren't related by blood, since he had reasons to avoid his biological family. Which made a pang of sympathy chime inside me. I hadn't known anything about Mark's childhood until now.

"Did Jocelyn do anything . . . proactive?" I asked. "Did she just send him angry texts, or did she, I don't know, slash his tires or something?"

"Nothing like that. But Jocelyn filed for divorce right away. We'd barely woken up after celebrating the new year when a process server showed up."

Part of me wanted to ask what celebrating the new year meant, since maybe it was innocent, but the "woken up" part made me suspicious. If Jocelyn had divorce papers ready that quickly, perhaps she'd already been planning on divorcing Mark and had the paperwork ready. Maybe his actions over Christmas had convinced her to finally file instead of holding off, hoping their relationship would change.

My brother sometimes volunteers at drop-ins for a local agency that helps people get free brief legal advice, usually referrals to services that can help them. He told me that the stress of Thanksgiving and Christmas triggers many decisions to divorce, and the rates of people filing for divorce spike in January.

I decided to switch gears. "Did you hear about a minority investor wanting out of Mark's company?"

"That was terrible. Mark vented to me about that when it happened. This dude had invested to help Mark go national but got cold feet and wanted his money back instead of waiting for the inevitable payday. Because you know if he'd held on, Mark would've made it big. Mark scraped together enough money to partially pay the investor back. He also had to spin off a couple of locations to a different company the investor is part of. So now they're snooty tea shops."

If Melissa was right, that explained why a small local chain of tea shops had taken over two of the old Left Coast Grinds locations. I wondered why Ramona hadn't mentioned this. Maybe Mark had kept this part of the business deal from his employees, but not his first ex-wife. Or Ramona was keeping her own secrets.

"If you want to know more about the minority investor, you should talk to Jocelyn. She introduced them. I'm sure she convinced him to do what he could to ruin Mark's business out of spite, too. When Mark asked Jocelyn about it over a phone call—he was staying at my place, because she kicked him out of the condo they shared—she denied it. The harpy."

"I don't know anything about Jocelyn." Except that Melissa clearly hated her.

"She sold the condo and didn't even share any of the profit with Mark, even though he'd lived there and helped pay the mortgage for two years."

"But she owned the condo?"

"Only because Mark helped with the mortgage. From what I heard, she is now unemployed and living with her parents somewhere out in Timbuktu. Else, I'm sure she'd be the prime suspect," Melissa said. "You know, someone should check out Jocelyn's alibi. Maybe she's here incognito."

"Have you seen her?"

"Note I said incognito. Maybe she has a disguise. I'm sure, if she's here, that she'd do her best to avoid me. The last time we saw each other, she threatened to staple 'my hippy boho crap to my forehead.' She's unhinged."

As a threat, that was definitely odd. But also hilarious.

Melissa stopped walking and held out a hand. "You know, Ramona said Mark argued publicly with that roaster he trained. Hailey?"

"Harley?" I said.

"That's the one. Mark took her from the gutter and trained her up to work in the roastery, and she stabbed him in the back."

The gutter? Harley had been a reluctant chemistry major when she'd started working for Left Coast Grinds. Which was hardly the gutter.

Melissa's tone took on a confidential note, making me wonder if she enjoyed gossiping a little too much. "Then, once she was finally an independent employee and Mark could finally trust her and quit holding her hand, she left."

Melissa clearly hadn't made the connection between Harley, Ground Rules, and me. Should I say something?

But Melissa kept talking. "Someone should ask what she was doing last night. Maybe she snapped and killed Mark out of jealousy."

"Jealousy?"

"It's hard when someone's a better roaster than you are, so it makes sense she'd be jealous of Mark."

It'd be obvious now if I hadn't known Melissa was biased before. Despite everything, she was Team Mark to the end.

We reached the end of the property and were next to the parking lot. Melissa turned and smiled, but it was sad and filled with grief. "Mark just wanted to build a lasting legacy. It's so unfair that he's gone."

We started walking back the way we came.

What would Mark's legacy be? His award-winning coffee company; his passion for quality.

His myriad of issues with female employees.

"I was surprised to see him here at the festival," I said. Maybe if
he hadn't snuck in, he'd still be alive.

Harley would be one of my primary suspects if I followed that
train of thought to the logical conclusion, along with me.

The sun was out in full force, and the temperature was rising into
the eighties. It was almost a perfect summer day, except for the emotional shadow Mark's murder was casting on my world.

I nodded at Hannah, who stood in the shade outside the booths,
drinking from a large water bottle. She nodded back, a quizzical look
on her face as she took in Melissa's overalls.

"Dulcie and Mark go way, way back," Melissa said. "One of her
older sisters used to be one of my best friends. So when Dulcie called
Mark, asking for help because she was nervous running a booth by
herself, he couldn't say no. And his new product is revolutionary. A
surefire hit."

Hmm, that wasn't the feeling I'd gotten from Dulcie yesterday.
But maybe she'd wanted to save face with me, considering I was here
as part of Ground Rules and part of the reason for the festival.

Or maybe Mark had lied to Melissa.

"Wait, did Ramona say you once worked for Mark? You know
the young girls always wanted his attention. He just had that fatherly
air," Melissa said. "So, of course, Dulcie wanted his help."

Okay, Melissa would clearly believe anything Mark told her.

"Why do you say that?" I asked. Going for innocent felt like my
best play here.

As we approached Melissa's booth, four women were inside, holding up skirts, and Ramona was gesturing to them.

"Customers; gotta run." Melissa beelined for the customers, and
I took a moment to think.

Melissa had looked for the best in Mark and clearly saw him as a
hero in the world, while to me, he felt like a villain.

Regardless of how I felt about him, he'd been recast as a victim.

And he'd never had a chance for a redemptive arc, provided he was capable of one.

Before returning to the coffee cart, I checked out Melissa's social media feeds, which I found by clicking on Ramona's Insta account. When we were walking, I realized Melissa had been in one of Ramona's pictures from when I checked last night.

Ramona's photo was from eight months ago. The caption: "High school besties reunite!" Four women, all in their mid-forties, smiled at the camera while holding glasses of wine. Neither of the other women looked familiar to me.

The photo made me realize that Ramona and Mark had been connected for a long time if Ramona had been a high school BFF with Melissa. Since Melissa had said she and Mark were high school sweethearts. I hadn't realized Ramona and Mark had that long of a history together. That could be one reason she'd continued working with him.

And I wondered, again, what would happen to the ownership of Left Coast Grinds. Were there other minority owners or investors who'd claim their piece of the business?

If Melissa and Mark were still as close as she claimed, would he have left his estate to her? If he'd started the company when they were married, did she have a current minority stake?

Ramona and Melissa seemed to be tight. Could they have planned Mark's death in some weird play to take over the company he created? The idea felt outlandish but as realistic as anything I'd thought of so far.

Maybe Melissa rubbed me the wrong way because she spoke so glowingly of Mark, slammed Harley, and indirectly cast aspersions on young female employees. Everyone says love is blind, but she took the concept to the extreme.

Unless she was lying.

But when we spoke, Melissa's emotions felt real. She seemed to love Mark. She'd sounded devastated, like her world had just tipped on its side, and she wasn't sure when it'd feel normal again.

Although she was at a festival right after his death. But people grieve in different ways, and it's not up to me to judge. There's no right way to grieve.

Even if I really, really want to.

Ramona had tagged Melissa in a photo, so I clicked on her name.

Most of Melissa's accounts showed a mix of dresses and skirts, all part of her "Fresh Pines Style by Melissa" business. The orange overalls she wore were from her current line. So, like Mark, she'd been entrepreneurial. When I followed the link in her bio to her website, she had a flowery bio, talking about how she'd always loved sewing. She had been working as a sales rep for a regional potato-chip company when she'd started designing clothes for herself, which led to others wanting to buy her original designs. This caused her to launch her clothing company, which was carried by a few eco-friendly retailers nationwide. I noted the list of small local boutiques that carried her products. I was pretty sure I'd once tried on one of her dresses, which was designed for someone much taller than me. The sales rep and I had joked about it before I put the dress back. It wasn't something I'd liked enough to make it worth tailoring to fit, although I'd liked the embroidery on the collar.

Melissa had talked up the fair in her social media feeds, offering a mix of promos, like a raffle, for people who dropped by. She was also launching a few new products in person here before adding them to her website.

Maybe Melissa had decided to put aside her grief since she'd already committed to the fair.

Or maybe she couldn't afford to stay home, regardless of how devastated she felt.

Chapter 11

Maybe an hour later, the influencer, Astrid, showed up at the coffee cart. She'd put away the camera she'd been filming with earlier, but her phone was in her hand. But given the angle she held it, she wasn't recording. Or if she was, she was getting footage of the inside of her hand. She eyed the menu board before stepping up to the order window.

"I'd love to try one of your espresso tonics!" Astrid said. She handed over a dented coffee tumbler layered with stickers. I couldn't fault her order; coffee tonics were one of my current obsessions.

Astrid tilted her head slightly as she looked at me, and I recognized what she was doing. The tilt made her seem nonthreatening, while the eye contact was designed to create a sense of empathy, like we were connected. She wasn't necessarily doing it on purpose, but I noted it. As I turned away to pour her double shot of espresso, I wondered if Astrid was manipulative or just instinctively creating a sense of intimacy. As I combined it with a can of tonic water and ice in a glass, I suspected it was the former, that she was naturally friendly. But I wouldn't bet I was right.

As I handed over her drink, Astrid asked, "Can I interview you for my social media feeds?"

"I hate being on camera," I said.

"If it helps, my goal is to make everything look beautiful." Astrid leaned in again, and her tone was warm. "My social media showcases the sort of vacation and experiences people aspire to, since the videos are curated to only show the fun moments. I'd never show myself sitting in an airport for five hours when my flight was canceled, or the time a bug crawled out of my salad while I was about to take my third bite."

She straightened up, but kept the smile in her voice. "Although I have used a few of those to create 'I made lemonade' videos, which are always popular. If you stammer or don't like your answer, I can edit it. Just say you want to restart and wait a few seconds, then answer again."

It was my turn to lean forward. My tone was purposefully light. "Tell you what. I'll let you interview me, as long as you let me see the footage you filmed yesterday, especially in the evening. I promise I won't repost it."

"Why?" she asked. She took a sip of her espresso tonic. "This is excellent. The slight bitterness of the quinine of the tonic balances out nicely against the espresso. I wasn't sure I'd like it."

Astrid's comments on the espresso drink felt honest, and it was the sort of observation sure to make inroads with me. But I didn't let myself fall for her charm.

"I'm glad you like the drink. I've been drinking at least one per day for weeks," I said. "About the videos. I'm curious about what was going on while I was onstage."

"I can send the videos your way, but I'm trusting you'll keep your word and not post them online, or share them with anyone else who would use them."

"That's not a problem. I solemnly promise I won't share or use the videos online."

"Then we have a deal." Astrid held up her glass, like she was toasting our agreement.

After adding a fresh layer of lip gloss, I joined Astrid outside the cart. We set up alongside the distillery, with the Doyle's logo strategically behind us.

As Astrid set her camera up on a tripod, I remembered when a true-crime podcaster had done something similar in the Ground Rules shop. Hopefully, no one would die this time around.

"Stand right there," Astrid said. She came around next to me, clicked the tiny remote in her hand, then returned to her camera. "Perfect. Don't move."

Astrid rejoined me and took a moment to fluff her hair. "Hopefully, I have a camera crew with me someday."

"Is that your goal?"

"I've been diligently manifesting starring in my own travel show. We'll see if it comes to fruition, but I have a good feeling about it.

"Okay, I'm about to start filming." Astrid was about six inches taller than me, which made me wonder if I'd look childlike beside her glossy presence.

A moment later, she smiled widely at the camera. "I'm here at the Doyles' Fourth of July Festival with Sage, the owner—"

It was hard not to interrupt her and say co-owner.

"—of the Ground Rules Coffee Roastery that partnered with Doyle's Oregon Whiskey to create the reason we're all here this weekend. This entire festival was set up to celebrate the launch of Irish-To-Go, which is a very tasty canned Irish Whiskey cocktail. But I have to tell you, I hope this festival continues, because it's pretty spectacular, as you'll see in my footage from the weekend."

Astrid turned to me. "How did you decide to partner with the Doyles?"

I pulled my Ground Rules spokesperson persona over me like a mostly comfortable hooded sweatshirt. "Tierney and Shay—the owners of Doyle's—approached Ground Rules about providing the coffee for the new product under development, which eventually turned into Irish To-Go. We saw the potential immediately and suggested a few of our blends or single-origin options that would work well with whiskey. Our relationship evolved from there."

"Tell me about that! Which coffee works best with whiskey?"

"Deciding which coffee works was a really fun part of the process. We did a lot of taste tests to see which of our coffees matched well with Doyle's Whiskey. We didn't want the finer notes of the coffee to clash with the whiskey and vice versa," I said. Astrid nodded along as I got into the weeds of the selection process. She either legitimately thought this was interesting, or she has a future as an actress. "We decided the dark fruit and chocolate notes of our Taste the Northwest blend end up paired perfectly with the smooth honey notes of their whiskey."

"Tell me about your coffee business. Where can people find it in Portland?"

We chatted for a while, and I appreciated the softball, but not pointless, questions. Astrid seemed interested in the questions she asked, and I bet she looked great onscreen.

I hoped I sounded intelligent, or at least not like a total idiot. This was a nice change from my previous experience with aspiring podcasters and journalists.

After we wrapped up the interview, Astrid turned to me with a smile.

"Now we're off camera. You did great! I knew you would. I'm putting together a series of segments of the festival, so expect to see this live in a week or so. Unless I get bored tonight and decide this will fit in nicely with my on-the-go teaser content rather than the full-blown recap."

I nodded. "If you tag Ground Rules in the posts, we'll reshare." As long as I didn't look like an idiot.

"I'll upload my footage to a shared folder, and I'll send you the link later today," Astrid said.

"Thanks."

As I headed back to the coffee cart, I saw Detectives Ortega and Moore walk by toward the barn. Ortega looked as bouncy as I've ever seen a police officer look. Moore shambled along behind slowly, seemingly performing an impression of Eeyore.

Was he that pessimistic about solving this case? Or was I projecting my feelings his way?

Chapter 12

Even though I'd been in and out of the cart all morning, leaving Kendall to hold down the fort, I took my late lunch when Bax and Jackson were scheduled to play in the cornhole tournament. Everyone who registered was divided and put into a bracket and division mostly randomly, except the under-twenty-one brackets were divided into under-ten, under-sixteen, and under-twenty, with another division for parent-child teams. Niko was in the Corn Chips, while Bax and Jackson, with a team name "Catching Corn," had been placed in the Last Bag Standing division.

As I was about to enter the makeshift cornhole arena, which featured six playing fields with room spectators alongside, I paused to let a llama and his handler slope by. This was a good omen: no Portland-area event is a success without a no-drama llama's appearance.

As I walked up, Niko still wore his fedora. He'd snagged a spot to the side of the playing field and was sitting cross-legged with his notebook in his hand.

"Are Catching Corn ready to play?" I asked him.

Niko closed his notebook and tucked it under his arm, holding it close to his chest. "Dad said he was going to warm up."

I glanced around and saw my brother downing a bottle of water with a pint of beer in his other hand, while Bax held a warrior pose. He slowly shifted into warrior pose two.

"How's your investigation going?" I said.

"Nothing to report yet, but it's early days." Niko looked too earnest to be a jaded PI, but he had the lingo down.

I wondered how many mystery novels Niko had read in the past year. "If your goat and cat crime-fighting team were here, what'd be their first investigative step?"

Niko studied for a moment. "They have an advantage, because they could smell the scene and pick up things we can't. But they also can't talk to humans. They'd first stake out the spot of the crime and see who avoids it or spends too much time looking at it. But Dad won't let me set up camp there."

"Honestly, Niko, hanging out in the parking lot would be dull."

"You don't know that for sure. It could be the key to cracking this case."

We needed to add some variety to his reading, which was self-guided by Niko's current interests. Bax and his ex, Laurel, didn't care what Niko read, as long as he spent time reading. But maybe if I pretended to be interested in sports, like something by Jason Reynolds or Matt Christopher, he'd follow along.

Or he'd see through my ploy.

Two people with familiar faces walked up as Bax and Jackson started their match against the Diva Duo.

My father and my Uncle Jimmy.

Together.

I couldn't remember the last time I'd seen them in the same place at the same time. Maybe my college graduation.

Was the world ending?

"Hi," I said as they walked up.

"Bug," my uncle said, using the nickname popular with his side of the family.

"Pumpkin," my dad said.

This was going to be interesting.

"I didn't expect to see you two here." I didn't add the word together to the end of the statement. Jimmy is technically my great-uncle on my maternal side, meaning he's my mother's uncle. So he's related to Jackson and me, but his only connection to this father is me. When my mother absconded with me, Uncle Jimmy tried to help my dad. I knew my father was also thankful that my uncle helped pay for my college like he had for all his assorted nieces and nephews. My uncle had employed my mother's cousin Miles for years, which made sense, since Miles is an excellent general manager of the Tav. He'd sent Miles's siblings through college, too. And Jackson had finished law school with no debt.

So it's not like my father and uncle dislike each other. But my father, being an Army veteran and retired police officer, is more strait-laced than my uncle, who runs his business empire out of the back of a dive bar.

My uncle looked as unflappable as always. "I ran into your father looking for you at the Ground Rules booth, and since Jackson texted you were going to watch their cornhole match, I figured we'd find you here."

Standing there with them made me feel like a high-school student who'd done something wrong.

"In your text, you said you have questions about the nightclub fire," my uncle said.

I glanced over at Niko, who was focused on his dad's game. We stepped a few feet away, and I spoke quietly. "I thought both of you might remember the fire. What happened? Was anyone arrested?"

My uncle and father glanced at each other, and both seemed grim.

My father finally spoke. "It was controversial at the time, but no one faced criminal charges for the fire."

"Even though people died?" I asked.

My father nodded. "The manager on duty, supposedly, was responsible for the fire escapes being locked and bolted. Which meant when the fire started, the panicked crowds couldn't escape through the emergency exits. And since the manager lost his life trying to evacuate the club, there wasn't anyone to prosecute."

"I never bought the scenario," my uncle said.

"What part?" I glanced at my uncle, who was watching the Diva Duo slap hands after a round, while Bax and Jackson spoke together urgently.

My uncle glanced my way. "I've never believed that the manager ordered the fire escapes locked. I'm sure that decision rested on the shoulders of the owners of the club, who were trying to keep kids high on who-knows-what from wandering out into an industrial area. I'd be willing to bet whoever made the order thought they were keeping their customers safe, but it backfired horribly when the fire started."

"How did it start?" I asked.

"The venue wasn't designed to be a concert space, and they hadn't updated their electrical system in decades. Add in a band with slip-shod equipment, with cables spliced together with duct tape and hope, and something in the electrical sparked and caused a fire under the stage. Something else quickly caught fire—" my uncle said.

"Hairspray." We both looked at my dad. "The fire started next to one of the band member's bags, and he had a couple bottles of aerosol hairspray. When the cans burst, they created a couple of fire-balls, which ignited the foam sound absorbers and curtains on the walls. It was truly unlucky."

"If the electrical system wasn't up to code, doesn't that make the business at fault?" I asked.

Niko cheered and jumped up and down. On the field, Bax and Jackson slapped hands while the Diva Duo wore matching frowns. I clapped, even though I wasn't sure what had happened.

"You'd think so. But the civil case was thrown out, and like I said, the manager on duty was used as a scapegoat."

"There was a huge sense of injustice afterward," my uncle added. "Including in the local business community. Some of us have always taken the safety of our event venues seriously. I was offended on a personal level, since it was avoidable, and people died. As a business owner, I was highly annoyed. Because the city's reaction was to start changing regulations in response, even if it didn't make events any safer. Because they needed to be seen as doing something in response to the tragedy."

"It was rather too little, too late," my father said.

"I've always been willing to invest in safety measures and follow the best safety practices. I consider it my moral duty and obligation to my staff and customers. The fire marshal is welcome to inspect my buildings at any time. But I've never been a fan of busy work. Most of the city inspectors were reasonable, and I've always agreed that we needed to ensure a tragedy like that never happens again. But a few were on power trips, and I struck them off my Christmas card list."

I wouldn't be surprised if my uncle sent Christmas cards to everyone who'd ever professionally interacted with his business, even city officials. "Someone told me that Mark Jeffries was involved in the nightclub, somehow," I said.

Both my father and uncle looked thoughtful for a moment.

My father's tone was thoughtful. "If I remember correctly—it's been a long time since I thought about this—Mark booked the bands for the venue. He had no real decision-making power over the business and wasn't considered responsible. He wasn't on site when the fire happened."

"Mark was pretty much blacklisted from the local entertainment field after the nightclub fire," Uncle Jimmy said.

We both turned to him. "I told you people were upset. There was speculation that Mark was a financial partner, not just an employee, and he'd somehow slithered his way out of trouble. Not that anyone had proof. But no one wanted to work with him when he tried to get involved in other nightclubs. Then a few years later, Mark was focused on his coffee company. I don't know if he was forgiven or if people willingly forgot. But I guess there's a reason why local music festivals, like Campathon, have never been willing to bring Left Coast Grinds on as a vendor."

"Yes, Dad!" Niko's chirpy voice tore through our dark conversation.

Bax and Jackson had won their first round. I cheered for them as they shook hands with the Diva Duo and triumphantly returned to the spectator area, ceding the field to the next matchup.

When Bax and Jackson walked up, one of the tournament referees was alongside. "We just updated the bracket on our website, so you'll see the opponent and time of your next match once this round is finished, so within an hour, I'd guess. If you have questions, check in with the official cornhole booth. Do you need directions to the booth?"

"Is it the same booth where we picked up our numbers about an hour ago?" Jackson said. His tone was deadpan.

"Exactly!" The referee danced away. He seemed to doing a modified version of the robot.

"Are people getting paid to be cornhole referees?" Jackson asked me. Next to us, Niko held up his fist for his father to bump it.

"Yes, but I'm reminded of a quote," I said. We both watched the referee dance inside the playing area, then over to one of the cornhole boards to check it was still on its marked spot. He stood up and danced across to the other one.

"I have a guess, but which quote?" my brother asked.

"If you do what you love, you'll never work a day in your life."

"I was thinking, 'Sometimes the best part of my job is that the chair swivels.'"

I laughed, but I knew Jackson loved his job, as much as it frustrated him. For him, it was a calling, not just a paycheck.

I turned to Bax. I lowered my voice like I was interviewing him for TV. "Mr. Lukas Evan Baxter, how does it feel now that your first round is in the bag?"

He matched my energy. "It was a tough-fought match. I'm glad our diligent practice and belief in ourselves allowed us to persevere."

We chatted for a moment, and I took a moment to appreciate the matching T-shirts of the Atoms, one of the next teams, which said, "Think like a proton: always positive." If I came to the festival next year, I'd have to enter a team with the name "cruising for a brewsing," with maybe "see you later, percolator," on the back.

Jackson, my dad, Bax, and Niko decided to head to the music area, since the first band was scheduled to start. I headed back to the cart with my uncle walking alongside me. Given the thoughtful look on my uncle's face, he had something to tell me, so I stayed quiet.

"Back when we were starting Ground Rules"—my uncle was a silent partner and financial backer of my business, so the we was appropriate—"Mark approached me for a loan. He was looking for an investor and offered a stake in his business to sweeten the deal."

"You turned him down?"

"After looking at his books, yes," my uncle said.

Had my uncle considered hedging his bets against Ground Rules? Or had he been willing to invest in local businesses, even if they conflicted with others in his portfolio?

My uncle continued talking. "I ran into Mark a few weeks later, and he . . . informed . . . me that he'd found a different investor."

From the way my uncle said informed, it hadn't been a pleasant conversation. Had Mark mocked my uncle? Argued with him?

"That conversation with Mark made me even happier that I'd declined to invest, especially since I was impressed by your and Harley's early steps of launching Ground Rules. But I have to wonder who Mark found to invest in his company. Because Mark was taking a few risks with national expansion that I had doubts about, and I was proven right. His plans didn't pan out. And as an investor, that would've made me nervous. I understand calculated risks, but his felt more like optimism that wasn't backed by enough data."

"From the outside, it seemed like he had a good shot at national expansion," I said. "I thought he'd do well."

"I can see why someone who hadn't looked at his books in depth would think that. Maybe a year ago, maybe more like two, Mark came back to me, looking for another investor, but I turned him down. Again."

"Did that coincide with him starting to spend too much time at the Rail Yard?" We paused alongside one side of the distillery, in the no-man's land between the craft fair and small tasting area for the cocktail. Given how the distillery's bar was hopping, most people were taking their drinks to the patio, where they could see the bands.

"I believe so, since he was looking for reasons to encourage me to sell Ground Rules to him."

"Mark knew you are our financial backer."

"Yes, I mentioned it to him the first time I turned him down. For what it's worth, Mark was convinced his brand was superior to yours, but I wholeheartedly disagreed."

"Have you known Mark long?"

"For longer than you've been alive," my uncle said. "His father was a friend, although not someone I considered to be in my inner circle. Despite my disinclination, I ended up one of the trustees of his estate. When Mark turned twenty-five, I thought I was done with Mark Jeffries forever. But Mark would sometimes show up and ask for advice, although I never knew why, as he rarely heeded anything I said. But in honor of the memory of his father, I did my best to give good advice."

"You never mentioned this, including when I started working for Left Coast Grinds. Or when I quit." I'd been so angry at the time I quit and offended. Plus, slightly grossed out. I'd talked about it several times with my cousin Miles, who managed the Tav. But it'd never come up between my uncle and me.

"I'd hoped Mark's pass at you was a one-off, and at the time, I wondered if it was because of our prior association, like if he wanted to use you to get closer to me, which I know sounds pompous. I'd been invited to his wedding and heard about his divorce, so I wondered if he was trying to get close to someone with a connection, however slight, to his past. It wasn't until a few years ago that I started hearing rumors about Mark being sketchy with his female employees."

"His young female employees," I said.

"Which is one of the reasons he wasn't able to find any backers."

Something about my uncle's expression made me wonder if he'd helped that piece of info make it into the right ears. And I wondered if it was the morality of hitting on female employees that made backers shy away, or the potential social media fallout of being associated with a company with "me too" issues.

"Why didn't Mark get a traditional bank loan?" I asked. "Surely he had collateral, since he owned at least one of the Left Coast Grinds buildings, not to mention the other capital investments in his company."

Coffee roasters, for example, are durable and maintain their resale value. Unlike the way a car does as soon as you buy it and drive it off the lot.

"No idea. You'd have to ask Mark. Or maybe his accountant," Uncle Jimmy said.

I noted Trevor walking over to the security trailer. So I told my uncle I needed to grab the security footage from last night and hustled after Trevor. When I glanced backward, my uncle had disappeared.

Chapter 13

"Trevor!"

I caught up to the security lead about ten feet from the white security building parked on the far side of the distillery, away from the bustle of the festival. Trevor glanced my way. "Oh, it's you."

"Is it a good time to get the security footage?"

Based on the narrowed-eye stare he sent my direction, I suspected Trevor wanted to tell me to get lost. But then he paused.

"Fine." He climbed the handful of metal stairs to the office's small porch and held up his phone against a keypad on the door. The keypad flashed green, and the door unlocked with a click. I followed him inside.

The security office was a temporary setup, with a hitch at one end that showed it could be pulled behind a truck, like the Ground Rules coffee cart. But unlike my cart, the trailer's exterior was a dull white, and the inside wasn't much better. The trailer was about twenty feet long and narrow, maybe eight feet wide. The door opened close to the center of the trailer, and inside was an L-shaped desk to the right. The left held a row of lockers, a mini-fridge and water cooler, and a short bench. A window at either end let in light, along with a window facing the door.

Everything was industrial gray except for the computer on one of the desks. It didn't add much variety to the ambiance, since the computer was a classic black. The setup looked expensive, and the three monitors looked like a gamer's dream setup. A remote with a small screen sat next to the mouse. It caught my eye, because it wasn't for a video game console I recognized.

Trevor refilled his stainless-steel water bottle, which had a sticker with a logo that said BRIGHT SECURITY on the side, then ambled over to the desktop setup. He stashed the remote in a desk drawer.

Other than the computer equipment and Trevor's water bottle, the only thing on the desk was a box with the words "lost & found" neatly printed on it. Trevor rummaged in the box for a moment, the clicked his walkie-talkie and spoke. "Has anyone found any lost cell phones? Remember the police are looking for one."

They were? Interesting. I pictured Mark's body and had no idea what could've been in his pockets. Had someone taken his mobile phone?

Trevor sat down at the desk. I watched over his shoulder as he opened the security footage of the festival.

"You really want all of last night's footage?" Trevor said. He sounded skeptical, as if letting the footage out of his hands was the stupidest idea he'd ever heard. "We already turned all of this over to the police."

"Maybe we'll see something they miss," I said. I could hear the doubt in my voice. "And as I told Tierney, we might need it for insurance purposes."

I really hoped we wouldn't end up in a wrongful-death lawsuit. If one happened, Tierney and Doyle's Oregon Whiskey would be more likely to be defendants, even if Ground Rules were prominently listed in the marketing, because the festival was hosted on the distillery's land, and they'd taken out the insurance coverage. Technically, Ground Rules was just a vendor.

But it was worth taking a gander at the footage. Who knows what I'd find, and if it kept Harley out of trouble, it was worth the time. You never know what you'll find when you kick over a rock—or, in this case, review hours and hours of security footage.

"I've already reviewed the footage, and you won't find anything."

Trevor's confident tone rankled me, and I got the sense that he was humoring me, like I was a small child pestering him. Like, of course I wouldn't find anything useful, especially since his greatness hadn't spotted anything.

And unlike me, Trevor didn't know all the actors in this scenario. What if Melissa was somewhere she shouldn't have been? It could be the clue that blew open the whole case.

Trevor's tone was self-satisfied. "Considering Tierney's background with Mark Jeffries, I thought I should take a close look at the footage. Just in case. So I came in early."

Mark and Tierney had history? I eyed Trevor, who, with a couple of clicks, was copying security footage to a file in the cloud.

From prior conversations, I knew the Doyle brothers had met up with Left Coast Grinds and a couple of other local coffee roasters before deciding to partner with us. Creating the proposal had been a challenge, since I wanted to show why we were the best without trying too hard or coming off desperate. I subtly made it clear I needed the brothers to prove they were worth partnering with, as I showed them why we should be their top choice.

"What sort of history?"

Trevor turned back to the screen, as if my question wasn't important.

I'd tackle Tierney later. "When your security guards escorted Mark out of the festival, how far did they accompany him? Just to the parking lot?"

Trevor's chest puffed up. "I, accompanied by one of my team members, escorted Mark to his car. A dark green CR-V, last year's model, with a scratch on the right passenger's-side door. I even noted down the license plate. We watched him get into his car and drive away."

Hmm, had Mark left and then turned around to come back? The venue had security around the festival, but anyone could drive into the parking areas.

I pictured the scene last night and couldn't remember a CR-V anywhere near the Ground Rules Subaru. But I hadn't tried to memorize all of the cars.

Besides, Mark could've parked outside the property and snuck back in.

"Does the video footage include the parking lot?" I asked.

Trevor huffed and then clicked around a few more times, presumably adding all the parking lot cameras to the footage he'd already compiled.

Trevor pushed back his chair a few inches. "Enter your email address here."

His weird amber and musk scent annoyed me, partially because it reminded me of my high-school classmates who'd doused themselves in the same body spray. And because he was purposefully making me invade his personal space to get the security footage. I didn't inhale as I typed in my address. Something told me he enjoyed annoying me.

I stood back up. "There." I enjoyed a breath of non-scented air.

"Before I hit send, you need to promise me you won't tell anyone where the security cameras are located."

"Why would I?"

"I spent hours analyzing this site for ideal camera placement. I don't want you spreading around any possible dead zones."

"Again, why would I?"

Trevor turned and made eye contact with me. "This festival is important to my business. I don't want my name ruined because someone self-important barista thought telling her friends how to avoid the cameras would be funny."

"You still haven't told me why I would try to harm the festival. You've seen my company name on the banners, right?"

"Please. You're not invested in this festival like the Doyles are. If it goes belly up, what have you risked? The Doyles could lose everything; I could lose everything. You'll just keep on making mochas and telling dumb jokes."

From the expression in his eyes, as Trevor looked back at me, he clearly didn't trust me. Or like me. Which was identical to how I felt about him.

At least we agreed on something.

On my way back from the security booth, there wasn't a line at the Ground Rules cart, so Kendall either had everything in control or we were, metaphorically, dead, meaning bereft of customers. So, I detoured into the craft fair. Shoppers mingled in the aisles, checking out the wares on offer. Before I returned to the cart, I needed to stop for a sample at the ginger beer booth.

"Are you a fan of ginger beer?" the woman working the booth asked me, and she looked familiar. At a guess, I'd say she was in her early fifties. She was about my height, barely over five feet, with blond hair pulled back into a ponytail. Her T-shirt listed the name of her company, PNW Sunshine Soda, and I wondered if this was like looking into a mirror of my future.

"I'm a big fan." I didn't mention it was a recent obsession fueled by trying a ginger beer that wasn't sweet like ginger ale.

"I hope you love ours. Would you like to try a sample?"

I nodded, and she pulled a small four-ounce bottle of ginger beer out of a bucket of ice and used a bottle opener to pop the top off. She poured me a sample into a small shot glass, and I noted the bin of dirty shot glasses behind her. They were going the eco-friendly mode and not using disposable cups.

"We offer our ginger beer in multiple-sized bottles, although the four-ounce size is perfect for cocktails." She handed the shot glass over.

"If you need to wash your shot glasses, let me know. I'm the co-owner of the coffee cart, and we have running water."

"I have boxes and boxes of glasses from my days owning a catering company, and I doubt we'll run out," she said. "But I will absolutely take you up on that if needed."

I took a small sip.

The intense flavor coated my tongue. It reminded me of a ginger chew but in liquid form.

"I love it," I said, and took another sip.

"I visit your shop in the Button Building regularly, and I met Harley a while back," she said. "If you ever want to offer one of our products in your store, we have wholesale rates and can deliver."

"I'll keep that in mind, since we're always looking for local options to stock." Hmm, I wondered what her ginger beer would taste like mixed with our house-made lemonade. Something told me it would taste like sunshine in a glass.

"Let me give you a flier and my card." After rummaging in a red pouch on the table behind her, she handed me a collection of promo material. "I'm Alicia, and I run PNW Sunshine Soda with my son."

"It's an interesting name."

"We thought up the name on a rainy day. I cracked open one of our sodas for inspiration, and it was like a small bottle of sunshine."

Okay, we were destined to be friends or mortal enemies, since her slogan was similar to the tagline I'd written for our Puddle Jumper house coffee.

We briefly talked about their other offerings, which included a sparkling marionberry soda, a seasonal hood strawberry soda ("seasonal because we keep selling out"), and a hazelnut soda that sounded strange but tasted nutty and refreshing.

"You know, I saw Harley arguing with the guy who died," Alicia said.

"That was unfortunate timing," I said.

"For what it's worth, he also got into it with the kid running the chocolate booth."

"Dulcie?"

"They were going at it while they were setting up. She was not happy with him, and he egged her on. It started out with him wanting more table space for products, and they just kept bickering."

Interesting, although needing a few more feet of table was an unlikely reason for murder, unless it was just the tipping point of frustration that culminated in an explosion of anger.

"Did you hear anything specific?" I asked.

"Just that Dulcie regretted agreeing to let Mark join her. He asked if she wanted to renege on their deal, and oh, the glare on that girl. Talk about laser eyes. But Mark just laughed."

Their deal, huh? I needed to look into Dulcie in more depth when I had a moment.

We chatted for a moment, then I moved on, making a note to contact the soda company after the festival about doing a trial run of their sodas in the Ground Rules café.

Even though I didn't want to, I thought about finding Mark's body. Had that been a crime of passion? Anger gone wrong? Or had it been planned?

Had someone killed Mark there on purpose? Maybe the killer saw Harley and Mark's argument or heard about it and lured him there to cast suspicion on us.

"Sage!" a voice called out.

Great. What fire did I need to put out now?

Chapter 14

Ramona waved me into the Bagatha booth. She looked urgent but turned away from me when a woman strode up to her, holding a sunflower-yellow purse with a poppy-red tag.

I paused a few feet into the booth when a waxed canvas satchel with bronze hardware caught my eye. Big enough to carry a sketch pad and magnifying glass but not too big for a burgeoning sleuth who'd yet to finish elementary school.

Ramona was answering questions about leather care. I was tempted to move on, but her voice sounded urgent.

I picked up the bag, unlatched the flap, and looked inside. There were two internal pockets, and a key strap was designed to tuck into one of them.

Simple, but classic.

"That should last for years," a familiar voice said behind my shoulder.

I glanced back. Ramona.

"It's a bit different from most of your products," I said. Most of Bagatha's stock was leather that tiptoed the border of classic and stylish. But they were slightly bland to my taste. But I wasn't an expensive purse sort of person, which meant I wasn't the target market the company was aiming for.

Ramona straightened a rectangular leather purse a little smaller than a toaster on the display beside me. "We tried offering a line of more masculine products, like that bag and a leather messenger bag, which turned into a solid seller. We played around with a few waxed canvas purses and a few accessories, but they didn't do as well. So if you want that, I'd buy it soon, since I'm not sure we'll keep making them. If cared for, that bag should last for years."

"I'd love to buy my fiancé's son a replacement satchel. He bought a cheap bag for an Indiana Jones-inspired costume and uses it so much that it's starting to fall apart." It might be a good birthday gift, since Niko's big day is coming up soon. I checked out the price tag, which was slightly higher than I planned to spend, but not egregiously so.

"If you promise to good faith investigate Mark's murder, I'll get you a discount."

"Honestly, I'd do that without a discount," I said.

"Plus, my boss really wants to move those. She always thought it was a stupid idea, and given the lack of marketing support, I'm not surprised sales were sluggish. Plus, men aren't our target market, unless it's the type of item a wife buys her husband as a gift. We move a decent amount of Dopp kits and wallets, but it's not our primary focus."

I hoped Ramona was playing straight with me, and I couldn't resist asking, "What sort of discount?"

"A good one."

She took the bag from my hands and carried it to the table they were using for checking out customers. She entered something on their tablet and then turned it to face me so I could see the price.

Forty percent off.

"It's my employee discount. We can each use it twice this weekend at our discretion, as long as it's not on a best-selling product."

"I'm in as long as you don't expect me to perform miracles. I can't make any promises." Niko would adore the bag.

"Just try." She tapped on her booth tablet and then turned it around so I could run my credit card.

"Why did you call me over?" I asked.

"I really shouldn't be here today," she said. "I guess you're one of the people who understands what I'm going through."

Was Ramona really that invested in solving Mark's murder? So much that she'd tried to bribe me to continue sticking my nose into everything?

Or was she that motivated to sell one of the satchels?

Or maybe she was bored.

Could she be trying to get me into trouble with the police by interfering?

"By the way, did anyone tell you about Dulcie and Mark's argument yesterday?" Ramona asked. She handed over Niko's bag, now wrapped in a linen drawstring bag that would be perfect for storing a leather purse.

Maybe she had another reason. I paused. "What argument?"

"I only heard about most of it secondhand, but they were snippy with each other. I was trying to stay out of Mark's view, since he'd have comments about me working here when I was his employee, and I wasn't in the mood to deal with his twaddle. But I did hear him tell Dulcie to chin up that it could be so much worse."

Hmm. I wouldn't want to share a booth with Mark.

"Mark's words struck me because it felt like a threat," Ramona said. "He would occasionally warn people of his limits in the same way. And if people didn't notice, they'd usually regret it."

"You've known Mark a long time, right?" I asked.

Ramona's smile was rueful. "Since I was a kid, but I don't think I ever talked to him until high school. But we weren't close, not exactly. We went our separate ways until I needed a job, and Melissa connected me with Mark. As you know, it's worked well enough out for me."

"Have you known Dulcie long?"

"Not really, although I used to be friends with her older sister. It was amusing to see her again, all grown up."

"Do you think she could've harmed Mark?" Ramona had told me about Dulcie's argument with Mark, so she was willing to throw

Dulcie under the bus. Dislike? Or was she trying to throw suspicion off of herself?

Ramona shrugged, and her eyes went to a display of cherry-red clutches. "If you'd asked me this yesterday, I wouldn't have thought anyone would harm Mark. Call him nasty names to his face, yes. But murder?"

Ramona made eye contact with me. "I don't know anyone who would have killed Mark, which scares me. Because it means that any one of us could have done it. Even you."

I should have returned to the coffee cart, but I dropped by Dulcie's chocolate booth instead. Half of the square footage was still dedicated to Mark's coffee products. The other half included print displays of Dulcie's offerings alongside jarred containers of chocolate sauce. But no truffles.

If you weren't offering many products, sharing a booth must be preferable to being alone.

Dulcie sat on a stool next to her display case.

"It's too hot, and my products keep melting if I leave them out," Dulcie said. She looked petulant. "I really shouldn't have come to a summer festival."

"I've seen local chocolatiers in the farmers' markets," I said. They'd had their hot weather systems dialed in.

"My products must be more delicate," Dulcie said. "I texted my mentor, but she hasn't gotten back to me yet."

"Maybe you'll come up with some solutions."

Dulcie waved her hand at the Left Coast Grinds side of the booth. "I'm not sure what I should do with all of that. Mark's new coffee product isn't bad, but I don't feel comfortable selling it. I'm sad he never saw how, as he'd say, his adoring public would react."

I still wasn't sold on the extreme coffee concentrate, even if I'd immediately seen the value and potential market. But I'm a purist.

"Maybe call Mark's second-in-command at Left Coast Grinds. Or make an executive decision and pack all of this up."

Dulcie brightened. "That's a good idea. Do you know who was second in command after Mark?"

I shook my head. "No idea. But you know Ramona, and she works for Mark. She's working at Bagatha's booth at the craft fair. She should know who to ask."

This made me wonder how my employees would react if we were at a festival and I became incapacitated. They'd probably run the cart flawlessly, properly clean it, and deliver it to the Ground Rules warehouse, all while telling me I didn't have anything to worry about.

My conversation with Melissa earlier popped into my head. She had said that Dulcie's sister was one of her best friends.

Was.

Past tense.

And it had seemed like Ramona hadn't seen Dulcie's sister for a while. I looked at the young chocolatier, who'd gone with a floral green sundress today with a pink apron that matched one of the accent colors of her dress. Her ballerina bun was tasteful, but it looked a bit tight.

"Did you know Mark well?" I asked.

Dulcie shook her head. "Just an acquaintance."

"But good enough to partner with?"

"For a weekend, like I said yesterday. But we weren't BFFs. We didn't hang out. He's almost old enough to be my dad."

"Him dying is such a sad situation. It's weird when you realize you know the last words you said to someone."

"That's deep. I hadn't even thought of that," Dulcie said. She scrunched her eyes like she was thinking. "The last I heard from Mark was when he texted me last night after he was kicked out. I messaged and asked if he was okay, and he responded he was fine, but he had to see a man about a horse. Did Mark even like horses?"

"I'm guessing the horse is a metaphor," I said. "Have you told the police about the text?"

Dulcie stiffened. "The police? No."

A woman and a teen girl entered the booth, and Dulcie jumped off her stool. "How are you two today? Can I help you with anything?"

From the way Dulcie turned her back to me, it was clear our conversation had ended.

At least for now. Something told me I'd be back to talk to Dulcie, as something about this situation didn't add up.

"Do you have any, like, chocolate?" the teenager asked.

Dulcie looked sad as I walked away.

Looking into Dulcie's past was next on my to-do list. I decided to check on Sophie, but I'd only taken a few steps when another voice yelled, "Sage!"

I turned and couldn't have stopped a big smile from spreading across my face, even if I wanted to. "Pike!"

A giant of a man, Pike McAdams, owner of my favorite coffee roastery out in the Columbia River Gorge, lifted me into the air in a hug. From the distance, Pike looked like someone you wouldn't want to cross. Sometimes, it's the leather jacket, which he wasn't wearing today as a nod to the summer weather, opting for a white T-shirt and blue jeans with a James Dean vibe. Or it's the double-full sleeve of tattoos combined with the bushy beard that gives a biker vibe instead of Portland hipster. But once you see the laugh line by his eyes, and realize most of the tattoos are homages to dogs, you'll get the sense he's actually a gentle giant.

And he's a dang good coffee roaster. He'd worked for several big names before setting up his own low-key shop. When we first set up Ground Rules, he dropped by and gave us a couple of suggestions on workflow, leading us to rearrange part of the roastery.

"When I heard about the festival, I had to come to sample the Irish coffee in a can. I was happy to hear you were collaborating," Pike said.

"You were one of the roasters the Doyles talked to, right?"

"I was, but I knew I wasn't the right choice. My focus is small batches and one-offs, and they wanted consistency. They made a smart choice when they brought you onboard."

"How are things going in the gorge?" I asked Pike. He gave me the lowdown on his coffee and roastery, which was in an old mini-mart attached to a gas station. He remodeled the space to be open and bright, with an outdoorsy feel that matched the wildness of the gorge. Being on a major freeway let him catch a lot of traffic, both repeat customers drawn in by his perfectly crafted espresso and strong house-brew coffee, and first-timers on a road trip. Whenever I travel out to the gorge, I include a trip to Pike's coffee shop for an after-hike recovery caffeine hit.

"Did I tell you about the new bakery that opened near me? A couple bakes in their house, but they upgraded their equipment to professional. They got certified to sell to businesses like mine. Their products are amazing and practically fly out of the store. I should've brought one of their cruffins for you. It's basically a croissant twisted into a muffin shape, and let me tell you, it's basically addictive." Pike looked around. "Is Harley here?"

The million-dollar question. "She's here somewhere, but I'm not sure where, exactly. I'm heading to the Ground Rules booth, and she might be there, but no promises."

"I'll tag along to see if she's there," Pike said.

The crowd parted as we walked toward Ground Rules, people making room for Pike instinctively in a way that never happens to me if I'm walking alone. I usually have to dodge and weave.

We chatted as we walked. The steady crowd holding shopping bags of goods was a great sign, although maybe it meant Mark's death hadn't made the news.

Hannah was chatting with a couple of women by her apothecary setup, so I was willing to bet she was about to make them both a custom blend. The Stonefield Beach Tea owner seemed chipper, almost bouncy, as she made notes on a small paper pad.

At least someone had the right summer energy for a festival like this. I was almost jealous since, for me, the weight of Mark's death had thrown a shadow over the entire weekend.

Sophie was adding a couple of bags of beans to a display, which was an excellent sign: she'd sold enough to warrant restocking. She also kept a subtle eye on the woman, who was inspecting the selection of camp mugs, picking up the teal cup, inspecting it before putting it down, and inspecting the black option with our logo printed in white.

But no Harley.

"Your booth looks great," Pike said. "I halfway thought about applying, but this was clearly going to be the Sage and Harley show."

A woman carried a mug and a bag of beans to Sophie, who quickly rang her up on the tablet and told her the total.

"Your accent! Are you Irish? Are you related to the Doyle brothers?"

Sophie's smile looked forced. "I'm Canadian. And the Doyles were born and raised here in Oregon."

"But your accent is Irish."

"It's from St. John's, Newfoundland," Sophie said. She held out the tablet so the woman could tap her credit card.

"Where's that?" The woman put her credit card back in her wallet.

"Canada." Sophie's voice was cheerful, but I could sense the frustration underneath.

"Oh." The woman sounded slightly confused. "You sure sound Irish."

Sophie smiled as she handed the woman a paper bag with the mug and coffee beans. "I've added a flier about our mail-order program to your bag. I hope you love your coffee."

"She honestly does sound Irish," Pike murmured to me. He turned and looked at our display of merch.

"She's from a remote region of Canada that never lost the accent of their ancestors," I said quietly back. "But she gets tired of people asking if she's Irish and not believing her when she says no. Last week, someone insisted on telling her about every stop on their trip around the Emerald Isle."

Pike picked up one of the trucker hats. "I think I need this."

I checked him out, and we continued walking. We exited the craft fair and walked toward the coffee cart.

"If I tell you something, can you keep it quiet?" I asked.

"Are you pregnant?" Pike asked.

"Am I . . . no. Do I look pregnant?" I was the same size I'd always been, and the thought of gaining weight so my wedding dress wouldn't fit made my breath catch.

"You look as beautiful as always, but you're getting married. Officially. Legally. A lot of people do that when they've roasting a little bean inside."

"No, I'm not pregnant, and that's not what I wanted to talk about."

Pike turned and glanced down at me.

"Mark Jeffries died," I said.

"Mark? Really? Did the dude finally work himself into a heart attack?"

I shook my head. "It's worse than that. He was murdered."

"Jealous husband?" Pike asked.

"Why do you say that?"

"I didn't know him well, but he didn't seem to care about boundaries. Years ago, maybe a decade, maybe more, definitely before you were on the scene, a now-defunct coffee magazine awarded Roaster of the Year to my old employer, Mads, who has since closed shop and moved to Austin. Some of the other roasters in town threw a party for him, and Mark came. He kept hitting on Mads's wife and wouldn't stop."

"Why am I not surprised."

"Mark apologized later and said he was drunk and out of line. But I always thought he wanted to make some sort of point. He was purposefully picking at Mads, being annoying, trying to get a reaction. It could've turned nasty. Well, nastier."

"That sounds like Mark."

"He had his good points. Mark used to be helpful to other roasters. But when he thought he was the king of the local roasters, he started jealously protecting his empire and started treating former friends like spies. I understand, in part. I'd be upset if someone opened a coffee roastery next door to my shop. But it would just mean I'd need to up my game."

"If that happened, how would you act?"

"I'd grumble but keep my chin up and kill them with kindness. I have faith in myself, and my goal has never been to expand. I just want to make good coffee and enjoy my life," Pike said. "You're more aggressive about expanding, which I appreciate. And I'm sure Harley likes being able to roast and let you lead her into a bright future."

I nodded.

"Speaking of Harley, will you tell her I'm around? I'll drop by again later and try to track her down."

"Sure thing."

As Pike showed his pass and disappeared into the music area, I thought that he was right about Ground Rules being aggressive. Not cutthroat, but we were focused on building an empire. I loved seeing WE SERVE GROUND RULES COFFEE signs at local cafés and restaurants. Although my vision was focused on local expansion if we opened more cafés, with no desire for a branded chain or franchises across the country.

But Pike was wrong that I was the aggressive force between Harley and me. She's just as dedicated to the cause, although I'm more visible.

If anything, Harley might have more to prove.

I didn't want to think about how Mark's comments could have touched a sensitive spot deep inside my business partner. The sort of deep area that people will lash out to protect.

Chapter 15

After Pike left to listen to the bands, I returned to the cart and promptly sent Kendall off on a well-deserved break.

Harley walked up, her steps dragging like she was ready to crash. She climbed into the booth and leaned against the door frame.

"Where've you been? People have been asking for you," I said.

"Like the police? I don't want to talk with them, and they can't make me."

"Also, Pike."

Harley straightened up a little bit, and she smiled. "Pike's here?"

"He was here for a while, then left to listen to the music." When the cart was quiet, I did what I always did: I cleaned. But my eyes kept straying to my business partner.

"I hope I find him before he takes off," Harley said.

"Pike said he'd come back and look for you." I put a cleaning rag down and turned to my business partner. "We need to talk about something."

"I'm sorry I took off today, but I just needed time to think. And I'm not scheduled to work until late afternoon."

"You're right, and I know you're not on the schedule. We also need to discuss how to communicate about serious issues in the future. But I have another question," I said. "I'm not claiming this will have any bearing on Mark's death, but you know how he crept on some of his female employees? Did he harass you?"

Harley looked up at the sliver of blue sky peeking through the row of booths, then shook her head. "I can't think of anything inappropriate, at least in that way. Maybe I just wasn't his type."

"That's an interesting take." Nina, our former barista who'd been involved in a physical relationship with Mark when she worked for him, had been confident, or at least presented as such. Ditto Ramona, who said she'd turned Mark down. I could see similarities between them and Melissa, Mark's first ex-wife. All presented themselves as bold and capable, even if it was a façade.

They were a contrast to Harley, who had always been a mix of shy and intense. She'd opened up to me in the past about her anxiety issues. She'd had a rough time as a teen. It could take a while for the real Harley to emerge, and I wondered how many people had dismissed Harley based on their first impressions. They hadn't gotten a chance to see the other facets of her personality emerge.

Maybe Mark had been drawn to women who'd veered into overconfident territory. The sort that can suck the air out of the room, even if it's not on purpose. From what Melissa said, Mark's childhood had been rough, and I wondered how much of his actions were overcompensation. Maybe he'd been attracted to women who seemed like they had it all under control. Like he'd feel better within the confines of their world.

Or maybe he liked tearing them down and feeling in control.

"When things were good at Left Coast Grinds, what was your relationship with Mark like?"

"Is that a way of asking if our relationship was ever functional, versus highly contentious?" Harley's smile was bitter. "In retrospect, there was always a lot of dysfunction. Although for a long time, I liked Mark. I thought he was a huge visionary in the world of coffee. Then, the more I roasted and earned my certifications with SCA, I started seeing that he was a good enough roaster, but he wasn't great, exactly. However, he is—was—extremely consistent, which is harder than it sounds. For a long time, he'd surrounded himself with people who turned Left Coast Grinds into a premier shop. Both in the roastery, but also in the shops, which is vital. If you serve a bad cup of coffee in your shop, who is going to buy beans to take home? Versus allowing people to feel aspirational when they buy your product."

Harley looked at the cart's ceiling. "Mark was good at setting the standard, if you know what I mean. He'd rather have us throw out a bad espresso than serve something less than our best. He was a pretty awesome barista, and when he wanted, he excelled at training new employees."

"I remember." I appreciated the shop's customer-first focus and commitment to quality. It'd been a good training ground despite Mark's flaws as a boss. "Mark accused you of stealing his ideas. Was there any validity to his claims?"

Harley's gaze shifted from the ceiling to the floor. She shook her head. "No, none. The closest you can claim is that I acquired my roasting skills while working for Left Coast Grinds. But all of our products are custom recipes I created versus borrowing the ratios Mark preferred in his signature blends. There's a reason our blends are more balanced. Obviously, when we source a single-origin bean, I use my judgment to determine which roast will bring out its flavors. That's not something I truly could copy, and each batch differs depending upon the bean. But hypothetically, Left Coast Grinds, or any one of our competitors, could create a roast similar enough that even the savviest coffee drinker could struggle to tell the difference."

I nodded, knowing that our single-origins are always sourced from small farms or cooperatives, so they're always unique. While the blends are magically consistent, showing Harley's skill as a roaster. And our blends are different than Left Coast Grinds, with unique flavor profiles, although not everyone who drinks a cup of our darkest French roast will be able to tell the difference between it and another craft roaster's version.

"Did you ever meet Mark's first wife?"

"Melissa?" Harley's lip curled up.

I nodded.

"She hated me. Melissa would come in, ask me a question, then talk over me before I could answer. It annoyed me, so I didn't talk to her, then she'd complain to Mark that I didn't respect her. Mark thought it was funny. But then they divorced, and it was a relief when she quit coming around every other day."

"Did you know he got married again?"

Harley laughed. "For real?"

"Someone named Jocelyn."

"Jocelyn . . . that name seems familiar, but I can't place why," Harley said. "Any other questions?"

"What'd you make of Ramona when you worked with her?"

"She can be fun to work with, especially during boring projects, because she'll dig in and get them done rather than procrastinate. But I wouldn't trust her with anything personal."

"What do you mean?"

"She has an element of a high-school mean girl who enjoys finding out someone's secret pain and then tease them about it publicly. Maybe I'm being unfair, but I always got the sense she was mocking me," Harley said.

"Did anything happen when you quit?"

"Other than Mark yelling at me?" Harley said.

"Well, yeah."

"It wasn't too dramatic, although I should've made it a bigger deal than I did. The flagship shop held a party to celebrate our winning the grand prize at the regional coffee championship. And Mark spent the entire day bragging about *his* roast, as if I hadn't created it. He kept making little digs at me, but they were subtle. When another roaster came in, Mark said that me doing the grunt work allowed him to shine, as if I was just around to clean up after him. But it sounded like praise to everyone else."

"That would've pissed me off." I'd been out of the country and missed the drama firsthand.

"I read his celebratory blog post while I was at the party, but he didn't credit me. It sounded like he'd spent hours developing the concept. I texted my sister, who was trying to calm me down, but when a few more roasters came in, including Pike, they all congratulated Mark. One asked how he'd managed to put the blend together. I interrupted and said the blend was mine. I'd created it."

"How did Mark react?"

"He said I was lying. That I needed time to develop my skills if I wanted to 'run with the big boys.' And one of the roasters laughed. It made me even angrier. I told Mark that he was the one lying. I sounded unhinged, but I couldn't stay silent. Although maybe I should have."

"Did anyone support you?"

"A few weeks before the contest, I'd talked with one of the roasters—Pike, who, by the way, is one of the roasters who didn't laugh—about the work I was doing to create a new blend. His boss—this was before Pike opened his own roastery—wasn't entering the competition. I'd been vague on the details, but I'd told Pike that I'd roasted a yirgacheffe with incredibly lemon notes, and I was deciding how to pair it. It was good as a single-origin, but I wanted to know if I could use the lemon notes to make something special."

I'd tried yirgacheffe before and knew it was an arabica bean from southern Ethiopia. The beans we'd briefly offered last year as a single roast had come from wild coffee plants over 1,300 years old.

"I joked about mixing it with hambela, which is very berry-forward, and calling the blend a raspberry lemonade. We decided that since it would be ridiculously expensive per pound, I might as well toss in kopi luwak and convince coffee snobs with more money than sense that the blend was the new thing. It'd be so hot, it'd be like printing money." Harley smiled at the memory.

I nodded. I knew the coffee beans Harley was talking about. Like yirgacheffe, hambela is grown in southern Ethiopia, but it has a fuller, deeper taste with berry notes. While kopi luwak, or civet coffee, is an Indonesian coffee that sometimes grosses people out. The palm civet, a cuddle-sized wild omnivorous animal native to south and southeast

Asia, eats the raw coffee cherry, and it passes through the wild animal's digestive system and is processed once it makes its way back out. Connoisseurs love it, but when I heard some entrepreneurs were caging civets and feeding them only a diet of coffee cherries, the thought of animal abuse involved made me sick. We'd debated trying to source wild-only produced kopi luwak, then decided it wasn't right for Ground Rules. It didn't meet our values.

"After talking with Pike, I decided to play around and mix the two. I managed to roast a hambela to have a lovely berry and vanilla profile. I experimented with blending it with yirgacheffe until I had the perfect blend of lemon and berry. I texted a photo of me drinking a cup to Pike, saying I'd created my raspberry-lemonade blend. He responded with appropriate emojis and asked if I'd send him a sample. And I did."

"Did he like it?"

"Pike loved it. And a few weeks later, the judges did, too. They highlighted the perfect lemon and berry notes in the blend. When he accepted the award, Mark claimed he was trying to recreate the flavors of his youth. That when he was small, his dad would make him blackberry lemonade with berries grown in their backyard. It would've been a heartwarming story if it was the truth."

Harley laughed with a bitter note. "I mean, maybe his dad did make him lemonade. But the coffee wasn't an homage to Mark's past. Then I realized I'd messed up when Mark insisted we call the coffee blend 'Tribute.' I thought he meant it was to honor the growing regions of Ethiopia. But then he spun it so the name honored his dad, and I was suddenly the lying harpy attacking Mark's brilliant blend that celebrated his beloved father taken from the world too soon."

"Ouch."

"I've never been that angry before in my life. If I was ever going to harm Mark, I would've done it then. But I quit at that party. My parting words were almost perfect, at least for me. I told Mark good luck defending his title without me."

The rumors I'd heard about Harley's last words matched her own recollection. "It must've felt good to leave."

"It was until I realized I desperately needed a job to make my rent. My sister helped me for a few months, since I'm pretty sure she decided the alternative was to let me sleep on her couch, and we're better together if we each have our own space."

Harley half-smiled. "There were rumors afterward, since roasters love to gossip. Some said Mark was a snake, but most people believed him. Or at least, they didn't stick up for me publicly, at least not then. Most have apologized to me now.

"But Pike stood by me. He tried to get me hired at the roastery he worked at, but the owner wasn't interested, because he'd heard I was 'difficult.' But he also closed down his Portland roastery a few months later and moved to Colorado, so it might've just been an excuse. He probably didn't want to get caught up between Mark and me, since Mark was determined that no one should hire me. He said that if I wanted to work in the industry again, I'd have to crawl back to him on my knees or leave the Pacific Northwest."

I flinched at the image, since I was sure Mark had intended the double entendre.

"But I found a job and a couple side hustles, since I was trying to save enough to start my own roastery, and then you came back, and we created Ground Rules together."

I wondered how many of the roasters who'd initially sided with Mark but had later apologized to Harley had tried our coffee and decided she'd been telling the truth about the award-winning blend.

"You know, Mark has tried to release the Tribute blend a few times as a special order, but it's not as good as it was," Harley said.

"I'm not surprised he couldn't recreate it without your brilliance."

"Or both of those roasts were a fluke. As I've told you many times, the notes in coffee beans can change yearly, depending upon weather conditions, like drought and a whole host of other factors. And that doesn't take into account how the coffee cherry is processed and how the bean is eventually roasted." A genuine smile crossed Harley's face. "And I might not have written down the exact proportions I'd been using. Talk about a happy accident. I'd meant to change the documentation, but then I quit before I had the chance."

Harley made eye contact with me. "I promise my Ground Rules records are perfect, because if something happens, I want them to be my legacy."

"We'll create a museum to coffee perfection," I said.

I wasn't sure if Harley's story would help me discover who killed Mark, but it linked a few threads in my mind.

Chapter 16

I told Kendall to call it quits for the day and that I'd work the cart until Aspen, one of our part-time baristas, showed up to work the closing shift with Harley.

"I'll see what I can find out from Naomi's friends," he said. "I'll see you back here when the festival ends."

I waved him off when a woman walked up and ordered a cup of house coffee, which I made fresh for her. When I handed it over, she added a splash of oat milk to her coffee. About fifty percent of our customers had switched to oat milk in the last year. It wasn't just because we're in Portland, although one local chain had even switched to oat milk as their default, and they carry cow milk for customers who request it. Customers across the entire world have adopted oat milk as a dairy alternative.

Then, the cart was quiet, so I did a few Google searches on Dulcie.

Opinions about Dulcie's shop were a mixed bag. While many praised her chocolate, they also found her shop to be a bit chaotic. For every person who commended Dulcie's warm customer service, someone else was frustrated with her inconsistent product offerings, with truffle cases sometimes empty with a promise of more chocolates on the way, and unpredictable opening hours.

A quick glance showed me Dulcie had no formal chocolate or candy-making training, unless she'd hidden it. Her personal Instagram account, which was public, showed a curated collection of beautiful truffles on shabby chic plates. At one point, she'd been obsessed with French-style macarons, with a brief foray into double-decker round cakes covered in whimsical fondant designs. The lack of education explained why she wasn't prepared for the summer heat. If Sophie was right, and Dulcie's wealthy parents were bankrolling her, they might have jumped a few steps and launched her business before she was ready. Making a batch of truffles at home is a fun hobby, but retail-quality chocolates made in bulk are a different, temperamental story.

It might be nothing, but something Dulcie said flickered in my brain. She'd said Mark joining her in the booth would allow her to leave the booth when necessary during the festival and that she was worried about turning a profit.

But she hadn't mentioned Mark paying to join her. I'd made the mental jump to subletting for pay, but Dulcie hadn't said that.

The music area of the festival started playing at noon, but the main crowds started showing up at four, with the bigger names scheduled to start playing at five. The headliner each night took the stage between eight and nine, with the music ending at ten.

In the Ground Rules cart, we'd emptied out the last remaining carafe of hot coffee and were ready to pull espresso drinks, although we expected to sell lemonades and our lineup of special naturally decaffeinated drinks, with my personal favorite being our blackberry herbal tea soda, made with fresh house-made blackberry syrup.

I left the cart in Harley and Aspen's joint hands and headed out. Barring any catastrophes, I was done for the day, but I'd keep my phone on me in case of "we need help" cart texts.

I noted that on the outside of the fence, close to the craft area, a few people had set up camp on blankets on the ground. When I heard the sounds of a well-known band warming up, I chuckled to myself. Just because you can't see the stage doesn't mean you won't be able to hear the music. Which I'd also been listening to, starting with the small local band popular with the under-ten-years-old set, all day. No cart radio needed when we had live music on tap.

The thought of listening to the music made me pause. Had anyone been stowing away here last night, listening to the opening bands from outside of the fence?

If yes, had any of them seen Harley leave? Or seen someone following Mark, even if they didn't realize the significance at the time? I doubted they'd seen Mark's final, fatal confrontation with his killer. But maybe they'd seen something they hadn't realized was important.

As I wasn't the only person who'd made this discovery.

A familiar small figure wearing a fedora and Indiana Jones-style satchel talked intently with two women sitting on a blanket. He was crouched down with his notebook perched on one knee and a pen in his hand, like a miniature journalist on the trail of a big scoop.

Although he did have a companion. Jackson's Australian Shepherd, Bentley, sat next to Niko, intently looking at the women as if he were gauging their trustworthiness.

Or maybe he could scent treats in their pockets.

Another glance around showed me that Bax wasn't in sight. Niko didn't have to be watched every minute, but there was no way his father would be happy that his son was interviewing people about a murder. Which I assumed he was doing.

When I walked up, Niko's eyes widened slightly.

Busted.

Niko straightened his shoulders but remained in a crouch. "This is my dad's fiancée, Sage," he told the women. "When they get married, I'm going to be a junior groomsman, but I wanted to be the ring bear."

I almost said, "bearer," but didn't speak. Niko still wanted to wear a bear costume and carry the ring down the aisle. He'd offered to throw flowers while doing it, since we weren't planning on having a flower girl.

"Hi," I said. I glanced at Niko. "Where's your dad?"

"He's with Jackson and Piper. I said I'd take Bentley on a walk," Niko said. "But listen, these women saw Harley last night!"

I glanced at them and raised my eyebrows. The older of the two women, who looked about sixty, smiled at me. Her companion looked enough like her that I bet they were mother and daughter. Bentley saddled up next to me and leaned against my leg.

"Our family owns Good Clean Suds, and we have a booth in the festival down the aisle from you. We met Harley while we were set-ting up. Yesterday evening, we saw her stalk out of the gate—"

"Harley is so intense," the younger woman added.

"—not long after the Doyle brothers opened the festival, and we couldn't help but notice her pace around by the booths for a while. Then she came over this way, and we invited her to sit with us." The older woman took a sip of her water bottle.

"She was so angry with someone. Mark?" the younger woman said. "She ranted a little bit."

Wait, Harley had stayed here? She didn't leave the festival imme-diately?

She'd told me that she'd left. That she'd gone for a drive and ended up at her sister's house in the gorge in the opposite direction of Portland.

Harley had lied to me?

More importantly, had Harley lied to the police?

Maybe, after listening to music for a while, Harley had been walking through the parking lot, unintentionally giving Mark time to sneak back on to wait by the Ground Rules Subaru. It was a fifty-fifty chance that either Harley or I would have driven that car to the fes-tival. Maybe she'd passed by the company car on her way to her own.

"How long did Harley stay with you?" I asked.

"She stayed for a band or two but kept ranting about Mark. She couldn't sit still," the younger woman said.

"So fidgety," the older woman agreed. "It was worse than when I taught kindergartners."

"He really got under her skin."

"He excelled at that," I said.

"Was he her ex or something?" the younger woman asked.

But before I could answer—or see if I could tease out an approx-
imate time Harley had left—a strident voice interrupted us.

"Dogs aren't allowed in the music festival!"

Trevor.

I turned. "True, dogs aren't allowed inside those fences," I said. I
pointed at the gates. "But we're on the craft festival side, where well-
behaved dogs are welcome."

"That dog is better behaved than most people we know," the
older woman said.

Trevor pulled his mirrored sunglasses down and looked at the
woman, taking in their picnic blanket, a flask of what looked like
lemonade, two glasses, a water bottle each, and a couple of Tupper-
ware containers of snacks.

Part of me was impressed. I've attended less-organized picnics.
And their deviled eggs, avocado salad, and watermelon slices looked
refreshing. My stomach rumbled.

"You need to move," Trevor said. He glared at the women like
they'd just offended his grandmother. Bentley shifted so Trevor was
on one side, and Niko and I were on the other.

"Actually, they don't," I said. "Review the vendor guidelines
and all of the rules we posted. Nothing says you can't sit on the
ground outside the fence. Feel free to call Tierney, but he will agree
with me."

We stared at each other, and Trevor blinked first.

"I'm going to talk to Tierney." Trevor pulled his cell phone out
of his pocket and stalked away.

"Talking bad about people isn't cool, but that security dude is
too much," the younger woman said.

"He seems to have a problem with women," the older one
added.

I pulled a teal business card out of my wallet and handed it to the
women. "If you have problems with Trevor—that's the security
guy—call or text me, and I'll handle it."

"Thanks." I glanced at Niko and nodded, and he responded in kind. We stood up, and the three of us walked way.

I glanced into the craft fair, which had shut down for the night. Most vendors had covered their displays in dark tablecloths, although a few had brought tent flaps that zipped closed. It felt spooky, but I knew it'd come back to life tomorrow.

"You know the women we talked to? And their company?" Niko said.

"Good Clean Suds?"

Niko nodded. "You should know they don't sell candy, even if their products look like they'd taste good."

"Some of their soaps do look like fudge," I said. I'd noted one of their soaps with gorgeous raspberry-red marbling. It reminded me of buying fudge at one of the ubiquitous candy shops on the Oregon Coast.

"They also have bath bombs that look like donuts," Niko added.

I glanced at Niko. "Did you go shopping today?"

"I was looking for clues," Niko said, but he blushed, like he always does when he's not being entirely truthful.

Before I could say anything else, Piper called my name. She held hands with Jackson, and they sat with Bax at a picnic table on the edge of the food cart zone.

"I didn't know you made it over," I said as we walked up. Piper, my brother's law school girlfriend who had broken up with him when she moved across the country after graduation, had transferred within the US Attorney's office to a local branch, and it hadn't taken long for her and my brother to resume their relationship.

"Bentley and I decided to drop by for dinner, but I have a red-eye flight tonight, so we can't stay too long."

We headed to the food carts and spiritedly debated what to order before Jackson left to get fish and chips from the Codfather. Piper grabbed something healthy-looking with tofu and alfalfa from Wrap-Tor. Bax grabbed burritos for him and Niko from Salsa Superstars, and I grabbed pad kee mao from Thai is Life.

As we settled back at the table together, Niko kept gazing longingly at the ice cream and cookies cart instead of his perfect-looking junior-sized burrito. My gaze kept drifting to the coffee cart, which was sending out a steady stream of iced drinks.

Fingers crossed, everyone loved the special menu I'd created for the festival.

"We were flawless during our first matches," Jackson said.

As Jackson and Bax updated Piper about their cornhole tournament, I kept thinking back to my conversation with the owners of Good Clean Suds.

Why had Harley lied to me?

Or was I remembering her story wrong? Had she left out stopping for a band or two, since it hadn't seemed important to her at the time? Had she mentioned it to the police? Because if she lied to them, she'd look guilty.

And the comment about Trevor having issues with women resonated with me. If we'd found a woman dead, he'd be my lead suspect.

"You're distracted," Jackson said to me.

"It's been a long day."

"Know what'll make it better? Ice cream. I bet Niko agrees with me."

"Yes!" Niko bounced in place.

After a round of ice-cream sandwiches and sorbet, it was clear my brief moment of normalcy was coming to an end. Piper said something quietly to Jackson, and he nodded. Niko tried to stifle a yawn.

My brother turned to me.

"I'd love to stay for the bands, but we have a few things to do at home before I drive Piper to the airport," Jackson said.

"Go, there will be more music tomorrow. Plus more cornhole." Different music, but that's life. We all have small choices we make or decide against. Or worse, we simply don't take action, and the opportunity passes us by.

"Don't get in trouble while I'm gone. Remember to call me if the police want to talk to you."

"Of course."

They left, with Bentley trotting at their heels (probably hoping he'd get another pup cup of vanilla ice cream if he was a good boy), and Bax turned to me.

"I think we need to split too," he said.

"Makes sense," I said.

Despite a valiant effort, Niko looked ready to fall asleep at any second.

"I'll see if I'm needed here, but I'd love to follow you home soon, unless I need to stay to collect the Ground Rules tablets and cashboxes."

They walked off, and I finally walked back over to Ground Rules.

The coffee cart looked quiet at the moment, so I asked Aspen if she'd be okay watching it alone for a moment while I talked with Harley.

"Of course," she said. Aspen was one of our newer baristas, and we'd trained her from scratch when she moved to Portland after she'd finished community college and enrolled in my alma mater. Last I heard, she'd decided to major in history.

"We'll be nearby. Call if you need us." Harley followed me outside, and I walked to a spot nearby, away from other people.

"Is something wrong?" Harley asked.

"Other than you lying to me?" I said.

"What lie?"

"You said that when you left the festival after your showdown with Mark, you drove to your sister's house in Hood River. But you didn't. You were here, next to the craft area, listening to music."

"I didn't lie; I just didn't tell you every single step of my movements. I did leave to blow off steam, then sat and listened to a few songs before leaving."

"Did you lie to the police, too?" She'd lied to Detective Ortega, at least. Maybe she'd tell the detective she just hadn't told her the entire story, too.

"Why are you grilling me? You're not a detective."

"Harley, do you want to be arrested for murdering Mark?"

"Of course not."

"I'm trying to keep you out of trouble. If the police think you're lying, it will look like you have something to hide. They're going to look at you even more closely."

"I know it looks bad for me. I argued with Mark, and I don't have an alibi. If I had stayed with the women listening to music by the craft area, then walked with someone to my car, I would've been fine. And maybe I could've stopped Mark from being harmed. Maybe I could've changed things. Instead, I was off driving alone. I should've stayed with you or our baristas and helped out. I should have done something useful. Instead, I flailed about mentally."

"We didn't blame you for wanting emotional space."

"I'm so angry with myself for rising to Mark's bait. No matter how often I reminded myself not to react, I couldn't stop myself. Which is why it was ironic."

"What?"

"Mark initially started in on me yesterday because he said I'd turned my back on him and his company when he needed my skills the most. He told me I'd do the same things to Ground Rules. That I'd crack, I'd run away, when things got tough, and suffer the consequences. And now I might've ruined the whole business."

"We're not ruined." Not yet, anyway. Harley being arrested—or worse, convicted—for murder would be a challenge we might not overcome. Although I could put out feelers for a roaster to do their best to fill her shoes until she was back with us.

Or I could prove she was innocent.

Which would have been easier if Harley had helped me out. I told myself to take a deep breath; it wasn't my job to prove my business partner and friend wasn't a killer.

"I can't believe this is really happening," Harley said. She tilted her head slightly and looked at me. "Why was Mark on site, anyway? He'd been kicked out. Why did he come back?"

"I think if we knew the answer to that, we'd know who killed him," I said.

"This is a nightmare," Harley said.

I nodded, trying to hold in my own yawn.

"I was here much later than planned last night because I had to talk to the police," I said.

"If you want to go home, I can drop by the tablets and cashboxes by the roastery on my way home," Harley said. "While I'm at it, I can package everything you'll need for tomorrow and leave it ready for you to pick up. Sophie already emailed us a list for the booth."

"That works for me."

"I didn't do it, Sage. I didn't harm Mark."

"I know, Harley."

"But what if the police arrest me?"

"We'll get you the best criminal defense lawyer in Portland and fight. But hopefully, that never happens."

After reassuring Harley for another minute, she returned to the cart, and I headed to the parking lot.

Harley had asked one of the questions I kept dwelling on. Did the police know, or had they any educated guesses, why Mark had snuck back into the festival grounds the night he died? He must have had a reason, and I doubted it was a good reason. He wasn't coming back to make the world a better place.

It'd be nice if I could check Mark's text messages or phone records, which might indicate why he'd come back. But I'm a barista, not a police detective able to get warrants for that sort of info.

And maybe if I figured out the answer to that question, I'd feel like the shadow of Mark's death wasn't threatening to block out all of the sun in my life.

Chapter 17

The refrain of music on the air made me slightly sad to leave. I'm sure the bands would be lovely to hear, but I was looking forward to the Monday night bands, which featured a musician I knew slightly who'd hit it big.

Someone I'd met when he was on the upswing, at a rather deadly music festival, which I decided was a point I didn't want to dwell on. After that fateful weekend, Ground Rules had worked at the same festival again, and it'd been low-drama. No murder. Just music under the trees, as intended.

Harley had driven her car, so I took the Ground Rules ride home. But before I turned my key in the ignition, I sent a couple of messages first. Then, I tucked my phone away in my bag and focused on driving.

When I arrived home in Southeast Portland, I didn't even need to check my texts to see that several of them had been received and acted upon. My father's hybrid subcompact SUV was parked in front of the house, but the car was empty.

When I walked inside, my dad lounged in my living room with a book. I noticed his empty water glass. From a murmur in the distance, Bax was supervising Niko's bedtime routine.

"Would you like more water?" I asked, and after he said yes, I headed to the kitchen.

"I can't believe Harley would harm anyone on purpose," my father said as I handed over his refilled glass. His book, *The Feather Thief: Beauty, Obsession, and the Natural History Heist of the Century*, sat neatly on the coffee table.

The "on purpose" hedge in his statement made me eye him. I suspected it resulted from his years as a police officer, including his final decade as a detective in the cold case unit. He'd probably seen a lot of people who'd snapped for whatever reason.

I sat down on the couch with my own glass. "Harley didn't do it."

"While I question how worthwhile it'll be for us to watch the security videos you acquired, do you want to get started?"

"Let's go with the boring footage first." Bax had already set my tablet to mirror on the wall-mounted TV, and I clicked open the security footage.

"I thought I'd left these days behind me," my father said, as we watched footage from the camera closest to where Mark was found. It covered the view of the side gate, which was staffed and allowed people to leave the venue, but if they wanted to come inside, they had to walk to the main gate.

Part of me knew that if there was something here, the police would've already found it.

I glanced at my notebook, which housed my bullet journal, and now a few pages for the investigation, starting with a timeline of Mark's movements. Under Friday, it had:

- Argues with Dulcie
- Argues with Harley—afternoon
- Argues again with Harley after the opening ceremony

Something flew in front of the camera. "Was that a bat?" I asked. I scrolled back, and something buzzed across the image.

"Maybe?"

I scrolled forward, since there wasn't anything happening on the screen, slowing back to real-time when a trio of women, maybe in their early twenties, walked into the festival, followed a moment later by Trevor, the security guard, who nodded at the two guards managing the gate.

I paused the video to note the time, then resumed.

Finally, Harley stalked out of the side gate, her fists clenched. She disappeared from view.

A few minutes later, Trevor and another security guard frog-marched Mark through the gate. Mark looked flushed but also a bit smug.

Which made me suspect Mark had meant to get thrown out. It'd been part of some master plan, which had clearly taken an unexpected twist. Since there's no way he planned his own murder.

But Mark had wanted to cause a scene, and he'd succeeded.

But why?

Bax walked into the room and sprawled onto the couch beside me. "Niko has a list of questions for you about police investigations," Bax said, looking at my dad.

"I look forward to it," my dad said. And he sounded sincere.

Bax eyed the screen and motioned to where Trevor was walking back up to the main music entrance. "Is that the guy who's in charge of security?"

"Yes, that's Trevor," I said. *Mark wasn't visible, nor was Trevor accompanied by the security guards who'd been with him,* I scrawled in my notebook, *twenty minutes before.*

"He's an odd one. He's blustered into the cornhole competition a few times and tried to order the referees around," Bax said. "The poor cornhole ref was doing exactly what she was supposed to do. And she was good. All of the cornhole referees are doing a great job."

"Trevor really wants to feel like he's in charge," I said.

We watched at double speed, and my eyes felt heavy as the festival zipped along the screen. Watching it reminded me of the time I walked through a local park and came across a dance party with a live DJ, but everyone attending was wearing headphones. The DJ was energetically doing his thing, but the party was silent to me as I walked by. I was the odd person out, someone who couldn't hear the beat of the music and feel the pulse of the crowd. Watching the festivalgoers felt voyeuristic, since most were living their lives without any suspicion they were on camera and that someone, probably multiple people, would watch the footage later because of a crime committed in their general vicinity.

Then my father paused the security video. "That's weird," he said.

"What?"

"Look at the time stamp." As the festivalgoers streamed out of the gates, the footage suddenly jumped forward an hour when the festival gates were quiet and dark.

When we checked the angles from all the cameras, they all had the same gap.

Why? Was it a blip? Had the power gone out?

Or the security footage had been tampered with. Who had access to it?

Tierney. Shay. Trevor.

Trevor.

Something about him rubbed me the wrong way. Maybe it's because he has a sort of weird macho air.

He seemed to be taking his job as festival security very seriously. So seriously, he was butting into the cornhole tournament, which had been a model of sportsmanship.

Maybe Trevor was taking his job too seriously?

Could Trevor have encountered Mark in the parking lot after the blowup? Had he argued with Mark, and the fight went too far? And he deleted the footage.

I brought us another round of waters, going all out with cans of grapefruit bubbly for the next round of videos.

"This will be more fun," I said. I opened the first video from the influencer, intending to work my way straight down.

The influencer's face filled the screen. "Hi, travelers. It's Astrid

Clementine here, and I'm at the Doyle's Oregon Whiskey Fourth of July Extravaganza near Portland, Oregon. It's going to be—oh, shoot!"

A bee buzzed into Astrid's face, and she laughed.

As I watched Astrid, I was impressed by her offbeat take but with a low-key glamour. I wasn't surprised to note she had several paid partnerships and sponsors, and I forgot why I was watching for a moment.

"Have you seen anything useful?" Bax said from beside me. He sounded sleepy, and I'd noted his eyes had stayed shut a few times before he'd darted awake.

"I think I just did."

DJ Helios, whom I'd last seen when he was introducing bands on the opening day, was talking to Astrid Clementine. The sun was bright overhead, so it was probably mid-afternoon. They stood with a bustling craft fair behind them.

"I'm not just an attendee checking out the craft fair. I'm actually emceeing the music festival later tonight."

"Will you be emceeing all weekend?" Astrid asked.

"No, just tonight, sadly, although I would've loved to work the whole festival. My coworkers are splitting the duties, with one DJ per night. We all work for the best rock station in Portland."

"How'd you get the gig? Presumably through your station?"

"When the email went out at our station about this gig, I offered immediately. It seemed like a great way to spend the long holiday weekend. Getting to hang out, listen to music, and entertain a crowd for a few minutes each hour? It's perfection."

"Have you been a DJ long?" Astrid asked.

"About six months full-time, although I interned and worked several other jobs at the station before getting on-air. It was a dream come true." The DJ's eyes suddenly narrowed, and he looked beyond the camera.

"Excuse me for a minute." DJ Helios quickly walked away from

Astrid, who turned while still recording. The DJ chased down a man walking by.

And it wasn't just any man.

Mark Jeffries.

DJ Helios reached out and grabbed Mark's shoulder.

"I told you to leave me alone," Mark said. He shook the DJ's hand off him, and swore. "Bother me again, and I'll call my lawyer."

"Avoiding me is just going to make things worse. You'll regret it in the long run, when a simple conversation could resolve this," DJ Helios said. His voice was suspiciously mild.

"Threaten me again, and you'll wish you'd never heard my name." Mark turned and walked away. He bumped into Hannah, barked an apology, then marched away as Hannah rubbed her shoulder with a thoughtful look on her face.

The DJ stood for a moment, staring in the direction Mark left. He pulled his phone out of his pocket, typed something into it angrily, and then walked away.

Astrid quit recording.

My father looked my way over the top of a sleeping Bax. "Do you have any idea about their relationship?"

"Not a clue," I said. "But I suspect this video should be considered one."

"In my professional opinion, yes, this is a clue."

I made a note on my list to send the footage to Detective Ortega before we watched the rest of the videos, but nothing else seemed relevant.

My father left, and I shook Bax awake, who wandered upstairs.

But I felt buzzed.

Something told me the video of DJ Helios and Mark was a gem in a bucket of glass beads that made the time we'd spent on this worth it.

I checked the DJ's social media, and scrolled through photos of bands and events, and quite a few work selfies.

Then I saw he'd posted on the anniversary of the North Portland nightclub fire, with an ode to the people who'd died.

From the comments, his followers had no idea what he was talking about, and he'd replied to almost every comment, telling them about the fire and the devastation it had caused.

He cared about the fire. But why? He was too young to have been in the crowd when it broke up, unless the nightclub had ignored their "no one under twenty-one" rule. While his answers all seemed factually correct, none hinted at his personal connection to the fire. And given his passion, he must have one.

I'd found my opening. Now, I just needed to figure out how to track the DJ down.

Chapter 18

The festival opened at noon, so after breakfast at home with Bax and Niko, I swung by the Ground Rules shop. The last time I was inside was Wednesday, and I missed it. An irrational part of my brain wanted to see it, to ensure it still existed. That it hadn't disappeared into the abyss while I'd been dealing with the festival and Mark's death.

When Bax and I leave for our honeymoon in a few weeks, I'd go two weeks without seeing the shop or our coffee carts. I knew they'd all flourish without me, but the thought of not being able to drop by made me nervous, hinting I might have control issues.

To my absolute not-surprise, Colton and Brooklyn, two of my baristas, had everything in the shop entirely in hand.

From the outside, the two didn't look like they'd be the perfect fit as coworkers. Colton's urban mountain man vibe, with lots of Carhartt, corduroy, and flannel, was a contrast to Brooklyn's sleek, androgynous style. But they worked together perfectly as a team. They reminded me of one of Ground Rules's goals: that we'd be a welcoming place for everyone, provided we treated everyone around us with a base level of respect, even if we disagreed on vital matters, like preferring instant to freshly ground coffee.

My gaze lingered on the pastry delivery, which looked delectable in the case customers stood next to as they waited in line. The smell of brewing coffee was the perfect perfume. Several tables were full of earlyish morning caffeine seekers. A woman showed up at the side-walk order window, and as Colton opened it, a black Lab popped up and rested his paws on the counter.

"Your coffee and a biscuit is coming right up," Colton said to the dog, who looked back with an openmouthed smile.

The dog, Hugo, and his human staff, known to us as Hugo's mom, are two regular customers lured in by the siren call of peanut-butter biscuits and fresh coffee on their daily walk.

Colton flashed a grin my way. "You had to check up on us, huh? You can't help but wonder if we will burn the store down in your absence."

"You know me too well."

"How's the festival going?" Colton pulled a peanut-butter dog biscuit out of the bin under the window and put it on a napkin before pouring a cup of coffee.

Only the best for Hugo.

Colton opened the window and put the cup down for Hugo's mom, before offering the Lab the biscuit. Hugo took the treat carefully and sat back down before munching enthusiastically.

When Colton turned back, I said, "Business at the festival has been brisk, and the music has been incredible."

"I have tickets for tomorrow night with some friends."

"Tomorrow's bands are the best lineup of the whole festival," I said. We'd assumed the Fourth would be the busiest day, with more people off work and booked bands that would draw the largest crowd.

"And there's fireworks. You can't celebrate the Fourth without watching explosions."

"Something like that." Apart from professional displays, Portland and a few counties on the coast have banned fireworks. Oregon has always had tighter firework restrictions than Washington State, and our close neighbors have their own firework stands just a short drive away over the Columbia River. Which led to another irrational fear that pinged in my brain. At one point, a local restaurant that had just been designated the best in Portland by a local paper, a coffee shop, and a web design firm had burned down one Fourth of July after being hit by illegal fireworks.

Mark's death must be preying on my mind even more than I realized if I was finding new, weird concerns to stress over.

Our shop wouldn't burn down because of illegal fireworks. Well, hopefully it wouldn't.

"Spill," Colton said. "Something is weighing on your mind."

"It's—"

"Whoa, check this out," Brooklyn said. Colton and I both turned to a man in a tuxedo, holding the door open for a woman in a white dress with a sweetheart neckline and one of the poofiest skirts known to humankind.

"They must be on their way to their wedding," I said.

"Thanks, Captain Obvious," Colton said. I elbowed him, and he responded gently and kindly.

Four women in pumpkin-colored dresses followed the bride, along with four men in tuxedos and a woman in a flowy pants suit carrying an expensive DSLR camera. Last but not least, a man with a clerical collar that didn't quite work with his fuchsia velvet suit entered the coffee shop.

"Even wedding parties need caffeine on their way to the big day," I told Colton.

Two bridesmaids started moving chairs, and the groomsmen moved two tables.

"Excuse me, but what are you doing?" I asked loudly.

"You could help us instead of watching, you know," one of the bridesmaids grumbled.

I glanced at Brooklyn and Colton, who had identical, openmouthed expressions.

A couple of people dressed in workout gear, with the telltale glistening of sweat that said they'd just finished a run, walked in.

The bride turned to them. "I don't think we have room for you," she said.

Her bridesmaids moved a few more chairs.

"You are welcome to come get a coffee," I told the workout enthusiasts. I stepped around the bar and ushered the two runners to the register while the bride glared at me.

"What's going on?" one of the runners asked.

"I have no idea," I said. I turned to the bridal party as Colton took the runners' orders. "What is going on?"

"We're getting married, duh." The bride turned away from me to face the photographer. She put a hand on her hip. "How's the lighting?"

I grabbed two of the chairs the bridesmaids had moved and shoved them into their original spot. "You do not have permission to rearrange our furniture."

One of the bridesmaids loudly told one of the occupied tables, "You need to move."

"No, you don't!" I hollered. The two women sitting with their laptops looked around with confused eyes. "Go back to your manuscripts. You know you're always welcome to work here." They were our Saturday-morning regulars who seemed to be getting an extra writing day in over the holiday weekend.

"But we don't have room with them in the way." The bridesmaid looked embarrassed and couldn't make eye contact with me.

"Room for what?" I asked, although I already knew where this was going. "This is a coffee shop, not a wedding chapel. Did you get lost on your way to the venue you booked?"

The rest of the occupied tables turned to watch. The runners stood by the counter, watching, while Brooklyn started making their drinks. The growl of the burr grinder was the perfect addition to the tense atmosphere.

Colton came around the edge of the corner, ready to be my backup.

"We're getting married," the bride said. She motioned to the groom.

"Good for you, but that doesn't explain why you want to take over my coffee shop. You're more than welcome to buy coffee to take with you on your way to your venue, provided you stop harassing my customers and leave the furniture alone."

"You don't get it. Our pop-up wedding is happening here." The groom finally spoke. His groomsmen were all edging backward toward the door.

I made eye contact with the groom, and he quickly glanced away.

I kept my voice level but firm. "That's news to me, as no one contacted me. If you'd requested to reserve our space, we might have been able to work something out. Even throw in some special pastries. But you can't just come into a busy shop and try to take over."

The groom looked at Colton, as if appealing for help.

Colton slowly crossed his arms over his chest and leaned against the counter. "You heard my boss," Colton said.

"If you'd showed up today and politely asked to use a corner of the shop, we probably would've said yes. But you can't try to kick out our customers."

"No, this is BS. We're here, and we need to get married!" The bride tried to stomp her foot but wobbled on her heels. She grabbed the photographer to keep from falling over. "And you made me break my heel!"

I glanced at the groom. His groomsmen were all by the door, looking ready to bolt. When a woman, who looked half asleep, walked up from the outside, one of them opened the door for her. "Welcome to the show," he said.

"Show?" The woman glanced at him. The excitement had made her look perkier. Based on her black cargo pants and green polo shirt, she'd been on night shift somewhere.

"Have a wonderful day," the groomsman said. He slipped outside before letting the door shut behind him.

One of his friends stared wistfully at the door, as if he also wanted to make a break for freedom.

The woman slowly walked up to the counter, eyeing the angry bride, groom with a red face and hunched shoulders, and the bridesmaids, who'd all sat slouched at a table, looking slightly dejected.

"I'd love a twelve-ounce decaf latte and one of your marionberry muffins," she said.

"We don't have time for muffins," the bride said. She glared at me again.

"Sweetie, we should go," the groom said.

The bridesmaids all popped up, like marionettes brought to life by a puppet master. The officiant rushed to open the door for them. They walked toward the door, while three of the four groomsmen walked alongside them, although one had to walk alone, since one of the groomsmen had already escaped. Sadly, they weren't accompanied by a stirring instrumental, but instead one of the rock songs I'd added to the coffeehouse playlist we use in the shop.

The bride turned to me one last time. "You ruined my wedding."

"Let's go, sweetie." The groom tried to put his arm on his bride-to-be. But she pushed away and strode out of the shop, her heels clicking with each step.

Including the allegedly broken heel.

"I'm sorry," the groom said, and almost ran out of the shop.

I looked at my baristas. "Just another day at the juxtaposition of entitlement and reality."

"Why did this . . . how?" Brooklyn asked.

"The bride is the main character, and we're just background extras," Colton said.

One of the groomsmen ran back into the shop. "Hey, I noticed your suspended coffee board. As an apology, can you apply this to whatever's most needed?" He handed me a fifty-dollar bill and rushed out.

I handed the cash over to Colton, who added a series of hashes to the suspended coffee board's sections for drip coffee and prepackaged oatmeal cups (just add hot water).

At least something good came from this.

Chapter 19

After I parked at the festival, I paused in my car momentarily. A quick glance at the Ground Rules social media feeds showed that if the pop-up wedding had complained about getting kicked out of my shop, they hadn't done so on social media.

Or, if they had, they hadn't tagged us in their comments.

Or they hadn't gotten around to posting yet.

Or it just had yet to go viral.

User reviews are a double-edged sword for us. Good reviews help us grow, since people want to check out the places their friends loved, or they're inspired to visit by a photo of a perfect latte next to a decadent pastry on a sunny day.

It's impossible to please every customer, and sometimes, that's my fault, meaning Ground Rules's fault. But sometimes, it's just someone who's going to be unhappy regardless, takes it out on us, and writes a scathing review because their experience didn't match the pictures in their mind.

Then I googled a name that had been poking at the back of my brain.

Dulcinea.

Which I should know, but I kept drawing a blank. But Wikipedia saved me.

Dulcinea was the golden-haired, beautiful, highborn woman Don Quixote wanted to perform brave deeds for as her paladin. The name generally means mistress or sweetheart.

Hopefully, Dulcie was aiming for sweetheart versus mistress when she named her chocolate company. Maybe she could argue that regardless of who you love, her chocolate was like a mistress to your taste buds and, therefore, your heart.

And something told me Mark wasn't a paladin, a champion, for Dulcie.

Whatever. I needed to get to work.

The coffee wasn't going to brew itself.

After grabbing several totes from the back of the car, I headed to the coffee cart. The morning was cool, still in the sixties, and I knew to enjoy this moment. The day promised to heat up to a manageable eighty-four.

Temps over ninety were miserable in the cart, even with our portable air-conditioner. When the weather hits 100, we close for safety reasons, since I can't put my baristas at risk of dehydrating or getting heatstroke.

As I got the cart ready to open, I hoped we wouldn't get a repeat of the wedding crew. I didn't think someone would try to take over the food cart zone, but I hoped we'd have regular customers seeking caffeine versus whatever the bride had envisioned.

Which still didn't make sense to me. If the wedding party had been respectful, we would've given them a corner of the shop for their quick I dos. If they'd booked ahead, we would've gone all-out.

I was glad I was there to handle things, instead of my baristas needing to deal with the wedding situation. They weren't paid enough to deal with that.

A thought struck me. Hopefully, as the clock clicked down to my big day, I wouldn't act as unhinged.

Kendall showed up just when the cart was ready to go, five minutes before we were scheduled to open.

"Good timing; I just finished the hard part," I said.

"Colton texted me that you chased a bride out of the Ground Rules shop?"

I shook my head, covered my eyes with my hand, and then told Kendall the whole story, taking a few breathers to serve customers.

About fifteen minutes after opening, Detective Ortega showed up. For once, she was alone. No grumpy-looking shadow.

"A large drip coffee, please," she said.

Even though I wanted to make jokes about her trusting me not to poison her, I kept them inside. As she tapped her credit card against our tablet, I poured her coffee, which smelled like coffee heaven.

"When you gossip with your coworkers about Mark Jeffries, what do you say?" the detective asked, after I handed over our largest to-go cup of coffee. She added cream and several sugar packets to it and stirred.

I glanced at the detective. "You're barking up the wrong tree. We didn't spend our time at work talking about Mark Jeffries. We had better things to discuss, like our plans to increase our mail-order club and our dream of opening a second shop or maybe buying another cart if we're sure the investment would make sense. We had better things to talk about."

"Mark must've been an impediment. He was a rival, correct?" She snapped the lid on top of her cup.

"We have a town full of rival coffee shops and roasters, and we get along with almost all of them. Some of the shops even carry our beans, so calling them a rival is a stretch," I said. My tone shifted into sadness when I said, "But you make a long list of people who had it out for Mark."

"Like who?" Her tone was slightly salty, which made me want to like her. But for now, we were on opposite sides of a problem.

"I heard he'd been receiving persistent angry phone calls from a woman who didn't leave her name. I'd start there. Maybe she snapped. Supposedly Mark and his second wife had a cantankerous divorce, and I heard it was heated. It was so bad that, if Mark's first ex-wife is right, one of Mark's minority investors bailed on him over the divorce, creating a ton of bitterness on both sides. That's not to mention multiple female former employees whom he'd, let's say, showed questionable business-appropriate boundaries toward."

"Does that include you?" the detective asked.

"I never had that type of personal relationship with Mark. We were just employee-employer, although I quit working for him years ago when he made a pass at me. But Ramona might have insight. She mentioned that Mark had briefly hired an outside HR firm, which didn't work out, because they were horrified by Mark's behavior."

I paused. "And that's all. I heard he skated on being charged with revenge porn and blackmail. But if he was willing to blackmail someone once, do you think that's the only time?"

The blackmail comment was off the cuff, but something about it rang true.

The detective scrawled something in her notebook, so I kept talking.

"You should also talk to Austen Smith. He worked for Mark for years, but now he's out at a new coffee roastery in St. Helens."

"Do you know the name?"

I shook my head. "But there can't be too many roasters out there. It's not a big town."

Business was brisk, and a little before lunchtime, I started to prepare to hike to the Ground Rules Subaru to grab some of the restock bins in the back. I'd misjudged how much to carry over this morning.

But then my dad walked up, and a plan formed.

"Hi, Dad."

"Hi, Pumpkin. Sophie needs a restock of Puddle Jumper for the booth."

That was a good sign. "Would you consider doing a double favor for me?"

"It depends." Which was a vintage answer for my dad.

I showed him the list of cups, coffee beans, and oat milk and then said, "And I'd like to see if Trevor, the head of the festival security, will give you a ride on his golf cart. That way, you can feel him out while using the cart to transport all of this back. The oat milk gets heavy."

"And why would I do that?" My father eyed me skeptically, as if I were trying to sneak something past him like the guilty fifteen-year-old I once was.

I explained why Trevor made my Spidey senses tingle. "Something tells me he'll treat you differently than me, especially if you mention that you're retired police." Just being male might help, since Trevor seemed more at ease with Tierney. So maybe I made him nervous.

"I'll give it a shot."

I texted Trevor and Tierney, asking if Trevor could drive my dad to help him restock, and Tierney replied almost instantly. *Trevor would love to help.*

Trevor replied about thirty seconds after I received his boss's text. *On my way, but please remember I'm in charge of security, not running errands.*

"Success," I said.

Not long after Trevor drove my dad away on a golf cart, DJ Helios, who'd hosted the music festival on opening night, walked up.

My back straightened. I needed to find a way to talk with the DJ. Should I try to charm him now?

"Are you emceeing the bands today?" I asked. He looked casual in perfectly distressed jeans and a vintage-looking Nirvana T-shirt. Plus, classic aviator shades.

He shook his head. "I'm just here to enjoy the tunes."

"Can I ask you something that might seem odd, but I promise I have a reason?"

"That sounds ominous."

"It's about the NoPo nightclub fire. Someone told me you know a lot about it." That someone was the small voice in the back of my brain that had analyzed the DJ's Instagram post, but I didn't need to tell him that.

"Oh, that."

"Yeah."

"As long as you first give me a giant cup of coffee." He handed over a well-used tumbler so covered in band stickers that I wouldn't have been able to tell its original color if a sliver of orange wasn't peeking out at the very top, where the sides met the lid.

"It's on the house, and I'll meet you outside with your coffee."

I joined DJ Helios at a nearby picnic table and handed over his coffee. Up close, without the sunglasses, he was about my age, maybe a year younger. His dark brown hair was purposefully tousled, with a small streak of wax he'd neglected to work in.

"What do you know about the nightclub fire?" the DJ asked.

"It was tragic," I said.

"It was more than tragic; it was criminal. But someone covered it up," DJ Helios said. His lips tightened until he forced himself to take a deep breath.

He continued speaking. "The fiasco wasn't an accident."

"You think it was arson?"

He shook his head. "No, I think the cause of the fire itself was legitimately an accident. But everything afterward? That wasn't a mistake. It was an avoidable tragedy waiting to happen."

"How so?"

"The crowd was locked in the room on purpose. The police blamed the manager on duty, but there's no way he was responsible. He was just a guy a few years out of college, doing what he was told. He was stuck inside with everyone else. But someone ordered him to keep the doors locked, and he made the mistake of listening instead of doing what he knew was right."

"Are you sure about this?"

"Yes, and I'm going to make sure the truth comes to light," DJ Helios said.

I studied his angry face. "This is personal to you."

"Very." He took a drink of his coffee. "My father was one of the bartenders that night. He was working a second job because my little sister had cancer, and the medical bills were piling up. He didn't make it home."

"I'm so sorry."

"When I had my daughter last year, I realized how my dad must've felt in his final moments when he realized he wasn't going to see me or my sister grow up. It infuriates me that no one paid for his death, or the others. And he was friends with the manager—Phoenix—whom everyone blamed. And I overheard a conversation about a week before when they were talking about work. My dad asked Phoenix if he was sure about their safety protocols. And Phoenix said, of course, it'd be fine, and if they didn't do as they were told, they'd be fired."

"Did you tell anyone this at the time?"

"I tried to tell the police, but no one wanted to listen to a kid when they could just sweep all of this under the rug. Make a big deal about how the city created new laws about event spaces to ensure nothing like this happened again."

"Who do you think covered it up?"

"The LLC of a few guys who owned the club. I've been working on an exposé to blow the lid on this situation and show who was responsible for covering up multiple deaths."

"You're working on this by yourself?"

He shook his head. "I found an investigative journalist who believes there's more to this story. We've been working together. My name, or at least being able to say I work for a local radio station, opens doors, and if he can't be there to ask the hard questions, he preps me. People always agree to let me record, since they think this is for a fluff radio piece, before I lay the hammer down."

"Did you interview Mark Jeffries? He was involved."

The DJ nodded. "Supposedly, he was just the scheduler as a side hustle. But I think he had more skin in the game than he wanted to admit. I've been trying to interview him, and he keeps evading me, but he finally texted me on Thursday afternoon. We were supposed to sit down next week."

"Dang." Thursday afternoon? After the confrontation that Astrid Clementine recorded?

"I doubt Mark would've been forthright with me, but my partner uncovered some archived business records that might've put Mark on the spot. I'm so angry he's dead, since it means I might not find the truth."

Did someone kill Mark to keep him from talking? Or was the nightclub truly just a tragic accident that DJ Helios refused to accept?

Was the DJ lying about his scheduled interview with Mark?

"Are you debating if this is why Mark was murdered?" the DJ asked.

I nodded. "It's logical."

"I hope not, because if someone killed Mark over it, then I'm on the right track. Which means I'm also a target. But if that's true, there's also a silver lining. I might get justice for my father and everyone else."

"Have you seen anything in your research or interviews that would give someone a motive to kill Mark?"

"Hmm, I can't think of anything. But we've recorded all of our interviews. If I think something in them is relevant in regard to Mark's death, I'll talk to my partner about sharing them."

I nodded. The DJ stood up. "I need to meet up with someone. Thanks for the coffee."

Before I stood up, I unlocked my phone. I sent a quick FYI text message to Detective Ortega, summarizing what I'd found out. I mentioned that Astrid Clementine, social influencer extraordinaire, had a video of Mark and DJ Helios arguing.

Would Jackson be annoyed if he found out I'd texted the detective without him approving the message?

Signs point to yes.

Whatever. Nothing in the message incriminated me or Ground

Rules. I'd made it clear the DJ had come to my coffee cart versus me hunting him down at his house or something equally creepy.

I started to put my phone away but then popped open a new text and summarized the situation for my father. He had opinions about the fire and experience investigating local cold cases. He still volunteers with his old unit two days a week and gets lunch with the other retirees-slash-volunteers who help out. Maybe one of them would be interested in assisting DJ Helios if his journalist pal seemed legit.

At least if one of them came across information relevant to Mark's murder, they wouldn't suppress it. They might see connections that the DJ would unknowingly discard.

Hmm, was the DJ working with a legitimate journalist or someone focused on crackpot conspiracy theories? But I doubted I could get the DJ to tell me his partner's name, unless I could offer helpful information on the fire.

As I returned to the cart, Trevor pulled up in his golf cart, and my father climbed out.

Trevor even helped my dad carry the reusable grocery bags of supplies to the door of the cart.

"Thanks for your help," my father said.

"Anytime."

After hovering momentarily while my dad and I pulled sealed coffee beans for the cart out of one bag so he could take the rest to the booth to sell, Trevor zoomed away in his cart while barking into his walkie-talkie.

"It looks like Trevor likes you," I said.

"He's definitely awkward," my dad said. "But he's former Army, so we had that in common, and it broke the ice."

"Oh yeah?"

"He just retired a few years ago before opening his security company," my dad said. "I think he's just obsessive about doing a good job. I doubt there's anything sinister that you should worry about."

Maybe. But Trevor still rubbed me the wrong way.

"Have you checked your texts?"

My dad read the message I sent, then stared at me. "You interviewed DJ Helios?"

"He came by the cart for coffee."

"He could be a murderer."

"We were maybe fifteen feet from the coffee cart in a busy festival."

"But you won't always be in a crowd," my dad said. "And anyone who could cold-bloodedly kill Mark won't be physically intimated by you."

At least he qualified his statement with the word physically.

"I'll be careful."

My father studied me for a moment and looked like he'd bit back something he wanted to say before walking away with the totes for the coffee stand.

I took a moment and googled *Bright Security*, aka Trevor's company.

Trevor's company was one of the top results, and I clicked through his site, which was slick with lots of dark colors and white text. They focused on events and corporate security, and highlighted their focus on cutting-edge tech. Trevor's bio mentioned his twenty-year stint in the Army, although he was vague about what he'd done. I wondered if that meant he'd been in catering, or something important, but not flashy.

His site highlighted that he had a hiring preference for veterans, and donated to charities that helped veterans who'd fallen on hard times get back on their feet. Like Tierney and Shay, Trevor had professional reasons to ensure the festival was a success, and Mark could've been getting in the way.

But would that be enough of a reason for murder?

Chapter 20

A while later, I saw the familiar comedy act, or rather, detective duo, walking through the craft fair when I was on my way to send Sophie on her break.

Detective Ortega seemed to be taking everything in, while Detective Moore looked tired as always.

The detective stepped in my way when she saw me. "Your text," she said.

"Yes."

"Thanks for it, although you should keep your nose out of police business."

Images of me worrying about Niko investigating the crime flashed through my brain. The detective probably saw me the way I saw the intrepid elementary schooler. Someone shorter than her, sticking her nose where it didn't belong, putting herself at risk, and potentially ruining leads versus acquiring them.

"If I come across anything else that seems relevant while working in my cart, I'll let you know."

"You haven't heard any more rumors about Mark in the coffee industry, have you?"

I paused. "Did you read the *Oregonian* article about Left Coast Grinds losing market share? It was a while ago, at least a year. Ground Rules was mentioned, alongside some other up-and-coming roasters.

I bet the journalist who wrote the article is more up on the gossip than I am."

"Interesting." Detective Ortega made a note.

"Have fun at the festival," I said, and continued walking to my booth.

My route took me past Bagatha and Good Clean Suds before leading me past Fresh Pines Style by Melissa, which was empty of shoppers. Melissa stood by the aisle with her arms crossed over her chest. She stood up straighter when she saw me.

"If it isn't the snake herself," she sneered.

I made eye contact. Her sneer didn't match the tiered purple boho skirt made with layers of tulle, her light-green strappy tank top, or the careful pin curls in her hair pulled under a Rosie the Riveter-style bandana.

"You didn't say you work with Harley Yamazaki."

"Does that matter?" I asked.

"I thought you were sympathetic to Mark's plight instead of trying to orchestrate his downfall."

"Pardon?" I wanted to tell Melissa I didn't need to orchestrate anything, that if anyone had harmed Mark's business, it was Mark.

But her eyes were puffy, like she hadn't gotten much sleep. And the whites of her eyes were tinged red. Her anger toward me was probably grief, and she was ready to lash out at anyone she could find a reason to blame.

Even the innocent.

"You convinced me to talk because it seemed like you wanted to help solve Mark's death, but you were responsible for it. You didn't tell me you partnered with Harley the Unhinged to destroy Mark's livelihood." Melissa put her hands on her hips.

"Umm, neither of us had anything to do with Mark's death." I tried to make my voice gentle, but I could hear the sharp hint of annoyance underneath.

"You're lucky I haven't slapped you into next week." Melissa stepped toward me. "I could end you."

"Take a moment and think about what you're doing. Is this how you want to honor Mark?"

She stopped but was clearly at war with herself. I turned my head and walked on. You're never supposed to turn your back on wild bears or mountain lions when hiking, and I wondered if the same logic should apply here. Maybe I'd find a pair of seamstress scissors stuck in my back.

Nothing happened, and when I glanced back, Melissa retreated to her booth. She was still glaring at me.

And Detective Ortega was eyeing Melissa.

Had the detective heard Melissa threaten me?

Had Melissa gone on the attack because she was guilty? Was she trying to throw suspicion my way?

Melissa showed signs of extreme grief. But maybe she was just upset about what she'd done. The actions she'd taken had, maybe unintentionally, killed the man she saw as the love of her life.

Melissa had clearly loved Mark, and love can snap to hatred. There's a reason people say there's a thin line between love and hate. All of that emotion can build up and swing in either direction. And if Mark knew how to push Melissa's buttons, maybe he'd gone too far, and she snapped.

Hannah of Stonefield Beach Teas passed me and paused. "Do you have scissors I can borrow? Or a knife?"

"Umm, there's one with the Ground Rules gear."

But then Hannah scurried off when a voice said, "Sage!"

Detective Ortega walked up. "Are you okay? Let me know if that woman hassles you. Detective Moore is letting her know she threatened you in front of two police officers."

"I'm fine. You know that's Mark Jeffries's ex-wife, right?"

"Melissa Macina? She's been ducking my calls." Detective Ortega turned and looked down the aisle.

"As far as I know, Melissa's been at the festival every day, working her booth."

The detective's eyes gleamed. "Now that is also interesting.

Thanks, Sage." Detective Ortega strode away like she was on a mission.

Even if Melissa was innocent, hopefully, this investigative path would keep the detectives from assuming Harley was guilty. Hopefully the more potential suspects, the easier it would be to ignore Harley until they found the truth. Thankfully, there wasn't a shortage of suspects with as good of reasons and a lot more anger than Harley. Although the thought also made me sad.

When I got to the booth, Sophie was ringing someone up on the tablet, while my father was telling someone about the Puddle Jumper blend.

"I drink it every day," he told the woman. "I grind it at home for my morning French press."

The man Sophie had helped walked out with a large bag, so I sent my barista, who clearly had impressive sales skills, out on a break.

Should I see if Sophie was interested in the corporate sales side of the business? I had it covered at the moment, but a second set of hands would be helpful as we got busier.

But given Sophie's focus on grad school and my suspicion she wanted to return to Newfoundland when she graduated, I didn't want to pressure her into a new role when she was such a great asset as a barista.

My father rang up the woman's bags of Puddle Jumper, a pour-over cone, a matching glass carafe, and a Ground Rules camp mug. He carefully packed them into a branded paper bag.

Maybe Sophie wasn't the only natural salesperson I had on staff.

"I should check out the tea before I go," the woman said, and stepped over to Hannah's side of the booth. She picked up a mint blend, made from locally grown peppermint.

"How are things?" I asked my dad.

"Good." He sounded stiff, and from the awkwardness, I deduced he was still annoyed I'd interviewed DJ Helios. So I didn't mention my mini-showdown with Melissa, and went over to help the woman pick out a couple of teas.

★   ★   ★

My uncle Jimmy showing up at the festival for a second time surprised me. Sophie was still on her break, and I'd sent my dad to get lunch, saying I could handle the booth.

"I'm picking up a gift," Uncle Jimmy told me. "I saw something yesterday and regretted not buying it."

"If you'd texted, I could've grabbed it for you," I said.

"Yes, but I couldn't have checked in on you in person if I'd done that. How are you holding up?"

"I'm fine." And maybe my uncle was buying something he didn't want me to see.

Or he just wanted somewhere to go, something to do, on a lovely holiday weekend.

"You know," I said, and glanced at my uncle. "Do you remember when Mark had been hanging out around the Rail Yard, causing problems?"

"As I remember, you sent him a cease-and-desist letter." My uncle's tone was grim.

"I sent it after he knocked a hot latte over my hand, causing a minor burn." He'd been annoying me by hanging out around the Rail Yard, but an injury, even if it thankfully wasn't serious, had been the final straw. "I've always wondered why, exactly, Mark kept showing up. Seeing us in action must've been boring."

My uncle's gaze focused on Hannah's collection of apothecary jars. "I know one of the reasons," he said.

"Did I need to resort to torture tactics to get an answer?"

My uncle laughed. "No need for that. Mark was looking for dirt on you. He'd talked to me again about investing in Left Coast Grinds, and he said he saw something that concerned him at the Rail Yard. But when I asked him, all he could mention was people comparing you to the bikini barista cart somewhere in the outer Southeast."

I wanted to roll my eyes. "I think Mark is the only one who made that comparison."

"At its heart, I suspect Mark was offended that Harley left his company. He invested in training her. He saw her skills as an extension of himself."

"Harley worked hard for him for years."

"Yes, she did. I'm not criticizing her for moving on. That's always the risk when you take someone new under your wing. It must have been hard for Mark, since Harley developed into a better roaster than him, but at least she was roasting under his brand. She made him look brilliant. For Mark, he saw Harley leaving as a fundamental betrayal. He saw himself as molding Harley from raw talent, and he thought she should appreciate it and stick with his company. Plus, he had to find a way to make up for her absence, and it's difficult to find someone with her talent."

"Do you think her quitting tanked his company? He was a good roaster, and while Harley's amazing, there are some very talented roasters he could've hired." Or poached from competitors with offers of more money, better benefits, and being part of an established brand.

"I don't think any good company will fold because one of their rock stars left. Although it can be hard to recover, depending on the situation," my uncle said. "But Ground Rules could recover if you or Harley left, although the transition would be difficult. We'd have to do the one thing I suspected Mark was unwilling to do: appropriately compensate someone of Harley's skill. I suspect Mark underpaid Harley for years."

Which didn't answer my question. I narrowed my eyes, and my uncle half-smiled.

"Harley leaving might have been the final straw that turned Mark's fortunes around. But they could've been heading for a downturn regardless. And Mark's actions to right his ship didn't go as planned," my uncle said. "It's tough when you have a business that's been excelling, and suddenly things aren't going as well. You have to decide how to pivot, and hope you make the right decision."

"Given how Mark treated female employees, I'm surprised he trusted Harley."

"As an owner of a business, it'd be silly to ignore the skills of an employee solely because of gender. But I bet Mark kept a close eye on the roastery, since it's vital to much of his business, including his wholesale dreams."

"Mark was so inconsistent," I said.

"I'm not saying Mark's actions make—made—sense. And when you quit working for him, I hadn't realized him asking out female employees was a habit. I thought he'd just liked you."

"More than asking out," I said. Mark had rubbed his hands on my hips and asked me to dinner, but the situation made me feel skeeved out, especially when Mark chided me for saying no and said I should be flattered. He usually preferred taller women, but he'd make an exception for me. My father had always told me to listen to my gut, so I did, and I quit. Later, I learned that Mark had most likely been trying to "neg" me, meaning, put me down while asking me out, trying to weaken my self-confidence.

"If I remember correctly, Mark asked you out, but you later heard about behavior that, at least as you got older, you saw as sexual harassment. And I listened to you. That was another reason I turned Mark down. I talked with a few former employees, and it seemed like his behavior was getting worse or more noticeable."

That could have been a function of age. When I'd worked for Mark, he'd felt ancient to my twenty-year-old self, but he'd been in his thirties. The gap between him and college-aged baristas had continued to grow.

A group of customers came in, and I greeted them.

"Do you have any espresso roasts?" one asked.

When I was done helping her, I realized my uncle had left without saying goodbye.

Chapter 21

At least one thing was going right this weekend: Jackson and Bax had made the semifinals of the "Last Bag Standing" division of the cornhole tournament. So I ducked out of the coffee cart to watch their match and settled beside Niko on a red plaid blanket.

Niko, sadly, hadn't made it past the first round of the Corn Chips, and he'd washed out of the Connect Four tournament early, as well.

"I'm happy for my dad and Uncle Jackson," Niko promised me. He had his battered satchel cradled to his stomach like it was something he was protecting, and he'd forgone the jaunty fedora in favor of a blue trucker's cap that contrasted with his orange T-shirt. But he still had his sketchbook, which he tucked out of sight into his bag when he saw me.

Jackson and Bax were drinking water like they were intently hydrating before their big match. Their matching bright-orange Catching Corn T-shirts made me laugh. Bax had drawn the logo a few weeks ago, and Jackson took it to a custom T-shirt shop downtown that can digitally print one-offs and small batches of designs onto clothing. They'd said all along they were saving the shirts for the semis and finals, and it'd worked.

At least they hadn't bought matching shorts or footwear, as Bax had a sliver of forest green "no show" socks peeking out of his running shoes, while my brother was in his favorite Chacos.

Bax knelt down beside me.

"We're ready to rumble," Bax told me.

"Are you maybe taking this a tad too seriously?" I asked.

"Blasphemy," Bax said, but then laughed and put his arm around my shoulder. "Although I am missing the Tour de France for this."

"You were going to go to France?" I joked.

"No, just watch a repeat of today's stage on TV this afternoon. Although I would love to see a stage in person."

"Maybe someday we'll go." If I quit falling over bodies long enough to take another vacation.

"Cornholios and Catching Corn!" The referee called the teams for the semifinals over.

"Good luck!" I gave a Bax a good-luck kiss.

"Gross," Niko said. "Good luck, Dad!"

Niko was studying the field like he was calibrating wind resistance for the beanbags, so I took a moment to breathe and enjoy sitting outdoors on a sunny July day. But nothing could untangle the knot of tension inside me.

A woman approached me and stood beside us, casting a shadow over Niko and me.

Naomi, aka Kendall's ex. I'd only met her once or twice, but I recognized her from her weirdly sulky aura. Like she was perpetually disappointed, even when she said she was happy.

And like everyone Kendall had dated, she was gorgeous. Tall, maybe five foot ten, with a slender build, like she used to be a ballerina. Her glossy thick hair, the same shade as a dark roast, swung around her face.

"Kendall said I should talk to you," she said.

"You used to work for Left Coast Grinds, right?" I asked.

"Yeah, while I was in school—"

Mark always had an ever-changing roster of college kids on his staff.

"—but I started my first 'real' job, so I quit."

"Feel free to sit down," I said, and motioned to the striped blanket we were sitting cross-legged on. "Did you enjoy it? What did you do for LCG?"

She plopped next to me and stretched out her long legs. I'm a fan of people wearing whatever they think is comfortable, but I couldn't understand her jeans and long-sleeved flannel, which she'd paired with a pair of flip-flops. She shook her hair back away from her face, and it caused a small breeze. "I was just a barista. Nothing special."

"There's nothing wrong with that. I was a barista for Left Coast as an undergrad." I glanced at Niko, who seemed to ignore us as he watched the match.

"I loved it there. I miss it. My coworkers were great, and I didn't even need to think about work until my next shift, when I was done for the day. Now, I feel I can't escape my job. I even dream about it." A half-smile brightened Naomi's face, and she leaned back on her hands. "And our coffee at work is terrible. Think stale coffee beans in an industrial drip coffee maker with a questionable cleaning history."

"Once you get used to good coffee, it's hard to go back."

"Impossible, you mean. I started packing a thermos, and one of my coworkers asked for a sample once. I made the mistake of saying yes. Now, she expects me to make her coffee daily and pouts when I say no. Which is every day. Literally, every single day. It's ridiculous." She laughed.

The glimpse of the true Naomi shone through here, and I started to see why she and Kendall had connected. After seeing this side of her, I also expected Naomi's languid air to be harnessed into stellar customer service in a calm, efficient sort of style.

"What do you do now?" I asked.

"I'm an aerospace systems engineer," she said.

I blinked. "I'm not even sure if I know what that is."

She laughed, and the remaining sulkiness fled from her face. "No one knows what I do. I did my PhD in Applied Physics. I'm just here for the holiday to see my family. I took a job out of state, which led to Kendall and me breaking up. He's not into long distance and didn't want to move with me. Grad school is too important to him."

Given the wistful note in her voice, she regretted breaking up with him.

"Are you catching up with any of your old coworkers?"

Naomi shook her head. "I saw Ramona walking around. She nodded hello. I thought about driving into the store to see some old coworkers, but I'll probably stay here with my sister and mom instead. We can't meet for our weekly mani-pedi date anymore, so I should spend as much time with them this weekend as possible."

I glanced at Niko, who was still intently watching Jackson and his dad. They were up eight to two, which meant they'd gotten the bean-bag through the hole twice and onto the board twice on their two throws. While their opponents had only managed to get the beanbag onto the board once. The first to reach twenty-one would win.

Maybe their opponents were intimidated by the growing crowd watching the semifinals. Or Jackson and Bax's focus was the distraction, or more likely, the glow of their Catching Corn T-shirts.

Naomi nodded at the field. "I don't get this as a sport. I mean, is it standardized?"

"The American Cornhole Association says the boards should be twenty-seven feet apart. The hole on the board is always nine inches down from the top."

"What about the slope of the board?"

I smiled. "No idea. We looked into getting this sanctioned as an official tournament but didn't go through with it. But maybe next year. We were surprised by the number of entries."

If there was a next year for the festival.

"Kendall's news about Mark was shocking. You never think someone you know will be the victim of a crime like that," Naomi said.

"Did you work with Mark often?"

She shook her head. "No, he dropped by the shop I worked at every few days, usually for an espresso or to meet with the store manager. He expected us to treat him like a rock star."

"How, exactly?"

On the field, the Cornholios groaned. Their final throw was

blocked by one of their own bags, which knocked both beanbags off of the board. Jackson and Bax high-fived over their growing lead, then got ready for their next throws.

"Mark expected us to greet him by name and pull a double shot for him as soon as he walked in, regardless of what else we were already doing. On her first day, some poor new girl didn't recognize him, and he started to fire her, but the manager stuck up for her."

There was some cornfusion over the score on the field, but the referee was adamant he'd counted correctly. One of the Cornholio players looked annoyed as he got ready to throw.

Naomi's eyes weren't on the game. "It wasn't unreasonable for Mark to expect us to greet him, but if we were slammed, it could be easy to not see him immediately, and he'd get snappy with everyone. But he was usually charming, as long as everyone fed his ego. And it was easy to go through shifts without seeing him."

"You weren't a fan of him, huh?"

"Not really." Naomi smiled again. "Especially not after the day Mark's wife—ex-wife now, I think—came in."

"Melissa?"

"That doesn't sound right."

"She's a willowy brunette with boho style? About your height?"

Naomi shook her head. "No, this woman wasn't short, but she wasn't tall—maybe five-foot-five? With bright pink hair. It was so intense, it probably glowed in the dark."

I tried to remember the name Melissa had said when she was ranting about how poorly Mark's second wife had treated him. "Jocelyn?"

"That could be it? I really can't remember. She had a cat in a carrier and said she needed to get home. She'd only come to Portland for an emergency vet appointment, but she saw Mark's car and hoped to catch him. She asked Mark for some document he was supposed to sign. He started screaming at her, and the cat started yowling like a fire engine. I decided the cat might be on to something, but I was already biased."

Naomi smiled again. "And I really like cats."

"We have a cat," Niko said. "His name is Kaldi."

"Kaldi, huh?" Naomi said.

"Yes, he's named after the goat herder who discovered coffee."

Niko kept his eyes on the field, and I wondered if he was planning to record notes of our conversation in his notebook.

Naomi joined Niko and me when we cheered for Catching Corn when they won.

"We're going to the finals!" Bax and Jackson high-fived.

Regardless of what happened this weekend, at least we were finding joy in the small things, like winning cornhole matches.

Chapter 22

Not long after I returned to the cart, a woman with shiny black hair cut into a perfect lob asked from the cart window if she could talk with me.

I glanced at my barista, and he nodded.

"I can step out for a moment, since Kendall is fine covering the cart," I said.

"I've got this." Kendall flashed me his usual smile. Two twenty-something-year-old men walked up to the order window, so I stepped back and stepped out of the cart.

I didn't recognize the woman. Could she have been a barista at Left Coast Grinds? Had the word gotten out that I wanted to talk to Mark's former employees and friends?

The woman waited for me by the cart entrance. She was barely taller than me, and her burgundy sundress wasn't soaked with coffee, unlike a few spots on my Ground Rules T-shirt.

"Hi, I'm Ariel Mai. I'm launching a specialized coffee company, mostly focused on gear."

She handed me a small box. "This is my premier product. It's a Phin filter, the most common way to make coffee in Vietnam."

"I've used one before," I said. The Phin filter is smaller than the pour-over cones we use, which is on purpose, since they use a smaller

water-to-beans ratio and produce an intense cup of coffee that's closer
to espresso than a pour-over, which is more like drip coffee. Brews
made with a Phin filter are perfect for iced coffee.

"Then you know it makes excellent iced coffee," Ariel said.

"For sure." I remembered walking into a Vietnamese-themed
café while visiting Houston and seeing a woman making five of these
at once for waiting customers. The result was excellent, although I
wasn't a fan of mixing it with condensed milk, since it was too sweet
for me. Given the number of customers buying it, my preference
against condensed milk was at odds with their bustling clientele. I'd
had a second one with regular milk and loved it.

"I don't plan on roasting my own beans, although I'd love to talk
to you about importing and roasting some Vietnamese beans for me
to sell. Robusta is the wave of the future. Well, robusta that has been
roasted to perfection, ideally by a talented roaster with vision."

Ariel had a point. As climate change impacted the growing regions of arabica beans, the lower-altitude and heartier robusta bean
was primed to become a coffee staple. I'd tried a few blends that
mixed arabica at about fifty percent to an equal amount of robusta to
include the sweeter and deeper flavor of arabica, which has more natural fat and sugar, to balance the natural bitterness of robusta.

"We can talk about this later when I'm not at a festival," I said.
"My business partner Harley is the roasting mastermind behind our
operation. We can schedule a time for you to drop by the roastery,
and we talk about your needs and our abilities."

"I had thought about approaching Left Coast Grinds but heard
they're in difficulties."

"Their owner died, so yeah." Had the news been officially an-
nounced? I mentally kicked myself.

"Is that why they've closed shops? I hadn't heard about Mark Jeffries's death."

"No, his death is more recent." Less than forty-eight hours ago.
"I don't have an inside scoop about all the ins and outs of their shop
closures. But if you want to talk to multiple roasters, I have sugges-

tions of places I'd consider collaborating with if we weren't roasting in-house."

Ariel leaned toward me like she was telling me a secret. "One of my friends works for the company that Mark contracts with to design and print the labels on his products. I heard one of Mark's investors called in his loan. Mark scraped up the money to pay him back, but I heard it was close, and he almost had to sell his entire business. It caused a major financial shortfall, and they're supposedly struggling to make payroll."

So, rumors about Mark's financial issues had been floating around widely.

Ramona hadn't mentioned the loans. Had she kept that quiet on purpose? Or had Mark tried to keep the news from his employees? When my employees had questions, I always answered them. I even held a staff meeting in May that I jokingly called "the state of the coffee union" when we finalized our summer plans, with the brick-and-mortar store, full-time coffee cart, and event cart in play.

If we'd had to cut out part of our business, I'd never hide it from my baristas.

But Mark's style had been more of an all-knowing guru. He was always in control.

If he'd felt like he was losing control . . . he'd snap.

But that didn't explain why he'd been killed here.

"Let's talk soon," Ariel said, and we agreed to text to schedule a time for next week.

Acquiring new business while under the shadow of Mark's death felt wrong, and I wondered again what would happen to his company. As much as I disliked Mark, I'd be sad to see his brand disappear.

But I'd also hate to see it sold to the wrong new ownership.

Hannah walked up as I was returning to the cart. I took a moment to admire the illustration on the front of her retro baseball shirt,

which featured a tea bag. The label on the end of the bag's string read
Tea Shirt.

"Are you on the hunt for coffee?" I asked her.

"I desperately need fish and chips, but I decided to check out
your tea menu on the way. I've heard some good things from attendees and realized I should check how you're using my products this
weekend."

"The blackberry tea soda is summer in a glass." I motioned to the
menu. "Hannah, when you were trying to set up wholesale accounts
in Portland, you talked to quite a few coffee shops, right?"

She nodded. "As many as I could find."

"What did you think of Left Coast Grinds when you approached
them?"

"I didn't. You couldn't pay me to have my tea in their shops."

"That's exactly what people do when they want to carry your
teas."

"I should've said there's no amount of money that would convince me to work with them," Hannah said.

"You've had a bad experience with them?"

"My sister and Mark Jeffries are sworn enemies, so keeping our
distance is better. Like Florin and Guilder."

"Who?" The names sounded familiar, but I couldn't place them.

"The fictional countries in *The Princess Bride*."

"Oh."

"You know, I made a custom 'Miracle Max' tea blend earlier
today with rooibos, dried apple, and rose petals. I'm still debating if I
should've added ginger and vanilla, so I've had the movie on my
mind ever since. I might make up a new one named Inconceivable,
because I really want to play with this idea."

Before I could ask about Mark, Hannah put her hand on her flat
belly. "I've got to get food. I'll come back for a tea soda later."

She left at a trot.

Why hadn't Hannah mentioned that she knew Mark Jeffries?
Maybe there hadn't been a reason for Mark to come up? We must

have mentioned that Harley was a Left Coast Grinds roaster. It's frequently brought up when we talk about our backgrounds and how we developed the skills to make our company successful.

And maybe it hadn't come up because most people didn't care about Left Coast Grinds versus Ground Rules. They just wanted a tasty cup of coffee that worked with their schedule. Location sometimes trumps quality.

After all, some people prefer instant coffee.

Because it takes all kinds.

Chapter 23

"You won't believe it, but we're almost out of cups. Again," Kendall said as I reentered the cart. "I wish everyone brought their own mug like they do at Campathon."

"Way less waste," I agreed. The environmental impact of to-go coffee cups weighs on me, and there's only so much we can do to encourage reusable cups, like offering a discount.

Instead of leaning on Tierney to loan me Trevor and his golf cart again, I hoofed it to the parking lot and loaded a tote bag with cups.

Right after I shut the back hatch of the Subaru, a buzzing caught my ear. I looked up, and a drone darted at my head. I ducked and felt the breeze of the drone as it buzzed my head.

I wished I'd tried to swat the drone instead of ducking.

But there was something I could do. I pulled my phone out of my back pocket and started recording the drone, which continued to buzz a few feet from me.

The drone flew up and zoomed away. It circled above a couple of people putting shopping bags in the back of a sedan, then dropped to about hip height behind them and flew away.

I shook my head. Was someone using a drone to illicitly get footage of festivalgoers?

Could it be more nefarious? Or innocent, for that matter.

I texted the footage to Tierney. *What's with the drones?*

My phone buzzed on my walk back to the cart.

The only drones I know of are the ones the festival security is playing with. I'm pretty sure we said no outside drones allowed in the terms of service when buying a ticket, but it's not like people actually read the TOS.

Is there a reason they're buzzing people? And flying around at hip height?

I typed out a quick explanation, hoping Tierney would understand the potential creepiness factor without me being explicit, and then added one final note.

If the drone's recording, can I get the footage?

On it.

Kendall and I worked the cart together, and a while later, Trevor stopped by the cart. He looked stiffer than usual.

"I'm here to apologize for getting too close to you with my drone earlier today. I didn't intend to alarm you or get that close to you. Please note I was doing a routine check of the parking lot. No offense to anyone was intended." His voice was formal, but I sensed a note underneath. Of hurt, maybe? Like he was offended, I'd think he'd been up to something nefarious while on his mission to keep the festival safe from evildoers?

"Okay," I said.

"Per Tierney's request, I have uploaded all of the drone footage to the same folder I sent you with all of the security footage."

"Thank you, Trevor," I said. He stared at me for a moment, then marched off.

I'd definitely made an enemy there.

Did he honestly not see that filming people in the parking lot at close range felt creepy, at least to the person being filmed?

A few customers walked up, and after Kendall and I served them, I stepped to the back of the cart, near the door, and pulled out my phone to check out the footage Trevor had sent.

The first files were lovely, high-view shots of the festival once it was set up, but vendors and the crowds had yet to arrive. This would be fantastic promo footage for next year's festival.

If next year's festival happened. Maybe the Doyles would decide the festival was more trouble than it's worth.

I scrolled through the footage of the parking lots, which had to be when the festival's vendors were setting up, given the empty lots, except for the closest one to the festival. I could see the Ground Rules Subaru. The drone dropped lower over a yellow Mini Cooper.

I stood up straighter.

Dulcie and Mark. She was clearly angry, and the drone had caught their conversation.

"I've kept it a secret all this time," Mark said. His voice was barely audible over the buzz of the drone.

They both looked up at the drone.

"C'mon, I'll help you get all of this to the booth before I unload my gear," Mark said.

Dulcie looked angry but still nodded yes.

They walked off, and the drone zoomed upward. I watched Dulcie and Mark disappear into the craft fair.

Hmm. I messaged Detective Ortega and asked if she'd received copies of the festival security's drone footage.

I wondered if she'd be able to use it if she decided it was relevant. Oregon is a two-party consent state, so technically, if you want to record someone, you have to tell them. But there are exceptions, and everyone who came to the festival had been notified there were security cameras on site. But did that include drones, even if they were operated by the head of security?

I continued watching the footage, but none of it was as sketchy as I'd been afraid, with no upskirts or extended recordings of attendees. Unless Trevor had deleted chunks of the footage, as there were time gaps. Which could also be explained, as Trevor was working and not using his drone at those times.

And the footage of Mark and Dulcie was a gold mine.

★ ★ ★

Even though I wanted to confront Dulcie, I stayed to work the cart.

Ground Rules first, after all.

Especially since Kendall needed a quick moment to himself, which was a euphemism for using the nearby bathroom.

As soon as he left, the chattiest customer of the day showed up, and I found myself speaking quickly, trying to keep up with her.

"Something's just different about getting coffee at home versus out. I know light roast has more caffeine, but I buy dark roast," the woman said.

I paused. "That's true, but it's not the full story. While there's a difference in the amount of caffeine between light and dark roasts on a per-bean level, the biggest impact is the huge difference in density between light and dark roast. And most home coffee brewers tend to brew by volume. I do when I'm just brewing for me at home."

"You've lost me." She tilted her head as she looked at me like Bentley does when something interests him or he really wants a biscuit.

I really wanted to go confront Dulcie, but I struggled to focus on the now. This customer deserved my time. "Let's say you have a favorite coffee scoop. I mean, I do. If you take one scoop of dark roast and put it in a pour-over cone, and then put the same-sized scoop of light roast in a different pour-over cone, and then exactly the same amount of water to each, there will be more caffeine in the light roast, because the light roast is denser. It's why we weigh the grounds while making a pour-over."

"Now I feel dense."

"There are other factors, too. The type of coffee bean you're using. Even among Arabica, there are hundreds of regional cultivators, meaning different bean types. And they have varying amounts of caffeine. If the coffee cherries are picked but not processed quickly, that can affect the caffeine level and flavor. Plus, storage matters. Both how the beans are stored before being sold to the customer, where the customer keeps the beans at home, and the time between when the beans are ground versus used. And the type of grind and how the coffee is prepared makes a difference."

"You should offer a coffee class."

I laughed. "You might be a fan of our newsletter. We talk about coffee minutiae."

"I had this coffee once in Italy, and it was so good. Do you know what I'm talking about?" The woman told me a long story about walking around a town in Italy, maybe Florence, Bologna, or somewhere on the Amalfi coast, and getting a perfect cappuccino that she'd drunk at a table on the sidewalk in sunny weather.

"And I've been chasing that drink ever since."

Something told me it wasn't the drink she was chasing but the whole experience. The joy of traveling and not having to worry about your day-to-day life. Of eating fresh pasta and drinking Italian wines and deciding where to explore tomorrow.

"Would you like a cappuccino?" I asked.

Then Kendall walked up, and relief flowed through me.

"Kendall makes a mean cappuccino. I need to go deal with something, so Kendall will care for you."

I left.

Because I was on a mission.

I had a murderer to confront.

Chapter 24

The craft festival wasn't as busy as yesterday, but it could be an afternoon lull before the bigger bands were scheduled to play this evening. I said hello to several vendors and waved at Ramona, who was unpacking a box and adding colorful purses to a display. Bagatha must be doing well if they needed to restock.

Luckily, Dulcie's booth was empty, except for the young chocolatier. The bottles of coffee juice had been boxed and were stacked in the corner, along with a few boxes of Left Coast Grinds gear. Sadly, the chocolate side was equally empty, except for a few tins of fancy cocoas.

Dulcie sat on a camp stool, looking rather pathetic. The left side of her yellow sundress was streaked with drying chocolate.

"Today is not my day," she told me. "If I ever sign up for a summer festival again, I will invest in thermoelectric coolers. They'd keep the chocolate cool and dehumidify at the same time."

"Did your chocolate get wet?" I asked.

Dulcie nodded sadly. "It's a mess. So I brought in some ganache and chocolate sauce today, thinking I could do something with fruit, but then I had a slight situation with the jars."

A quick glance showed me a few broken jars of chocolate sauce piled up in a recycling bin.

"At least I've sold a few jars of cocoa mix, probably to people who feel sorry for me."

Given her tone, Dulcie seemed deep in the pit of feeling sorry for herself. While I can understand going with the flow, I still couldn't figure out why she had come to the festival and was unprepared to handle the typical weather conditions. It's not like we were in an unexpected heat dome, even if it was a warmer Fourth of July than some previous years.

"Maybe I'll stick to winter events or just sell from my shop," Dulcie said.

I metaphorically geared up for battle. I pushed aside any sympathy I had and decided to, in the immortal words of Oregon-based company Nike, just do it.

"Mark had something on you. Something you don't want to get out, so I'm guessing it's highly embarrassing or criminal."

Dulcie shook her head. "Why would you think that?" she said. But I could hear the lie in her voice. And her gaze skittered away from me, like she couldn't make eye contact.

"There's footage of you arguing about it," I said. "Which makes me believe you didn't offer Mark half of your booth out of the goodness of your heart. I know he's blackmailed at least one person to get what he wanted."

"You're making this up." Dulcie still couldn't maintain eye contact with me and looked away.

"You're also terrified to talk to the police. I can understand being reluctant, since that's logical, but your reaction is too extreme. You're afraid you'll be arrested. So you either killed Mark or know you could get in trouble for something else."

From how Dulcie flinched, I'd hit home with my second statement.

I made my voice sound gentle and caring. And I spoke the truth. "What did you do, Dulcie? Is it worth carrying the guilt around with you?"

Tears filled Dulcie's eyes. "It was an accident. It wasn't supposed to happen."

I nodded and kept eye contact.

"It was my fault, but it wasn't malicious." Dulcie covered her face with her hands. like she was trying to hide from her actions. "It was raining, and she just ran out of nowhere."

"She?" Raining? The holiday weekend was dry.

We definitely weren't talking about Mark.

"The girl. She was a high-school kid, just a freshman. Wearing a black raincoat. I was running late and feeling hungover, so I pulled over to pound a bottle of water and scarf down an energy bar on my way to school. She ran in front of my car when I pulled back into traffic. I didn't even see her until she bounced off my bumper. I panicked and fled. I told my friend's older brother I'd bumped a pole in a parking garage, and he fixed my front bumper for me on the downlow, so my parents never knew I'd been in an accident." Dulcie dropped her hands and looked at me again. She seemed devastated.

I focused on the "you hit the girl and left the scene" part of Dulcie's story.

Dulcie nodded. "I kept waiting for the police to knock on my door. Someone must have caught my license plate, or caught me on a security camera. But no one came. I've waited for the axe to descend every day for over three years."

"You never thought it would be better to come forward and tell the truth?" I asked. I tried to imagine if I'd caused an accident and fled the scene. Saying my father would be disappointed in me was an understatement. But never coming forward? Would be worse.

Dulcie looked away. "Maybe it wasn't a huge priority because the girl didn't die."

That's one way to justify your actions. "How injured was she?"

"I've tried to make amends. I anonymously donated to her family's GoFundMe when they needed to buy her a wheelchair because she was paralyzed in the accident. Just from the waist down."

Just. I held in an annoyed huff. The girl's whole life had changed in an instant. If Dulcie were telling the truth, and the girl had run out in front of her car, maybe both of them had been at fault. By fleeing, Dulcie had, perhaps unwittingly, assumed full responsibility.

And while Dulcie claimed she'd been hungover, could she still have been drunk? Or just unwilling to take responsibility?

Or she'd been a kid who'd panicked and made the wrong choice and hadn't been brave enough to face the consequences.

"Mark was blackmailing you over this? How?" I asked.

"Mark was a childhood friend of my sister. Like childhood BFFs, she was good friends with his ex-wife, Melissa, although they're not friends anymore. My sister lives in Alaska now, but when she visited last year, some of us got together to hang out. A few bottles of wine later, my sister was zonked. Melissa had left in a huff, angry about something. Which is totally on brand for her. Mark kept refilling my glass, and I mistakenly told him about the deep, dark secret that's kept me awake at two a.m. for years."

"And he blackmailed you."

"Sort of. I mean, Mark didn't ask for money. When I sold a cocoa mix to a local shop, he wanted me to lean on them to ask them to sell his coffee, too. And when he heard about my booth here, he wanted in. And it's not like he blatantly said, 'Do this, or I'll turn you in.' He just inferred it. Or implied it? I always get those mixed up."

"He implied it, you inferred it." My words were automatic as my mind whirled.

Dulcie could still be the murderer, even if she'd admitted this dark secret. If Mark had continued to threaten her, she could've snapped. Or when she saw Mark and Harley's public blowup, maybe she saw her chance. Since if she killed Mark, she had a suspect in the spotlight.

But I doubted Dulcie had killed Mark. If I could get Dulcie off the suspect board, the truth might come to light.

And the poor teen girl she'd paralyzed deserved closure.

The more this muddled the issue, with lots of potential suspects, could be better for Harley if she needed a criminal defense. I assume throwing up a host of possible suspects is a way to create reasonable doubt, but I'm not a lawyer.

I texted Detective Ortega and asked her to come to the Dulcinea booth ASAP.

Then, I made eye contact with Dulcie again. "You can't keep living with this secret. You need to handle the consequences."

"Which are going to be so much worse, because I fled." Dulcie stared at her hands. Her yellow polka-dot manicure was chipped on the thumb. "You don't know what it's like to have a crime cast a shadow on your entire life."

Actually, I did know. Intimately. Although I'd been an unwitting pawn. But I'd made the decision to always do the right thing, regardless the personal cost.

"Maybe I don't deserve success," Dulcie said.

"Maybe you need to just be brave," I said. And do more research.

Detective Ortega strode into the booth, followed by her partner.

"You rang?" Detective Ortega said, in a slightly sarcastic tone. If we'd met during other circumstances, I'd adore her edge.

I motioned to Dulcie. "This is Dulcie, and she needs to tell you about a hit-and-run accident a few years ago."

Dulcie burst into tears.

A while later, Dulcie was escorted out of the festival by a pair of uniformed police officers, followed by Detective Ortega. The detective changed course and strode up to the coffee cart.

The smile she beamed my way felt authentic. "I wasn't expecting to solve a hit-and-run today."

I raised my eyebrows at her.

"Okay, you solved a hit-and-run that I will get to take professional credit for. My boss will be impressed. We're sending Dulcie to the Portland Police's traffic division, since the accident occurred in city limits, and they handle hit-and-runs."

"The poor girl she hit."

"I don't understand why Dulcie didn't stop. I can't imagine just leaving someone in the street like that, especially a kid. The girl she hit was only fourteen," the detective said.

"Me, neither," I said. "At least it looks good for you, solving the hit-and-run while investigating a murder."

Detective Ortega leaned toward me and whispered, "I've only been a detective for a week."

"That's all?"

She straightened back up. "I've been a police officer for five years and just got promoted to detective," she said.

"That's why you're part of a double act." That explained her ever-present detective shadow.

"Moore is one of the best detectives in the department. I'm lucky he's mentoring me."

"He seems . . . gruff, maybe?" And sleepy.

"He's Multnomah County's answer to Columbo." Detective Ortega snorted. "Don't tell him I said that, but it's true. But don't let the grumpy exterior fool you; he doesn't miss anything."

"Well, congratulations on the promotion."

"Thanks. I better go make sure everything is processed. Please don't confront any murderers until I get back." Detective Ortega sounded like she was joking, but we both heard the truth layered under her words.

As she walked away, I thought about all sorts of random things I know, like how a company in Eastern Oregon, Ore-Ida, invented the tater tot so they'd have a use for leftover potato scraps after making potato-based products, like frozen fries.

But my investigation into the murder felt like it was floundering. I still hadn't found the right reason for someone to harm Mark, although I'd solved a surprise cold case. One sticking point was that I wouldn't have been surprised if a series of people had walked up and slapped Mark, but I still couldn't find a reason for murder that felt right.

Although I'd found plenty of reasons why Mark had angered

people. Dulcie had felt like my best, most straightforward solution, with video footage to prove it, and I'd been wrong.

Mostly wrong.

At least I'd gotten justice for a teenage girl whose life had been forever changed because of Dulcie.

And I wasn't a police officer, and I shouldn't be sticking my nose into the investigation.

The rest of the day felt slow, even anticlimactic, and leaving the cart in the hands of Harley and Aspen didn't lessen the feeling that there was something I should be doing.

"I'll drop the tablets and cashboxes off at the roastery again," Harley said. She shooed me away from the cart, promising she could handle this.

So I headed home.

Tomorrow could bring about a new set of clues.

But I felt like this case was destined to never be solved.

Chapter 25

My phone rang at four a.m.

It rang.

Not a beep for a text or a message notification.

An actual phone call that made me flinch.

Someone I'd set for my nighttime Do Not Disturb to let through must be calling.

Tierney's name flashed on the screen.

A tiny sliver of relief flowed through me that this wasn't an emergency call from my dad or brother.

"It's four a.m.," I said.

"Sage, I have some bad news," he said.

Bax stirred beside me. Kaldi chirped from behind my head on my pillow, as if he were asking what was wrong, since I should be in Dreamland.

"Did someone else die?" My brain was still booting back up.

"No, but your coffee cart is on fire. I mean, it was on fire. There's a fire truck here now, and they've extinguished the flames."

I bolted upright, the sleepy haze burning off my brain.

"How bad does it look?"

Tierney paused. "You should come see for yourself."

"I'm on my way."

I jumped out of bed and grabbed a shirt and a pair of jean shorts from the closet.

"Did someone else die?" Bax sat up in bed, so Kaldi jumped into his lap in an example of orange-cat logic.

"The coffee cart was on fire. I need to go check things out."

Bax picked up Kaldi and put him on my pillow. He started to stand up. "I can drive you," he said.

"No, stay here with Niko. But maybe, if I don't get home in time, you can pick up Sophie and Kendall for work if they need a ride? They are supposed to carpool with me." If they needed to report to work, given my business might have literally burned to the ground.

"Of course." Bax gave me a hug.

"I'll text when I know what's up."

I rushed out, thankful I'd driven the Ground Rules Subaru home instead of leaving it at the roastery and riding my bike home.

Before I started the drive, I called Harley, and once the call was ringing through the car speakers, I pulled away from the curb.

Harley's phone rang a few times as I navigated the dark streets of our neighborhood.

"You've reached Harley Yamazaki. Please leave a message."

"Harley, it's Sage. Call me back; it's an emergency." I clicked the button on the steering wheel to hang up, knowing my tone sounded frustrated with my business partner. But I couldn't blame her for sleeping through a phone call in the middle of the night. Part of me wished I was still blissfully asleep, getting a few more hours of shut-eye instead of driving.

At least I-84 was as quiet as the Portland streets, so I didn't get stuck behind any traffic on my journey. On my way into the gorge, I only saw a handful of cars or long-haul trucks. The first rays of sunlight brightened the horizon, promising a beautiful day. Full sunrise this time of year was just before 5:30. As Kaldi thought sunrise equals breakfast, I'd bought him an automatic food dispenser to stop him from waking me up with the sunrise a few months ago. So he'd eat breakfast soon, then head back to bed for another eight hours of clearly needed sleep, unless he had errands to run on his busy to-do list.

With sunset around eight p.m., today was going to be long in more than one way.

The days start early in Portland during the summer, and the sun stays late, making long days. Something told me this would be a no-good, no-caffeine, horribly long day.

As I pulled into the long driveway leading up to the distillery, I passed a fire truck heading in the opposite direction. It looked like their job was over. They could head back to the station and do whatever it is that firefighters do when they're waiting to respond to calls.

The lots next the barn, and the food cart area, were mostly empty, since it wasn't yet five in the morning, except for one fire truck, a fire inspector's pickup truck, two police cars, and several other vehicles. I recognized Tierney's SUV, which I parked alongside. He and his brother Shay were talking to the police officers and a guy in jeans and a hard hat with a fire marshal logo.

Trevor, the security guard, was hovering behind Shay's shoulder, clearly wanting to be involved in the discussion.

Tierney waved me over. "This is Sage Caplin, one of the Ground Rules owners."

The officers acknowledged me; then one scribbled something on the back of a card and handed it to me. "Here's the report number for your insurance company."

The police left, and the fire marshal walked toward the ruin of my cart.

The ruin of my metaphorical child.

I turned to Tierney and Shay.

"What happened?"

"I can answer that," Trevor said. "A little after three hundred hours, I smelled smoke and came out of the security trailer, leading me to find your cart. I promptly called nine-one-one while acquiring a fire extinguisher, which I sprayed on your cart to keep the fire from spreading. I then called Tierney." His tone was overly formal, and I suspected he was trying to impress the Doyle brothers, aka his bosses.

"What were you doing here in the middle of the night?" I asked. Something didn't smell right, and I didn't mean the lingering notes of the burned coffee cart in the air.

"I set up a camp bed in the security trailer, since I don't feel comfortable leaving the site alone at night, even if we have two security guards on patrol." Trevor sounded faintly embarrassed but with a note of pride.

He'd kept the fire from spreading, even if he hadn't saved the Ground Rules cart.

That was something. The fire could've been a lot worse if it'd taken a few more carts and possibly spread to the distillery.

"I'll be back in a moment," Tierney said; then he and Shay walked away.

"Your guards didn't see anything?" I asked. My brain was whirling. If Trevor was sleeping in the trailer, the guards weren't sitting by the video monitors, watching the grounds. What had they been doing?

Trevor looked toward the distillery, and I followed his gaze. Two men, maybe in their mid-twenties, in orange shirts and black cargo pants like Trevor's, sat on a bench by the front door. They looked glum.

"They say they didn't see or hear anything. They claim they were patrolling the far side of the music area. But I think they were slacking off. When I review the security footage, I'll see what they were actually doing. But our footage has substantial coverage gaps, because Tierney and Shay didn't listen when I told them where to put cameras and that we needed more. They thought the entrances and major choke points were enough and that we didn't need to infringe on everyone's privacy. They wouldn't even let me message the craft-fair vendors that they should bring their own cameras to protect their booths.

"And you know what? Now there's been a murder and a major vandalism incident, which just shows they should've listened to me."

Trevor sounded angry, with an overconfident note layered underneath.

Hmm, Trevor just happened to find the cart on fire and called it in? Beating his employees patrolling the grounds to the scene of the crime?

Had he set the fire?

Then called it in to act like a hero?

"I am sorry about your cart," Trevor said. His tone was gruff. "That shouldn't have happened under my watch."

I tried to smile. "Thanks."

He walked away, and I turned and looked at the cart again.

The old horse-trailer-turned-coffee cart was ready for the scrap pile. The top and one of the sides were gone. A few firefighters still stood near it, and I wondered if they were making sure all of the hot spots were out so the cart wouldn't burst back into fire and threaten to take out the entire complex.

Hmm. A fire in the distillery would've been more dangerous with all of the alcohol around. Would a generic arsonist target my cart because it was easier to get into instead of the bigger, more impressive option?

Or did I get too close to the truth? Was the fire a warning?

Or was there a different reason someone would target the cart? Did someone want to punish Harley or me? Did the arsonist think one of us killed Mark and was trying to get their own form of revenge?

Or did they want to keep me and my baristas away from the festival? Or to distract me from the final day of the festival? To keep my focus elsewhere, so the villain could leave the festival without me noticing their actions?

Or was I being too egotistical by assuming someone was targeting me?

But if it was chance, why was it the coffee cart versus the burrito cart, for example? Unless our lock was easier to break.

No. The arson had to be on purpose.

Now, I just needed to figure out why.

Chapter 26

The festival was coming to life around us, while the Ground Rules cart was still taped off behind yellow caution tape, since the arson inspector with the local fire marshal had yet to finish his investigation. A lone uniformed police officer was on duty just outside the caution tape, looking bored.

Multiple craft-fair vendors came over to commiserate, and if I were less peppy than usual, no one seemed to mind.

One of the co-owners from Bagatha—Beryl—even offered to share some of the coffee in her old-school Stanley thermos, but I declined with a heartfelt no-thank-you. Tierney had already brought me several cups of coffee, which I suspected had been made from coffee pods, given the taste. I suspected he didn't know what else to do other than offer a hot beverage as a way of saying sorry.

I could've driven home.

I probably should have. Just left and taken the day off. It's not like Ground Rules could open today at the festival.

I'd already texted my baristas about what had happened and told them they could stay home. I could handle the booth.

Harley was still incommunicado.

As I looked at the cart and remembered what I saw inside, it was obvious: the fire was arson. It wasn't a fluke accident with propane, as we didn't use any flammable energy source; we used electricity. And it wasn't an electrical fire, since it was clearly started when someone threw some sort of Molotov cocktail through the cart's order window. I'm no expert, but it looked like the fire started on the floor in the middle of the cart.

The damage hurt my soul. We'd know later if the espresso machine was salvageable, although I had doubts. The burr grinders were a loss, as their hoppers had warped in the heat. I had yet to scope out the collection of pour-over filters and other equipment stored in the wall cabinet, but I assumed it was all destined to be recycled or sent to the dump. I'd already emailed our insurance agent, cc'ing my uncle, Harley, and Jackson. My brother wasn't technically part of the business, but he'd reviewed contracts for me in the past, and it would be easier for me to keep him in the loop.

Detective Ortega walked up, followed by Detective Moore and a man I didn't know. He was dressed in a county police polo shirt that matched the other two detectives, so I assumed he was one of their coworkers.

"What happened here?" Detective Ortega asked. She eyed me like she wanted to trap me in a lie.

Or maybe I was feeling paranoid, in addition to exhausted.

"There was a fire," I said.

"I've heard. Where were you when the fire started?"

I pulled my phone out of my pocket. "At home asleep. Let me text my lawyer and have him drop by if you want to ask me other questions."

"Do you have insurance on this cart?"

"Of course. We're a business."

"Interesting. Detective Moore was just telling me about an insurance fraud case when a guy burned down his workshop."

Of course, the police would suspect we'd set fire to the cart ourselves. Insurance fraud? Or an ineffective attempt to shift attention away from Mark and recast us as victims instead of murderers?

Life would've been easier if we hadn't come to this festival.

Then, a bright-pink Sprinter van honked at me, and my life brightened.

I recognized the driver and the peppy van. I smiled and walked away from the detectives without saying anything.

Callie, aka the Traveling Barista, had arrived. Her pink van was entirely self-contained, with minimal emissions, and she was proud of operating "off-grid." She stocked her coffee van with Ground Rules beans, and I'd always enjoyed chatting with her when she stopped by to pick up her wholesale orders. A few weeks ago, she'd told me she'd spent most of her winter set up around Mt. Hood, following her son's ski racing schedule. She'd planned to spend the summer at festivals and other outdoor events, including some of her children's baseball tournaments.

And evidently, popping up like a coffee superhero in times of trouble was part of her persona. I'm sure I wasn't the only one at the festival practically dying for a cup of excellent coffee.

"I heard you might need some help," Callie called out of the window.

"That's not untrue," I said. It was true on multiple levels, but I didn't want to think about the nitty-gritty details.

Callie laughed. "Do you want me to set up? I can show you or one of your baristas the ropes, and we can sell some coffee together. But if you'd prefer, I can leave. I don't want to drive over your toes."

"Please stay."

I helped Callie navigate to a spot near the Ground Rules cart, just a few feet from the yellow caution tape.

Trevor walked over, and I forced myself to smile at him. "I've got this."

Callie popped out of the driver's-side door and grinned as she skipped over to me. Her pink shirt and skirt matched the vibrant pink of her van, and I realized she had a matching headband holding back her chin-length brown hair. She was older than me, but not by much, maybe in her mid-thirties.

"Colton called and said you might need help, so I felt compelled to answer the call to adventure. Luckily, I'd just restocked my van since I'm going to a tournament next week, and you know you're the only coffee I carry. But I can make room for your Ground Rules gear if needed."

I half-smiled. "You mean if any of it or our gear hasn't gone up in smoke. I have extra cups and a few other supplies we'd been keeping in the back of the Subaru, along with our cashbox. And I can get more supplies if we need them."

Within half an hour, after I checked in with Tierney and got his enthusiastic consent, we were ready to brew. We'd rearranged the coffee area of the Traveling Barista van to show a mix of her bright-pink branded cups with the Ground Rules teal cups I'd snagged from the back of my company car. Her espresso machine was calibrated to both of our satisfaction. We couldn't offer the special drink menu I'd developed for the festival, but at least we could sell drinks. No caffeine at a festival can make attendees cranky.

A festival without caffeine sounded like torture. And from the looks of the people who'd gotten in line, festivalgoers agreed.

Not long after we'd opened for the day, Kendall and Sophie showed up, quickly followed by Bax and Niko.

I climbed out of the van and met my squad.

"Did the cart really burn down?" Sophie asked.

I nodded and walked around the van. Everyone followed me, like a sad barista version of the Pied Piper. We stood for a moment, staring at the remaining hulk of the Ground Rules horse trailer coffee cart.

"Darn, I loved that weird, quirky little cart," Kendall said.

Bax put his arm around my shoulders. "Do you know what happened?"

"The jury is still out," I said. I motioned to the investigator, who was videotaping something inside the cart. "But it looks like arson."

"Who'd want to burn down Ground Rules?" Sophie asked.

"Someone who thought we killed Mark?" Kendall said.

"Someone who wants to put pressure on us," I said.

"Someone who has something to hide," Kendall said.

"Someone who hates coffee?" Bax added.

"Someone mean," Niko said.

We stepped back over the van's order window and talked with Callie for a moment about who would cover the booth and who would help out in the van.

"I run this by myself all of the time, but a second set of hands would be welcome," Callie said. She left the discussion to take an order for an iced vanilla latte.

"Where's Niko?" I asked, and looked around.

Niko was crouched just outside the caution tape, looking at something with his magnifying glass. The police officer watched him warily, but with a posture that still screamed bored. I headed toward Niko, but the fire marshal got there first.

The fire marshal's words were kind when I walked up, with Bax hustling behind me.

"My investigation is based on four concepts: observe, hypothesize, test, and conclude. It's similar to the scientific method. Have you studied that yet?" The fire marshal sounded too happy to be investigating a crime scene this early in the day, but I could understand why having an eager young bystander would brighten his day.

And maybe his job brought him joy.

"No, sir," Niko said.

"Well, using your magnifying glass to observe is the first step, although I'm also using a video camera to record the scene before I disturb it any more than it's been disturbed by the firefighters who put out the fire. Next, I'll take samples of the scene."

"Can I do anything to help you?" Niko asked.

The fire marshal looked at Bax and me. "Is this delightful young chap yours?"

Beside me, Bax said, "Yes."

The fire marshal looked back at Niko. "In a few years, you could join the national junior firefighters' program, if you're still interested in investigating fires."

I returned to the cart as Bax, Niko, and the fire marshal talked.

The day was shaping up better than I'd hoped a few hours ago, but I still needed a nap.

Chapter 27

"So, what happened to the coffee cart?" a woman asked, as she swiped her credit card on the tablet in Callie's coffee van. I didn't recognize her.

"We're still waiting to hear the full story," I said.

"They probably left something turned on, and it shorted out. It's easy to do, especially in carts, since they're not checked for safety like traditional shops are. It's a tragedy waiting to happen," the woman said.

I held onto my temper, resisted the urge to correct her, and simply said, "Your coffee will be ready in a moment."

Most of our customers had asked about the Ground Rules cart, and a good number had recognized me, or Kendall, who was sitting just outside with a sandwich. Once he was done with his lunch, Callie would take her lunch break; then I'd leave the efficient coffee van in their hands and check on the booth.

Things were working almost like clockwork, thanks to Callie and her coffee van.

A woman walked up to Kendall. "Do you have a GoFundMe?" she asked.

"Excuse me?" Kendall looked up from his phone.

"Your coffee cart. Do you have a GoFundMe or some sort of fundraiser?"

"Not as far as I know, but you should talk to my boss."

"The cart's not yours? I've seen you in it before."

"I'm a loyal employee. If you want to talk to one of the owners, ask for Sage in the van right now."

"Sage owns the van, too?"

"No, the van's a different company, but we're all friends."

"The cart's really not yours? I thought you owned it. I'd love to donate."

"Please talk to Sage."

The woman wandered off. Kendall stood up and looked at me. "Do we have a GoFundMe?"

"No, but she's not the only person to ask."

Callie joined me. "And people are tipping really well today, which I assume is because of the fire."

"I'm uncomfortable soliciting donations, and it'd be premature now, since we don't even know the damages. I'll assess where we are when we get the insurance payout."

"The cart is definitely a loss," Kendall said.

"That's true. We'll have to look into a few options to fulfill our festival contracts for the summer," I said.

"If I'm free, I'm happy to help," Callie said. "I can work the festivals, or you can borrow my cart once we work out an official agreement."

"Thanks, Callie, I appreciate it."

Her van was set up well; something similar could work well for us as an events coffee van. But I liked the quirky look of our converted horse trailer.

Worry about this later, I told myself. I talked with Callie about Ground Rules needs during the rest of July to see if she could fill in, and then a rush of people showed up. Kendall joined me, and before Callie left to grab food, we agreed to formally sit down tomorrow and figure things out.

"This van is pretty awesome," Kendall said. "It's no horse trailer, but it's designed well. I'm impressed."

"Yeah, it really is a great setup." It was efficient and logical, but it lacked the charm of our torched cart.

Could a van like this be a suitable replacement for us? Painted teal, of course. We wouldn't need a second vehicle to tow the cart, and what it lacked in charm could be made up by efficiency.

And a good AC, which Callie had turned on early.

A short while later, it was my turn for lunch, and my plans revolved around food, checking on the Ground Rules booth, and watching the cornhole final.

Because Jackson and Bax had valiantly fought their way through the brackets and qualified for the final round. They might be the inaugural cornhole champions of the Doyles' Oregon Whiskey Fourth of July Festival.

After a quick debate, I ordered my portafoglio pizza from Pizza My Heart, even though I knew the fish and chips from the Codfather were excellent.

As I waited for my slice of accordion-folded pizza, I stepped to the side and pulled out my phone. I might as well check the Ground Rules social media accounts. Thankfully, no one had seemed to notice that we'd been in the proximity of another murder. Nor had the fire made the news. But news trucks had shown up, so it was just a matter of time before I saw our name and "breaking news" in the same segment.

"Smells like you've gotten part of what you deserve," a snide voice said behind me.

Melissa.

Dressed in orange stripes today, like an oversized, bitter creamsicle.

She smirked at me.

"The last text I received from Mark said he was going to see about a horse," Melissa said. "Hopefully, the last thing I'll see from Ground Rules is the smoldering remains of your stupid horse trailer coffee cart before you're carted off to jail."

"Don't hold your breath. We'll be back stronger than ever." Maybe in a teal van.

I ignored Melissa, and after "accidentally" bumping me, she sauntered away.

Her words stuck in my mind. Seeing a man about a horse? According to Dulcie, Mark had texted her the same thing. The phrase usually meant the person was stepping out to do something they didn't want to specify, like visiting the bathroom.

Something told me that Mark had come back on site for a specific reason, and if I could learn why, I'd know who'd killed him and why.

And I really hoped it was just chance that Mark had died near my car. Versus his joke about a horse being a veiled reference to our coffee cart.

I texted Detective Ortega about Melissa, feeling like a tattletale. But the detectives had heard Melissa threaten me, and if she escalated to anything more, she'd have a serious problem.

While I might be willing to turn the other cheek for grief, I'm not willing to be bullied.

Chapter 28

I made it over to the cornhole finals a few minutes before the match started. Two sets of kids, about twelve, were finishing up their final in the youth division. Tierney was waiting to give them their prize, which we'd chosen carefully. Hopefully, the booklet of passes to a local chain of "nickel" arcades with laser tag, mini golf, and at least one movie theater would be a hit.

Bax and Jackson were waiting in their matching Catching Corn T-shirts while a man and woman in striped T-shirts were talking intently together. I suspected they were getting ready to face off in the Last Bag Standing championship.

Niko had staked out a viewing spot, so I sat beside him, wondering if he cared that he'd been knocked out of the kids' single division early. From what I'd observed, Niko wasn't particularly competitive, but he could be hiding a cutthroat competitive streak.

Instead, I opted for, "How is your investigation?"

"It's good, I think; I've found out a lot," Niko said. "But I can't make sense of the clues."

"Would a second set of eyes help?"

Niko nodded, then opened his notebook. "This is where my investigation starts."

He handed it over and sat next to me as I read his notes on his investigation. He'd painstakingly made notes on his interviews, and I was surprised by the number of people he'd managed to talk to. He'd even inked a few sketches along the way, including a surprisingly good one of my barista, Sophie, drawn with anime flair.

"Sophie's really nice," Niko said.

"She is."

Niko had made a few notes about Hannah, accompanied by a sketch of a teacup and a Stonefield Beach Tea business card tucked into the page like a bookmark. I read his summary, which was written in block letters. I ignored the fact that his handwriting was neater than mine.

Hannah Clyde, 29. In business with her older sister, Josie, who isn't at the festival. Owns two cell phones (one black, one with a purple case with a Stonefield Beach logo). Likes strawberries. Doesn't like Trevor the security guard. (Sophie doesn't like him, either.)

"You've been reading a lot of mysteries, haven't you?" I pictured Niko's stack of books from his weekly library trip.

"They're research for my Kaldi and Ben story."

Wait . . . I looked back at Niko's notes. "Tell me about when you talked with Hannah."

"Well, she and Sophie were eating strawberries, and she offered me one. Which made it hard to take notes," Niko said. "So I put my notebook on her table and knocked over her tray. Hannah keeps a bunch of random stuff in it, including her phones. She got angry with me but tried to hide it, even though I helped her pick everything up."

"Hmm."

"But Sophie said it was just an accident, and Hannah should chill. I didn't know Trevor, the security guard, was watching the booth, and he told me that if I knocked anything else over, he'd kick me out of the festival. But Hannah defended me, told Trevor that he's a jerk and a big bully, and apologized for getting angry with me. She said she was just feeling hangry and needed to eat more. And then she ate a sandwich."

"Interesting."

"Hannah told Trevor to leave and quit hovering around her booth. That means hanging out, right? She also called him a creep."

"Yes."

Niko leaned over and wrote the definition of the word hover on the corner of his sketchbook while my mind was taking in these new pieces of information, and they clicked into a composite.

I knew who'd killed Mark.

And I knew why.

I wanted to do something with my newfound knowledge. If I told Detective Ortega, would she take me seriously? I texted her and asked if she was at the festival.

My mind was whirling as Niko and I watched the cornhole battle, cheering and groaning at the appropriate times. I snapped a few photos and texted them to Jackson's girlfriend.

Niceeee, Piper texted back, after I'd sent a hilarious photo of Jackson's studious face studying the cornhole playing field as he prepared for a throw, with a follow-up photo of his grimace as the bean-bag bounced off of the board and thudded to the ground below. *Gonna turn these into a series of magnets for the fridge. Or maybe a T-shirt.*

I laughed, suspecting Piper was telling the truth. She knew when to tease Jackson and when to let things go. And these photos were gold.

Niko groaned as the other team scored a twelve-pack, or four perfect throws in a row, getting maximum points that round.

It wasn't looking good for Catching Corn.

Trevor walked by, and I wanted to confront him. Instead, I settled for smiling at him, like I knew something he didn't.

Because I did.

When the match ended, I consoled my brother and fiancé.

"It was a hard-fought battle," I told Bax. He and Jackson had taken their second-place showing like champs.

Which was good, as this was supposed to be a fun tournament. Although they did look sad.

"I think those two are trying to go pro," Bax said.

"What did one call a professional cornhole player? Cornholists?"

"Just pro players. Like those two, 'cause they're awesome."

Tierney arrived to give the winners their prize: a case of Doyle's Irish-To-Go Whiskey.

I glanced at the runners-up. "Cheer up. I can get you unlimited amounts of their canned Irish whiskey."

"It's the principle," Jackson said.

Sophie texted and asked if I could relieve her at the booth quickly.

"Sorry, I've got to go; Sophie needs me. You two fought valiantly."

When I got to the booth, Sophie was the only one there.

"I'm working alone today, and I desperately need to use the bathroom," she said.

"No Hannah?"

Sophie shook her head. "She has a migraine, so I said I would handle the booth. Except I can't make the custom blends, which has disappointed a few customers."

Sophie headed out of the tent, and I took over. Since it was quiet, I took a few notes on my phone and made a plan.

Hmm. Detective Ortega still hadn't texted me back.

Her loss.

I mixed it up and had a grilled cheese and tomato sandwich from Cheese, Please for dinner with Jackson, Bax, and Niko, and then we staked out a spot in the music area. We set up four low-profile chairs on the hill, looking down at the stage in the meadow.

This should've been the perfect time to sit and watch excellent bands perform with the gorge as a backdrop. But I was too nervous to relax.

"You really had to send Piper photos of me playing cornhole?" Jackson asked during a break between bands.

"I had to share the experience with her, since she couldn't make it in person."

My phone warned me that its battery was ten percent depleted, so I tried pulling my charging block out of my bag.

But it wasn't there. I'd left it, charging, in the Ground Rules booth.

"I need to run back to the Ground Rules booth real quick. I left my charging block." And I really wanted Detective Ortega to respond to my text. I hadn't texted her again, not wanting to sound like I desperately wanted her attention.

But I needed to tell her what I'd found out.

"Want us to come with?" Bax asked.

"No, I'll just be a minute. Enjoy Maya's band." Maya had been friends with Bax for years and regularly wrote music for his video games. Her band headlining this festival was an example of her dreams finally coming true. She'd always been an exceptionally talented musician, able to play multiple instruments and with a deep knowledge of music theory and history. She was just now being recognized on a global stage. Her European tour had sold out, although she'd told me none of the venues had been giant. Her former band was also playing tonight, and I knew they'd ask her to come onstage for a song or two.

As I headed out of the music area, I needed to weave through crowds of people. The festival was busier than yesterday, which made sense. Today's bands were popular and top-notch, and the final two bands had both charted in the past year. The day would end with a Fourth of July fireworks display after the final band's encore.

Trevor stood at the gate leading to the craft fair, and when we made eye contact, I smirked at him again. Which made his eyes narrow, and I held in a laugh.

The craft fair was closed, and the lack of people felt relaxing, although I could hear Maya singing from the stage.

When I got to the booth, I quickly found my charging block, which I'd left on the back table, plugged into the power strip that had been provided for each booth as part of the registration fee. I unplugged, swapped out my device's charging cord for the phones, and connected my phone. I felt relieved as the battery started clicking upward from five percent.

As I glanced around the booth, I realized I needed to do something so I could fully relax.

I sat on the stool in the tent, texted Detective Ortega's phone number, and summarized what I'd learned and put together. I could be wrong, but something told me I was right.

I stood for a moment outside the tent. The last rays of the sun had faded, and the sky was dark. Music filled the air. I should join Bax, Niko, and my brother.

Or my baristas. Colton was here with a group of his friends, along with Kendall, Sophie, and a few more. I shouldn't hang out here alone when I should be enjoying the festival.

As I turned down a row on my way back to the music, I saw someone walking. I stepped into the shadows.

And the killer walked by.

Were they heading to the Ground Rules tent?

Was burning down the Ground Rules cart not enough, and they were going to sabotage the booth, too?

So I followed, pausing briefly to open my voice memo app and setting it to record.

Chapter 29

"What are you doing, Hannah?"

Hannah jumped and wheeled around to face me. "You scared me."

"Consider it a small payback for you burning down my coffee cart."

Hannah narrowed her eyes as she looked at me. One of her hands was wrapped in a gauze bandage.

"This has been the worst weekend. First you, then the miniature Hardy Boy running around, poking his nose into everything, but at least he's harmless. Unlike you, who doesn't know when to let things go."

"Why did you do it, Hannah?"

"It's not like I wanted to harm Mark," Hannah said. "But when he saw me at the festival, he asked how my psycho sister was doing. I could've lived with his stupid smirk. Then, before the music started, Mark told me he was going to screw me over. He'd reviewed his divorce papers with Josie—"

"Your sister was married to Mark?" Jocelyn? Josie for short?

"—and she owes him money that she doesn't have. If he sued her, it would sink our tea company. Josie has already tried to commit suicide once because of him, and I'm not going to let him harm her ever again.

"When I saw him fight with Harley, I knew someone had to stop him. So I messaged him and told him to meet me after the crowds thinned out, saying that I had something better than getting money from Josie, especially since she didn't have the amount of money he was looking for. I told him it would be grounds for a takeover, and the idiot jumped on it. He assumed I used 'grounds' as a pun." Hannah's face was half hidden in the shadows, and I realized this was how she'd been all weekend. Part of herself hiding from what she'd done, and the rest trying to brave the sunlight and get through the festival without attracting attention.

"And you killed him," I said.

"The irony of Mark meeting his maker at a makers' fair felt like fate," Hannah said. "I had my knife, and Mark didn't even notice it when he started to taunt me. Then I got the last laugh."

"Did you purposefully kill him next to the car I was driving?"

"It's not like I wanted to pin it on you or Harley, but I knew it'd distract the police. I knew if I kept my nose down, worked my booth, and disappeared when the festival ended, no one would connect me with his murder. But then you had to stick your nose in. I was going to pin it on Dulcie, but then you had to go and get her arrested for something else."

"So you burned down my cart."

"And singed my hand, so I had to stay away today. I thought I'd be safe to sneak in now to get my stuff, but of course, you're skulking around. Again."

Hannah assessed me, then asked, "How'd you know it was me?"

"You have two cell phones. One with your logo; one that's black. You stole Mark's phone."

"I couldn't let the police read our texts. I knew I could bluff and say Mark was threatening my sister if they realized we were texting. Wait, when did you see the second phone?"

I half-smiled. "You don't remember? You're not very good at this, are you? You should've thrown Mark's phone out of the window on I-84 or found a convenient dumpster."

A loud boom sounded, followed by a fizz and a swish.

The fireworks had started.

"I kept it in case I needed to plant it somewhere. And that place just occurred to me." Hannah stared at me again. "I'm sorry, but I won't let you ruin my life. No one will hear you over the fireworks."

She was taller than me and sturdier.

But something told me I was faster.

I splashed the contents of my water bottle in her face, then threw the bottle for good measure, aiming for her nose.

I wheeled around. I sprinted away, not letting myself enjoy the brief squeal Hannah had let out when the bottle smashed into her. It's too bad I was carrying a plastic Nalgene versus one of my heavier stainless-steel bottles.

When I turned the corner, I noted that Bagatha had only partially covered the entrance of their booth. So I slid under their table and bolted for the back wall. As I crawled under the canvas, I heard Hannah's lumbering steps run past.

Followed by another large boom.

I was next to Niko's favorite Good Clean Suds booth, so I ducked inside and snagged a bag of bath salts, in case I needed to throw some in Hannah's eyes.

When I peeked out, I saw Hannah at the end of the row, looking around like she was debating which way to go. She headed down the row toward me, so I scrambled back into the suds booth and headed back the way I'd initially run.

Maybe one of the security guards would see me over the cameras. Although the music and fireworks could sidetrack them, drawing their eyes to the sky instead of the drama unfolding on the ground.

But guards were at the gates, so I headed in that direction.

As I turned the corner, another boom filled the air, and red Catherine wheels exploded through the sky.

And I realized Hannah had spotted me, so I sprinted faster to the gates.

The two security guards saw me and straightened up from where they'd been leaning against the fence by the entrance to the music area.

"Call nine-one-one," I gasped out.

Given what I knew about Trevor, I lacked faith in his security staff. But there were two of them, both bigger than Hannah. And when they straightened out, they suddenly seemed capable instead of listless.

Hannah ran into sight, and I was a little proud a small stream of blood dripped from her nose. When she saw the security guards, she turned and fled, while one of the bouncers called 911 on his phone.

"Do you need water or anything?" the second security guard asked me.

I laughed.

It was over.

Well, mostly over.

Chapter 30

The fireworks show had garnered oohs and aahs from the crowd, which I listened to alongside my buddies, the security guards, while waiting for the detectives to show up.

It hadn't taken Detectives Ortega and Moore long to send out a bulletin on Hannah Clyde's car.

I didn't tell them I would need a new tea vendor for the Rail Yard cart and our shop. Maybe Hannah will rebrand her company CriminaliTEA if she ever gets out of the slammer.

I noted the pun on my phone to share with Bax later.

When the fireworks ended, I'd texted Bax, Jackson, my dad, and my baristas that I'd solved the crime and that I was with security at the craft fair gate. As the happy crowd streamed out, buzzing after an evening of music and fireworks, we staked out a spot not far from where the Good Clean Suds duo had listened to music, and I explained what had happened.

I glanced at my dad, the now retired cold case detective. "I solved a murder and a cold case hit-and-run in one weekend."

"Would you like a gold star?" His delivery was entirely deadpan.

I smiled when I got his joke. Police and sheriff's badges are shaped like stars. But I wasn't cut out to be a police officer.

I glanced around at my friends, families, and coworkers. Harley was holding a bottle of water, and she looked as relaxed as I'd seen her for the past few months. She'd always be a little bit tense, because that's the frequency she vibrated at. But at least she wasn't a murder suspect anymore.

"You want to know who gave me a vital clue?" I asked everyone. My gaze settled on Niko.

"Who?" Niko chirped.

"You did!" I held his gaze.

Niko straightened and adjusted his fedora. "Really? Which clue? My interview with the Good Clean Suds ladies?"

"You were interviewing strangers?" Bax asked.

I smiled at Niko. "No, you noted that Hannah had two cell phones."

Niko tilted his head slightly to the side, shifting his hat down over one eye. "Wait, that's weird? Last year, my teacher had two cell phones. I thought most adults did."

That sounded like a story for another day. "It stuck out to me, since Mark's phone was missing. Although you're right. Hannah could've had two phones for an innocent reason. But it also fits the bigger picture that suddenly clicked into place for me. Hannah hated Mark."

Niko turned and looked up at his dad. "Did you hear that?"

"We all heard it, buddy." Bax put his arm around Niko's shoulder.

"I'll use this as inspiration for my next Kaldi and Ben story," Niko said.

Jackson looked at me and raised his eyebrow.

"Niko's drawing a graphic novel about a crime-solving goat and cat," I said.

"That's sure to be a hit," Jackson said. "Was it just the second phone that led you to the truth?"

"No, that was just the final piece of the murky puzzle. There was another clue that stuck out. Hannah had an impressive knife when she set up, but asked to borrow a new one later. Either she'd broken hers, or she'd gotten rid of it."

"Do you know why she did it?" Jackson asked.

"Hannah's older sister, Josie, was married to Mark. Supposedly, Mark was going to lean on Josie for money that he'd been promised in their divorce decree. But Josie doesn't have the money, and Hannah was afraid it would ruin their company. Hannah kept her relationship with Mark secret, going so far as to try to distract me when I asked if she'd pitched her products to Left Coast Grinds. From what I heard, Josie and Mark's marriage was toxic. Hannah even blamed Mark for Josie trying to commit suicide."

"That's heavy," Colton said.

"Very heavy, but murder was clearly the wrong choice," I said.

"Hannah should've chosen someplace else to get revenge, although she might have been successful if it hadn't been for you lousy baristas," a voice said from behind me.

Detective Ortega.

She laughed. "I'm sorry, I just couldn't resist. I wanted to let you know that we arrested Hannah Clyde, so you're safe to go home."

"Thank you, Detective."

"You're welcome. Stay safe, and please stop sticking your nose into murders. It'd suck if you were the next victim."

"Maybe we should embroider that on a shirt for Sage," Jackson said.

We left as a group, although I was parked the closest, as I'd arrived at five a.m. yesterday.

The parking lot was mostly empty; most of the crowd had left after the fireworks, not knowing the real excitement was happening behind them in the craft fair.

Niko and Bax stopped by the Ground Rules Subaru as the rest of the group hiked on to the other parking lots, calling out goodbyes as they walked.

I came to a decision, but before I could say anything, Bax spoke.

"I can't believe you confronted a killer."

"It was instinctive."

"I'm so glad you're okay."

We made eye contact, and Bax's smile was soft. "Quit putting yourself in danger, Coffee Angel. I don't know how I could live without you."

Niko yawned, breaking the mood, and Bax ruffled his hair. It was late for Niko.

I yawned. It was late for me, too.

"I have something for you," I told Niko.

He looked at me with a mix of tiredness and the sort of wired feeling that keeps you awake from coffee or from the excitement of unmasking a murderer.

I opened the back of the car, pulled out the satchel I had bought, still wrapped in the linen drawstring bag, and handed it over to its new owner.

"This is for you," I said. "You did a great job investigating this weekend, but please don't do it again."

Niko loosened the drawstring of the linen bag and pulled the satchel out. He examined it in the glow of the security light above us.

"This is just like my bag, but better," Niko said.

"If you take care of it, this bag should last a long time."

"Thank you—I now have two new bags!"

Of course, Niko would be as enamored with the linen bag as much as the satchel itself.

As Niko pulled his sketchbook, water bottle, pen case, and a few other random items out of his old bag to put them into his new satchel, Bax glanced at me.

"Are you sure rewarding him for trying to solve a murder was the right idea?"

I shook my head. "I just knew he'd love the bag."

Chapter 31

A few weeks later, the festival had disappeared from sight in my rearview mirror, and I'd thrown all my attention into a different project.

And now it was time.

Despite a few minor hiccups, the wedding was on track. Months ago, we'd chosen an event center on seven acres outside of Portland, complete with a lake, stream, and gardens, as our wedding site. I'd gotten ready on site in a charming one-bedroom cabin with my bridesmaids. When it was thirty minutes until go time, the photographer led us across the grounds, stopping at a bridge that crossed a creek that led to the venue's private lake. She set us up for a photo, but when she walked off the bridge to a small landing I guessed was regularly used for photos, Erin, my photographer friend, followed her.

They had a brief conversation, and the photographer, who'd come with the venue, let Erin look over her shoulder as she did something with her camera. Once Erin decided the photographer knew what she was doing, she hustled to the bridge to join us.

All of my bridesmaids were in the same shade of deep purple, but they'd chosen the style of their airy chiffon dresses. Erin pulled up the hem of her A-line dress with an illusion neckline as she climbed onto the bridge.

In the photos, Piper, the bridesmaid next to Erin, had opted for a halter dress that showed off her toned arms. She double-checked Erin's hair, and the photographer adjusted Erin's stance and then took photos of us. The bride and her crew.

She took a few of me solo, several with my maid of honor, and then it was almost time.

We walked toward the pavilion, which was really a gazebo next to a large enough brick patio to seat one hundred people. We'd hold our ceremony in front of the gazebo, with the lush green forest of trees in the background.

My father and Jackson met us. The lodge hid us from the guests' view. One of the venue's event staff brought us small glasses of water.

"I have a mirror in case anyone needs to check their makeup," she added.

"Are you ready? Because if you change your mind, I can handle this," Jackson said.

"You like Bax. Sometimes, I suspect you like him more than you like me," I said.

"Nonsense, I love you more. But while I like Bax, marriage is a legal contract, and you know I always have your back."

"I'm good, Jackson."

My father linked my elbow with his. "Jackson stole my line."

"For real?"

"I, too, like Bax, but I'm Team Sage," my dad said.

"I'm making the choice I want to," I said.

"That's all I wanted to know."

"Are you done hassling your sister?" Piper asked. She linked arms with my brother. She glanced around. "It's too bad your sister found this venue first. It's gorgeous."

"You could still use it," I said. "Just tell everyone I'm the arbiter of what's hip to you."

"You wish," Jackson said.

We joked for a moment; then the musical quartet started playing the *Moonlight Sonata*. The prelude song meant it was almost go-time.

Jackson looked at Piper. "I'd kiss you, but I don't want to share your lipstick."

As my brother walked toward the ceremony, the wedding coordinator chivvied him to join the groomsmen.

I could hear the venue staff carefully encouraging attendees to take their seats as the venue's wedding coordinator had us line up.

"Didn't we already practice this?" Piper joked.

"It's always like herding cats," the wedding planner said.

As my dad and I took our place in the back of the line, I caught a glimpse of a blond-haired woman about my height. She stood off to the side, near the edge of the lodge, not quite in the shadows. But also not in the light. When I glanced back, she'd slipped away.

Maybe I'd imagined what I'd seen.

But as I closed my eyes for a second, double-checking I was ready, the woman I saw kept flashing through my mind.

Was my mother at my wedding?

But as the song changed and the processional started, my thoughts focused on the present.

It was time.

After a short and sweet ceremony, and in front of about one hundred of our closest friends and relatives, it was done.

Bax and I were married.

I couldn't wait to see what new adventures awaited us.

RECIPES

Blackberry Simple Syrup

Ingredients

½ cup water

½ cup sugar

½ cup blackberries (fresh or frozen)

Preparation

Add all three ingredients to a pan and bring to a boil, stirring occasionally. Simmer for about six minutes; you want the berries to start falling apart. When they soften, smoosh the berries with your spoon.

Once the simple syrup has simmered for six minutes, remove it from heat. Strain the syrup into a jar, ensuring none of the berries or seeds make it into the final syrup. Discard the fruit solids, and store the syrup in your refrigerator.

In addition to making a stellar Blackberry Tea Soda, you can use the simple syrup as a drink mixer (it goes great in champagne, lemonade, or sparkling water!).

Blackberry Herbal Tea Soda

For a naturally decaf drink, rooibos is a great choice. If you'd like a jolt of caffeine, you can use your favorite black or green tea.

Ingredients
Blackberry simple syrup
Club soda
Rooibos tea
Ice

Preparation
First, make your tea concentrate by brewing the rooibos with a higher ratio of tea to water than normal. For example, if you're using a bag of rooibos, only brew about one inch of water in your mug. Check the brewing time of your tea. You don't want to overbrew the tea, but you do want to make it stronger than normal.

Once brewed, you can let it cool for a few minutes or immediately add it to your favorite approximately sixteen-ounce glass or jar. Add a tablespoon of the blackberry simple syrup (or more to taste), along with the club soda. Stir carefully, then add ice. And enjoy!

Hazelnut Simple Syrup

Ingredients
½ cup hazelnuts, chopped coarsely
½ cup sugar
½ water

Preparation
Bring the water, sugar, and hazelnuts to boil in a pan. Cover and let it simmer for ten minutes; the syrup should thicken slightly. Remove from heat and let the mixture rest for thirty minutes, then strain the syrup into a jar.

You don't have to discard the hazelnuts—you can eat them! Add them to a salad or sprinkle them on ice cream.

Notes:
You can use a teaspoon of hazelnut extract if you don't have hazelnuts available.

You can easily double, triple, etc., the recipe; just keep the ratios intact.

Mason Jar Cold Brew Coffee

Kyoto coffee—aka cold brew—has been popular in Japan since the 1600s, and legend has it that Dutch coffee traders brought the practice with them from Indonesia. Nowadays, you can buy premade cold brew concentrate, but making your own is simple. You only need to mix coffee grounds and cold water together and let them sit in the fridge for 12 to 24 hours.

Cold brew is sweeter and less acidic than coffee made with hot water. You can buy fancy pitchers to make cold brew, but you can also make it in mason jars or a simple French press.

Making coffee is all about the proper ratio of coffee grounds to water. To make a cold brew concentrate, you'll need ¾ cup of coarse-ground coffee to 4 cups of water.

You can double, triple, quadruple, etc., this recipe; just keep the ¾ cups ground to 4 cups of water ratio intact.

Ingredients
¾ cup of coarse coffee grounds
4 cups of water

Preparation
Mix four cups of water and the ¾ cups of coffee grounds in an appropriately sized mason jar and screw on the lid. Place in the refrigerator for 12 to 24 hours.

When the coffee has been brewed to your liking, strain it into a clean pitcher or mason jar.

Serve over ice and dilute with water or milk at a 1:1 ratio or to taste. To sweeten, add in simple syrup.

Hazelnut Coffee Soda

Ingredients

¾ cup cold brew concentrate
1 tablespoon hazelnut simple syrup (or to taste)
¾ cup club soda
Ice

Preparation

Mix the cold brew concentrate and hazelnut simple syrup in a wide-mouth, pint-sized mason jar (or glass of your choosing). Add ice to the glass, then slowly pour in the club soda. Lightly mix, and your soda is ready.

Coffee Tonic

Coffee tonics are easy to make and very satisfying, especially on hot days.

Ingredients
⅓ cup of cold brew coffee (or more to taste), or a double shot of espresso

¾ cup (or six ounces) of tonic water

Ice

Slice of fresh orange, lemon, or lime (optional) to finish

Preparation
Add ice to your favorite glass, and pour the cold brew in. Tilt your glass to the side when adding the tonic water to keep it from fizzing. Stir lightly, then adorn with a slice of fresh citrus. And voilà!

Note:
You can swap in two espresso shots for the cold brew.

Ground Rules Frozen Hot Chocolate

Ground Rules has you covered if you're looking for a frozen chocolate drink on a hot day. The espresso powder and cinnamon are optional but delicious add-ins.

Ingredients
½ cup of chocolate chips or chopped-up chocolate (note: if you're making this dairy-free or vegan, be sure to check the ingredients of the chocolate you use)
1 tablespoon of cocoa powder
2 tablespoons granulated sugar (or more to taste)
¼ teaspoon espresso powder (optional)
¼ teaspoon cinnamon (optional)
Pinch of salt
1½ cups milk (I used Oatly; regular dairy will work)
3 cups ice cubes

Optional Ingredients
Whipped cream
Shaved chocolate
Cinnamon sugar
Whatever toppings sound delicious to you

Preparation
Melt the chocolate chips or other chocolate in the top of a double boiler. Once the chocolate is melted, stir in the cocoa powder, sugar, and pinch of salt. Add ½ cup milk and stir to combine. Let this cool to room temperature.

Add one cup of milk and ice to a blender once the chocolate mix is at room temperature. Pour in the chocolate mix you just made in the double broiler. Blend until smooth. If you'd like it thicker, add more ice cubes and blend. You can add more sugar at this point, as well, if needed.

Serve immediately. Feel free to top with whipped cream, chocolate curls, a sprinkle of cinnamon sugar, etc.

Notes:

You could also melt the chocolate in a microwave instead of using a double broiler.

Vanilla, caramel, or other flavors could be added at the same time as the cocoa powder.

The espresso powder doesn't add a ton of caffeine and really brings out the chocolate flavor.

You can add more if you'd like this to taste like a frozen mocha.

This doesn't store particularly well, although you could freeze and reblend it later.

Ground Rules Oatmeal Chocolate Chip Bars

Ingredients
¼ cup plus 2 tablespoons of oil

½ cup brown sugar

½ cup granulated sugar

1 egg

1 teaspoon vanilla extract

1 teaspoon cinnamon

¾ cup all-purpose flour (you can sub in an equal amount of oat flour to make it gluten-free)

½ teaspoon baking soda

¼ teaspoon salt

½ cups old-fashioned rolled oats

¾ cup chocolate chips (this recipe will be dairy-free if you use dairy-free chocolate chips!)

Preparation
Preheat your oven to 350 degrees Fahrenheit, and line an 8-by-8-inch pan with parchment paper.

Add the dry ingredients (salt, baking soda, flour, and rolled oats) to a bowl, mix, and set aside.

Combine the oil (or butter), brown sugar, and white sugar in a large mixing bowl. Mix until smooth and airy.

Add the eggs, mixing well; then add the vanilla. If you use oil, beat it until the mixture looks frothy. If you use butter, it will be denser (but still light).

Add the dry ingredients to the wet ingredients and stir until just combined. Mix in the chocolate chips.

Dump the cookie dough into the prepared pan and gently level it with your fingers or a spoon (don't press it down hard).

Bake for 25 to 30 minutes; the cookies should be golden brown on top.

Remove from oven and let the pan cool completely before cutting into bars.

Acknowledgments

I dedicated this book to the readers who've been with Ground Rules from the beginning and those who have joined along the way, because the series wouldn't exist without you. Thank you for your support.

As always, I should thank my writer friends. This includes everyone in my "dessert" group, my Shut Up and Write meetups, and my friends in my local writing organizations, like Sisters in Crime, MWA, and Willamette Writers. I also want to thank friends like Robin Herrera, Miriam Forester, Bill Cameron, and so many more who've been wonderfully supportive over the years.

And I owe another round of thank-yous to my agent, Joshua Bilmes, editor John Scognamiglio, publicist Larissa Ackerman, and the rest of the team at Kensington, who've brought Sage and the series to life. Tsukshi Kainuma's fantastic illustrations on the Ground Rules covers deserve a special shoutout.

Visit our website at
KensingtonBooks.com
to sign up for our newsletters, read
more from your favorite authors, see
books by series, view reading group
guides, and more!

Become a Part of Our
Between the Chapters Book Club
Community and Join the Conversation

Betweenthechapters.net

Submit your book review for a chance to win exclusive
Between the Chapters swag you can't get anywhere else!
https://www.kensingtonbooks.com/pages/review/